CH00829576

Discover other titles by

ANTHONY RYAN:

THE DRACONIS MEMORIA

The Waking Fire

The Legion of Flame

The Empire of Ashes

Sandrunners - A Draconis Memoria Short Story

THE RAVEN'S SHADOW SERIES

Blood Song

Tower Lord

Queen of Fire

THE RAVEN'S BLADE DUOLOGY

The Wolf's Call

The Black Song

THE SEVEN SWORDS SERIES

A Pilgrimage of Swords

The Kraken's Tooth

City of Songs

THE SLAB CITY BLUES SERIES

Slab City Blues: The Collected Stories

For information on where to find these books, free audio downloads, news and general wittering about stuff he likes, check out Anthony's website at: anthonyryan.net

Short Fiction from

THE WORLD OF RAVEN'S SHADOW

ANTHONY RYAN

SONGS OF THE DARK

Cover Illustration: Kevin Zamir Goeke
Cover/Interior Design: STK•Kreations
Interior Illustrations: Anthony Ryan

Contents

INTRODUCTION

On January 5th, 2012, I published my first novel, *Blood Song*, on the Amazon Kindle Store with, it must be said, no real expectations at all. I had been writing stories since my early teens and writing novels since my early twenties, enjoying the level of success typical of the novice writer, i.e. none. Calling *Blood Song* my first novel is, in reality, something of a misnomer. My first novel was actually a pretty terrible gangster crime epic set in 1980s London that fully deserved all the rejection it received from the publishing industry. Fortunately, this was in the pre-internet, pre-cloud storage, pre-'you can never forget or lose anything' age so there are no copies of this execrable opus hanging around to embarrass me now. The fact was that I had written a novel without really knowing how and the results were predictably awful. The more important fact, which I can only appreciate with the hindsight of twenty-plus years, is that I had written a novel. Bad as it was, I had actually completed a three hundred page story, learning a great deal in the process, the most salient lessons of all being:

Writing is hard.
No book ever writes itself.
(Also, try never to run out of tea, but that might just be me).

So, as I said, no real expectations, except that with *Blood Song* I had a dim, nebulous suspicion that I might just have… something.

I've been asked many times about the origins of this novel. What or who inspired Vaelin Al Sorna and his brothers in the Sixth Order? Where did the world come from? Why does he carry his sword on his back because I saw a YouTube video that says that's a stupid way to carry a sword? The honest answers to these questions are always somewhat underwhelming: I don't know exactly. Reading a lot of history. Because it looks cool.

The exact moment of inspiration for a story is never easy to pin down, and often impossible. What I do know is that it first began to gel in the post-911 era when notions of religious conflict where at the forefront of my mind and I had spent much of the previous decade reading a great deal of fantasy. Add my abiding love of history to the mix, stew for a few years and what would become the world of the *Raven's Shadow* series was born.

Six and a half years is a long time to spend writing a book, in fact it's a long time to spend doing anything. During the course of writing *Blood Song* there were protracted periods where I wrote very little or nothing at all. The pressures of having a job and living a life will do that, although I probably could have spent a little less time playing video games or bingeing Buffy and Angel box-sets on VHS (an ancient mechanical contrivance fashioned from magnetic tape and plastic, ask your parents or Google it). Did I mention this was a while ago?

Despite my many absences (and bouts of laziness), something always kept bringing me back to Vaelin's story. Other books had come and gone over the years, most unfinished it must be said, but this one stuck around. It took me a while to figure out why and in the end it came down to two things: curiosity as to what would happen next and an increasingly deep sense of connection to the world and characters I had created.

Other writers have spoken about the curious sense of discovery that comes from writing fiction. Put simply, it doesn't feel like you're making it up (even though you are), it feels like you're finding it out. So it was with *Blood Song*. I did have a plan of sorts when I started. It was about a page long and I didn't look at it again throughout all the years it took to finish the book. So, it could be said I knew what would happen in the end, except I didn't. Ultimately, I changed it because the original ending just didn't make sense. Also, if the ending came as a surprise to me, there was a decent chance it might also surprise the reader.

What followed is a familiar tale that requires little re-telling: author sends manuscript to numerous agents, author receives numerous rejection letters, author decides to take a chance on self-publishing. The seven years since have been a remarkably transformative experience that enabled me to become a full-time writer and sell over a million books worldwide, all largely because a lot of readers became as engaged with Vaelin's world as I did.

The unexpectedly swift success of *Blood Song* led to a publishing contract for a trilogy, the second volume of which brings us to the genesis of the stories you, dear reader, now hold in your hopefully un-sweaty hands. I had vaguely pondered the notion of writing short fiction set in the Raven's Shadow world but it was only when my UK editor raised the possibility of including addition material in *Tower Lord*, book two of the trilogy, that the first serious ideas began to come together.

Stories are a bit like an itch at first. You scratch them with a few moments attention every now and then but the itch only grows fiercer the more you scratch. As a consequence, the prospect of writing the suggested shorter works seemed more like a necessity as time went by, as the only way to banish this particular kind of itch is to excise the cause. Once written, the itch goes away. Naturally, it'll soon be replaced by another but that's the lot of being a writer. In this case the scratching produced a novella, *The Lord Collector*, and a short story, *A Duel of Evils*, of which more in the author's note that precedes each story.

For various reasons neither story actually made it into the Tower Lord hardcover which left me free to publish them elsewhere. The response from readers was sufficiently encouraging to set me thinking about other stories which would allow a deeper exploration of characters who hadn't received as much screen time in the main series as they perhaps deserved. This led me to write (when time allowed) two more novellas, *The Lady of Crows* and *Many Are the Dead.*

The stories are presented here in the order in which they fit into the timeline of the overall *Raven's Shadow* narrative rather than the order in which they appeared in print. Therefore, *A Duel of Evils* is placed first by virtue of the events it depicts taking place centuries before everything else. At present, I have only vague ideas for further short works in this world, but I'd be very surprised if there weren't more itches to scratch sooner or later.

Anthony Ryan, June 2019

Author's Note

The genesis of "A Duel of Evils" came from a historical anecdote related at one point in *Tower Lord*, Book 2 of the Raven's Shadow trilogy. Lord Verniers, a historian of some repute, briefly describes the fall of the city state of Kethia as an example of heroic leadership. I had originally wanted this section to be a bit longer but kept it short for pacing reasons. With *Tower Lord* complete and off to my editor, I started thinking about how Verniers would have approached telling the tale of Kethia's fall. History has been a passion of mine since childhood and it was a fun idea to present the imaginary history of the Raven's Shadow world through the prism of an historical text rather than the conventions of prose fiction. In doing so I drew a great deal of inspiration from the Punic Wars, which climaxed in one of the first true city-battles in history when mighty Carthage was raised to the ground after a protracted street-to-street and house-to-house assault by Roman legionaries. I also wanted to convey the depth of the backstory that comes to fruition in the main trilogy, so fans of the series will surely find a few nods to future events in the tale of Kethia's dark fate.

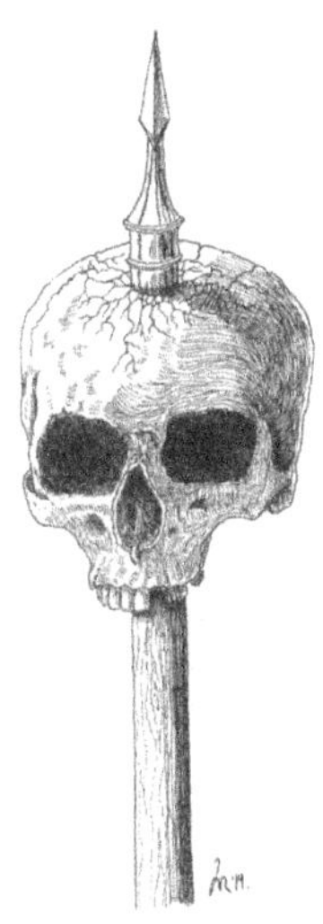

A DUEL OF EVILS
- OR -
THE FALL OF KETHIA

Being a true and unbiased account of the destruction of that city compiled at the order of Emperor Aluran Maxtor Selsus (blessed by the Gods for all the ages) by Lord Verniers Alishe Someren, Imperial Chronicler and First of the Learned.

In preparing this history I have been honoured to follow My Emperor's wise instruction to compose an account free from the vagaries of myth and legend, those cursed twins destined to forever obstruct the path of the rational scholar in his quest for truth. However, as you will see, all surviving sources relating to the events described below are riven, one might say sullied, by references to the bizarre and outright impossible. It is a singular mystery why an event of such import to the Volarian Empire, a culture renowned for promoting rationality with a vigour bordering on mania, should produce witnesses so lacking in that very quality. It is, of course, probable that these witnesses were delusional, the extremes of war having been known to strip reason from even the most stable mind. However, I have chosen not to exclude their more outlandish reportage, as it has ever been my contention that the perception of an event is at least as important as its true substance.

In considering how and why the once mighty city-state of Kethia came to its dreadful end, we must first understand its origins. The bulk of early Volarian history exists as a melange of legend and folklore, largely revolving around the deeds of various improbably mighty heroes, their myriad battles and betrayals performed in service to the now extinct Volarian pantheon. Much of the physical evidence to emerge from this period is limited to indecipherable tablet inscriptions and somewhat lurid illustrations from the few artifacts to survive, mostly pottery fragments and incomplete mosaics. The one unifying theme to these disparate images is that of destruction; cities burn, hordes of people are put to the sword by inhuman armies clad in blood-red armour, and beasts of unlikely configuration spring from the bowels of the earth to wreak all manner of havoc. Whilst these images are most certainly exaggerations or complete inventions, taken as a whole they do indicate that the landmass which now comprises the bulk of the Volarian Empire was once witness to a struggle of near genocidal proportions, a struggle that can only be said to have abated when recognisable settlements begin to reappear, generating trade and correspondence in the process.

The earliest reference to employ the modern name for Kethia dates back some sixteen hundred years, a full century in fact before the birth of our own (glorious and surely eternal) Empire. My prolonged sojourn through the imperial archives unearthed several ancient cargo manifests relating to the purchase and exchange of goods with a settlement situated on the western coast of what is now the Volarian province of Eskethia. The record of trade with this settlement increases in volume over successive centuries to the point where they attain sufficient wealth and sophistication to secure a formal treaty with Emperor Rahlun, the tenth chosen to sit on the Alpiran throne. The details of the treaty are fairly standard; an agreement to maintain existing tariffs and mutual protection of vessels from piracy. But it is clear from the preamble that by this point the Kethians were already engaged in a bitter rivalry with the port of Volar, situated over three hundred miles to the northeast.

A brief glance at any map of the north Volarian coast provides ample explanation as to why these two cities might come into conflict. Volar sits at the end of a long, narrow estuary known as the Cut of Lokar. A relatively easy waterway to navigate according to my seafaring sources, but providing markedly less ease of access to the Boraelin trade routes than that offered by Kethia, which also benefited from rich surrounding farmlands producing wine and cotton in substantial quantities. The decades preceding the Kethian treaty with Alpira had seen numerous border skirmishes and at least one major battle as the two ports competed for trade and prestige. However, events were to take a decidedly more serious turn with the advent of Volarian hegemony over much of the continent, a period known to history as The Forging

Age. Aided by a sophisticated military doctrine, and a ruthlessly practical approach to both diplomacy and warfare, the nascent Volarian Empire had become a recognisable entity some eight centuries ago, at which point our tale begins in earnest.

To understand the subsequent course of events requires a certain appreciation of both the differences and similarities between Kethian and Volarian culture. It is not my intention to laud one as superior to the other, as it will become clear to My Emperor that both peoples appear somewhat bestial in comparison to the unmatched excellence of Alpiran society. For example, each culture employed a code of justice that can only be described as barbaric; every crime, regardless of pettiness, was (and remains so in modern Volaria) punishable by execution, more serious criminals being required to undergo a series of prescribed tortures before receiving the, no doubt, blessed release of death. However, similar brutality between the two adversaries was not matched by similar governance. I will spare you, Sire, a recounting of the long and ugly history of the peculiar Volarian institution of slavery, except to relate that by the dawn of its ascendancy, slavery sat at the heart of all aspects of Volarian society.

Volaria, as My Emperor knows, is ruled by a council drawn from the wealthiest citizens in the empire. In modern times the path to Council-man status is a mysterious one, wreathed in labyrinthine intrigue and a complex system of patronage. In fact, it is never clear to outsiders who sits on the council, as it appears some families have occupied their seats for generations without troubling themselves to change the name to match the current occupant. But, in its earlier incarnation entry to the council was simply a matter of amassing wealth equivalent to the value of one hundred thousand slaves. The number of council seats throughout the ages is therefore a useful indicator of the overall size of the empire, or at least its slave population. By the advent of unrestricted war against Kethia, the council consisted of ten members and its control over the growing Volarian dominions was near absolute.

Kethia, by contrast, had no need of councils. For, like the savages inhabiting the damp land to the north, Kethia had a king. However, unlike the north-men, the king of Kethia did not ascend by virtue of birth but at the whim of his people. Every four years all men over the age of thirty, owning house or livestock, would gather at an impressive structure in the city's centre. The name of this building has been lost but, if the illustrations of Kethia's ruins are to be believed, it would have been a remarkable sight, standing thirty feet tall and ringed by marble columns some five feet in diameter. Every man would be given a single black stone and a vase would be placed before each of the candidates aspiring to kingship. Each man would come forward and reach his hand into every vase, keeping his fist closed when he drew it out, so none would know into which vase he had dropped his stone. Once all the gathered men had cast their stones, each vase would be emptied and the stones counted in full view of the assembly. The candidate whose vase contained the most stones would ascend to the throne.

Any man of suitable age and property could present himself for kingship, though the Kethian scholar and diplomat Karvalev provides an insight into the kind of individual who stood the best chance of success:

> *No farmer ever won the throne. Nor a drover, nor a smith, nor a wheelwright. Our kings have ever been merchants, or the*

sons of merchants. Or warriors of great renown, or the sons of warriors of great renown. And none have ever known poverty. Kethian mothers wishing to shame indolent sons will often resort to an old saying, 'Keep on like this and there'll never be a stone in your vase.'

Karvalev was fated, or cursed, to witness much of what follows, so naturally his account forms a principal source for this history. Many of his works have been lost to the ages but he appears to have been widely read in his lifetime, ensuring a considerable portion of his writings were copied and distributed, apparently to his great annoyance: '*The whole world benefits from the art of this poor scholar who must bargain for ink.*'

Volarian sources for this period are sparse and those that survive often biased to the point of uselessness, except to illustrate the depth of hatred many felt towards Kethia. *They are thieves*, one Volarian merchant wrote to a trading partner in far off Verehl. *Every chance for profit is stolen by guile and graft. A Kethian will sell at a loss if it means denying profit to a Volarian.*

However, it is Karvalev who provides the clearest illustration of Volarian antipathy to their wealthy neighbours at this time. The author of several fruitless missions to Volar in search of some form of peaceful accommodation, his final attempt produced this enlightening account of a brief meeting with an unnamed Council-man:

He stood regarding me with eyes of ice and face of stone, clad in robes of red silk and flanked on either side by guards with drawn swords. His every aspect seemed to convey the sense of a man suffering the worst indignity. Intent on my mission, I began to relate my message whereupon he spoke: 'The daggertooth does not bargain with the goat.'

Karvalev goes on to describe being seized by the Councilman's guards and marched back to his ship, his every step assailed by a baying mob *crammed into the streets to spit their bile at the hated Kethian.* Clearly, war with Volaria was becoming inevitable.

It should not be surmised, however, that trade was the only cause for antagonism between these rivals. Whilst they spoke much the same language and shared the same pantheon of gods, they pursued wildly differing modes of worship. As My Emperor will no doubt recall from my earlier treatise, *The Land of Nightmares—A Portrait of Pre-Imperial Volaria*, the long-vanished Volarian pantheon remains one of the most aggravating points of inquiry for the modern scholar, for only the priesthood were permitted to know the names of the gods. The common worshipper would look to the heroes of legend, quasi-godlike figures themselves, for inspiration and guidance, but direct appeals for divine intervention required the assistance of the priesthood, on payment of an offering of suitable value. Kethia, however, stood alone among the cultures to share this pantheon in having divested itself of a priesthood a century before its destruction. The Kethians, it is said, had committed the ultimate blasphemy in actually naming the gods and allowing any citizen, even women, to appeal to them directly. It is unsurprising, therefore, that the loudest Volarian voices to call for war came from the priesthood.

One of the few Volarian sources to offer a remotely unbiased account of the war comes from one Sevarik Entril, a junior officer at the war's commencement, set to rise to battalion commander by its end. Entril wrote a series of letters to his wife throughout the conflict, unwittingly providing a valuable narrative of the campaign. It seems he entrusted these missives to a neutral sea captain who was in fact a spy in Alpiran service, hence the presence of copies in the Imperial Archives. Entril records his entire division being paraded at the base of one of the tall towers common to the long since destroyed Volarian temple complexes:

> *A priest stood atop the tower, calling out in the language of the gods, his words translated by one of his brothers who stood before us. His brother had been blessed, he told us, by a vision from not one, but every god in the heavens: 'Kethia will tumble in flame and Volaria rise on its ashes!' As was custom the priest then cast himself from the tower, his life's work being complete and the gods sure to catch his soul as he fell. We raised our swords and cheered ourselves hoarse as his empty body shattered on the ground in bloody homage.*

An additional point of particular odium to the Volarians was the Kethian practice of child sacrifice. As already noted, these cultures were evenly matched in their barbarity but this facet of Kethian society does make it difficult to express much sympathy for their eventual fate. That such a practice took place, and is not a figment of Volarian prejudice, is confirmed by Karvalev and several other contemporary sources. It appears sacrifices occurred only on the ascension of a new king, Karvalev's account of one ceremony conveying a chilling sense of normalcy:

As the king took his throne he reached into a great glass bowl filled with wooden pegs onto which the name of every child in Kethia had been inscribed. No child was excluded, regardless of station, for what parent could forgo such an honour? Having chosen, the king stood and called out the name of the blessed child. On this occasion it was a boy of perhaps eight years, the son of a shipwright who proudly carried him forward, the boy bouncing on his father's shoulders, laughing happily. The king greeted the boy with a kiss to the forehead before leading him, knife in hand, to the font from which the gods would drink come the moon-rise. The gods have ever blessed us, but they are also ever hungry.

It was the ascension of this particular king that provided the spark to war, for this king was a warrior, known to history as Tavurek and described by Karvalev as *the apex of Kethia. His stature and prowess in battle matched by a mind keener than the sharpest blade. It seemed as if the gods saw our need and sent Tavurek from a prior age, for he was not made as other men.* The Volarians were very thorough in destroying all images and statues of Tavurek, so the accuracy of Karvalev's description cannot be judged, although Entril's portrait of the doomed warrior king is in broad agreement with most Volarian sources:

He towered over his men as they advanced on us, unhelmed and arms bared, wielding a great two-bladed axe as if it weighed no more than a twig. A fury of muscle and steel, inspiring those that followed him to unhesitant sacrifice.

We know little of Tavurek's early life, though Karvalev intimates he was born to a wealthy trading family and spent much of his boyhood at sea. There are various garish and frankly absurd legends surrounding Tavurek's seafaring days, from abduction and seduction at the hands of exotic island queens, to savage battles with pirates where it's said he learned his deadly skills. Surely the most outlandish of these fables is the future king's epic battle with a giant, many-tentacled monstrosity from the ocean depths. Naturally, he emerged the victor but with wounds so severe he lay near death for several days. Whatever the truth of these tales, it is clear that by the time Tavurek rose to prominence he was both widely travelled and physically formidable. To the Kethians, however, his most important virtue was not his martial prowess but his passionate hatred of the Volarians.

Karvalev has left us a record of Tavurek's first public address to the Kethian populace. Allowing for some poetic phrasing which can almost certainly be ascribed to the scholar's hand, the speech provides an unambiguous insight into Tavurek's virulent anti-Volarian stance:

> *Can they even be called men? These beasts, these curs, these wretches? Where is their honour, I ask you? Where is their courage? Where is their religion? They call us blasphemers. They say we dishonour the gods whilst their every act is an abomination. There is more religion in my dog!*

References to the gods abound in Tavurek's speeches. A Kethian ambassador to Alpira named him as the most devout man ever to sit on the throne, and we can say with some certainty that the new king considered his mission to be a divine one. *They have called to me, my friend*, Karvalev has him saying one evening as they shared a sparse meal of berries and water, it being the custom for Kethian kings to live frugally. *The gods . . . I have heard their voice, and they name me their instrument on earth. The Volarian filth must be wiped away.*

This does, of course, raise the possibility that Tavurek may have been insane, or at least partly delusional. If so, it was a shared delusion, for his people never wavered in their support, even unto death.

The first serious clash came barely two months after Tavurek's ascension to the throne when he led a fleet of warships directly into the Cut of Lokar. The king's express intention was to choke off Volarian commerce, weakening the city in advance of an invasion. This proved a wildly ambitious notion. It appears the Volarians may have had some forewarning of Tavurek's intentions, for his fleet soon found itself attacked in front and rear. A Verehlan sailor was witness to the subsequent debacle and gave the following account to an Alpiran associate several months later:

> *It all happened at night and at first I thought the gods had set both sky and sea afire. I saw many men tumbling from burning ships, alight and screaming as the Volarian mangonels did their work, the fireballs falling like a fiery rain. The Cut is rich in white-nosed sharks, small but vicious buggers they are, like to swarm on you in packs. There was so much for them to feed on it seemed the sea was boiling. By morning the shore was thick with wrecks, some Volarian but mostly Kethian, and the sharks were still busy feeding.*

Tavurek somehow managed to survive the calamity and return to Kethia with the remnants of his fleet. Oddly, for a king who had authored such a calamity he was greeted with universal acclaim and there is no record of any dissent among the Kethian populace. *He has a way about him*, Karvalev said of Tavurek in the aftermath of the disaster. *A means of capturing the souls of all men. I have never truly understood it, but even I find no room for doubt in my heart. I have never been more certain; this man is meant to lead us.*

After such naked aggression it was inevitable that the Volarian counterblow would be swift. Kethia was soon blockaded, the Volarian fleet forcing all ships to seek harbour elsewhere regardless of flag, even sinking a dozen neutral vessels when their captains proved deaf to intimidation. However, the main blow would be delivered by land rather than sea. There are various estimates of the size of the Volarian army that marched into Kethian territory barely three months later, from Karvalev's surely exaggerated half a million to Entril's more restrained but still barely credible two hundred thousand. However, it was surely a formidable force, possibly the largest army to take the field during the Forging Age, and certainly the most experienced.

The vile practice of employing slaves in Volarian armies would not take root for another four centuries, so their soldiers of this period were all free men. The basic Volarian military unit consisted of the infantry battalion with an official complement of one thousand men, though many would remain under strength in the field as battle and sickness inevitably took a toll. Most soldiers were conscripts aged between sixteen and twenty-five, their numbers swelled for the Kethian campaign by reservists called back to the army by emergency Council decree. Most battalions were a mix of youthful conscripts and veterans who had chosen a career in the army in preference to the often dire uncertainties of Volarian civilian life; the practice of enslaving impoverished debtors had been enshrined in law by this point, and life for those without wealthy family connections could be highly unpleasant. At the very least the army offered some measure of security. *Three meals a day, a whore twice a week and a battle every now and then to sate the belly and fill the purse with loot*, Entril records his senior sergeant saying. *The recipe for a happy soldier, Honoured Commander.*

Although life in the army may have been preferable to poverty, standards of discipline were so rigid as to border on sadism. The most lenient punishment prescribed by the Volarian military code consisted of ten strokes of a barbed whip, usually meted out for such crimes as an unpolished breastplate or tarnished belt buckle. Unauthorised drunkenness earned fifteen strokes, and disrespect to an officer twenty, which may well have been fatal for many recipients. The harshest punishment was reserved for deserters, who could expect to have their hands and feet cut off and the stumps coated in pitch before being set upon by a pack of slave-hounds. A particularly cruel, but undoubtedly effective disciplinary measure took the form of collective punishment for battalions deemed to have acted in a cowardly fashion. One hundred men would be chosen by lot and obliged to lead the charge in the next engagement, completely naked and armed only with a single sword. It is scarcely surprising, therefore, that those who fought the Volarians often spoke of their unmatched bravery.

In addition to the standard battalions the Volarians also maintained a number of elite, all-veteran formations, each with a long list of battle honours and bearing a name rather than the bland number afforded other units. These names were mostly derived from the heroes of legend, 'Livella's Blades' and 'The Sons of Korsev' being perhaps the most celebrated, having fought in every major engagement of the Forging Age without ever tasting defeat. In the struggle that followed, however, even such formidable soldiers would come to learn that invincibility in war is a myth.

Whilst the bulk of the Volarian army consisted of infantry, they did maintain strong cavalry contingents, mostly drawn from the sons of the wealthy merchant class, and a highly effective, perhaps crucial corps of military engineers. Via a remarkably swift series of bridging operations, it was these engineers that enabled the Volarians to cover more than one hundred miles of Kethian territory within the first five days of the campaign, all without meeting serious opposition or word of the invasion reaching Tavurek, now licking his wounds in Kethia. Once word arrived, however, the king lost no time in responding.

Kethia had a small standing army of perhaps twenty thousand men, though its strength had been severely denuded by the Battle of the Cut. To augment this meagre force Kethia had instituted a long-standing tradition of hiring mercenaries from far and wide, a practice that had increased tenfold with the advent of war. So it is unsurprising that the picture Karvalev paints of the force that marched out to confront the Volarians is a cosmopolitan one, as well as shedding more light on Tavurek's uncanny ability to inspire loyalty in even the most hardened heart:

> *Archers from the shores of the Jarven Sea took their place alongside dark-skinned slingers from Vehrel. Lancers from*

Atethia called 'brother' to savage pale-skinned axe-men from the northern mountains. And all bowed low to mighty Tavurek, giving solemn oath to follow him to the fire pit and fight the Dermos themselves should he so ask. That this oath was truly spoken, none can doubt, for these men no longer received pay. They came to us as mercenaries but stayed as loyal Kethians, and as such they died.

As ever, sources vary in estimating the size of the Kethian force, but it was almost certainly outnumbered by at least two to one. Despite the disparity in strength, the clash that followed four days later was anything but one-sided. The two armies met at a point some thirty miles from Kethia and barely a mile inland from the southern bank of the Cut of Lokar. The Volarians had wisely opted to keep close to the shore in order to enable constant resupply by their fleet, another factor in the swiftness of their march. Entril describes the battlefield as:

. . . merely rolling farmland, devoid of hill or landmark that might afford it a name. The Kethians came on in a solid mass, eschewing manoeuvre or feint for a charge aimed straight at the centre of our line. When the day was done we had a name for the field, The Spoiled Land, for what could grow on such corrupted earth?

Entril's own account of the fighting is a confused morass of close-quarters encounters with men he describes as *maddened beasts, void of reason or fear*. Therefore, we are obliged to refer to the report of the overall Volarian commander, one General Derilev, for a description of the battle as a whole. Derilev appears to have been an experienced officer of some renown, though his handling of the campaign speaks more of basic competence than inspired leadership. His account must be treated with considerable caution, conveying as it does the sense of a long-serving officer employing outlandish claims to avoid responsibility for near disaster:

> *There are several unquestionable reports from my most seasoned veterans firmly asserting that they saw Kethian soldiers continuing to fight on after suffering mortal wounds. Clearly, we have underestimated the vileness of our enemy, for it is my belief that they could only have effected a penetration of our centre through unnatural means. When the dead are seen to fight there can be only one conclusion: the Dermos are risen anew and now make their home in Kethia.*

The Dermos, My Emperor will surely recall from *Land of Nightmares*, are the legendary enemies of both gods and men, said to reside in a fiery pit beneath the earth. Derilev goes on to describe how the Kethian breakthrough was stemmed by the vaunted Sons of Korsev who threw themselves into the breach at the last moment, sacrificing two-thirds of their number but fighting with such ferocity that the Volarian line had time to reorganise. Derilev expends considerable ink in describing his deftly executed counterstroke, pulling back the battalions in the centre whilst reinforcing his flanks and sending his cavalry against the Kethian rear, thereby inflicting a crushing defeat. This must all be considered at best an exaggeration and at worst a desperate lie, for Karvalev describes the Kethian army retreating to the city in good order, albeit badly mauled. The length of the subsequent siege is also evidence that, regardless of Derilev's claims, Tavurek retained considerable military strength in the aftermath of defeat. It is also significant that Derilev would soon find himself replaced by a new commander. I searched in vain for further mention of him in any history, although the Council's notorious treatment of unsuccessful generals is probably ample explanation for his absence.

Entril wrote to his wife shortly after the battle, relating that he had lost a third of his men *most to battle, a few to madness*, and found himself elevated to battalion commander as all the officers senior to him were now dead. If losses on such a scale were typical it must have been a badly shaken army that laid siege to Kethia, but lay siege they did.

The Volarians were no strangers to siegecraft, the Forging Age being rich in tales of their expertise and patience in reducing enemy fortresses and cities. Initially, it appeared Kethia would be little different. Entril relates how the newly appointed Volarian commander gave a rousing speech to the assembled army soon after the siege began:

> *'A month of spadework, men,' he promised us, 'to earn a lifetime's worth of loot.'*

This new commander emerges as an even more obscure figure than the unfortunate Derilev, known to history only by the less-than-flattering title Entril has his men affording him when his optimistic speeches became tiresome—'The Lying Ape.' In fact it was more than two months before the first direct assault, The Ape having grown impatient at the meagre progress made by Volarian engineers as they inched their trenches closer to the walls. Over ten thousand men were ordered into the attack, charging forward with scaling ladders at three different places in the hope of dividing the defence sufficiently to allow a breakthrough. It proved an unmitigated disaster, barely three thousand men straggling back come nightfall. Entril described the survivors as:

> *Wide-eyed and black with soot. Babbling of unkillable enemies and the Kethian king appearing at will in their midst, wielding an axe that cut through armour as if it was rice paper. The Ape gave the coward's punishment to one in every ten, but the fear provoked by their rantings took root, and fear is the worst plague for any army.*

Clearly possessed of a stubborn streak, The Ape tried again three days later, doubling the size of the assault force and placing his elite battalions in the vanguard. Entril's men were ordered to support an assault on the main gate by the Spears of Morivek, one of the most celebrated formations in Volarian history. A palpable sense of shock, not to mention mystification at his own survival, is discernible in his next letter home:

> *Assailed from above by a ceaseless rain of arrow and rock, the Spears clawed their way onto the battlements on either side of the gate. How they fought, my dear—I do not have the words—it seemed as if I gazed upon men fashioned into rock, the Kethians breaking on them like a storm-driven tide. As*

ordered, we charged forward with our great iron-headed ram, pounding and pounding at the gate as the Spears held the wall above. All for nothing.

Entril describes his men breaking through the gate but finding their way blocked by a deep pit filled with what appeared to be water, revealed in fact as oil when a single torch fell from above *and soon all was flame*. Entril tried to rally his men but their waning courage shattered completely when the Kethians on the battlements above began to throw bodies into their midst:

. . . bodies in Volarian armour each bearing the crest of the Spears of Morivek, and every one was headless. The men ran, heedless of my exhortations, and soon I stood alone at the shattered gate. Knowing death would come swiftly, I straightened my back and resolved to meet my end with the dignity due my rank. On emerging from the gatehouse I forced myself to pause and raise a defiant gaze to the Kethians on the walls. I saw only one man, face lost to the gloom of gathering night, though I knew him by now. He looked at me for a long time, hands resting on the haft of his great axe, then raised his arm and pointed a finger at our own lines.

Curiously, Entril appears to have suffered no punishment as a result of his men's cowardice. This is perhaps due to the fact that The Ape was found dead by his own hand the following morning. This, of course, necessitated the appointment of a new commander, and he proved to be a man with a surfeit of patience.

Vartek Lovril remains the most celebrated figure of the Forging Age, and one of the few luminaries of the pre-imperial period not to be largely expunged from the visual and historical record during the Great Cleansing. His reputation had already begun to grow by the advent of the final Kethian war, but it was a renown built entirely on personal courage and fighting skill rather than command. Vartek had spent his early years in the northern port of Varral, until recently an independent city state. Vartek's father had been one of the principal conspirators in the coup which had unseated the previous regime and opened the way for Volarian annexation.

Being a third son, and therefore unlikely to receive more than a paltry inheritance, Vartek had enlisted in the Volarian army at an early age. This appears to have been done without his father's approval, for Vartek entered the ranks as a common soldier whereas his social standing should have been sufficient to secure a junior officer's commission. However, the myriad opportunities for distinction offered by the Forging Age soon saw Vartek's courage and skill vaunted throughout the empire, ensuring swift promotion. I'm sure My Emperor would find a complete list of all the battles and feats of martial prowess ascribed to Vartek somewhat tedious, so suffice it to say that he was quite possibly the most dangerous man to ever wear a Volarian uniform.

By the time of the Kethian war we find him commanding an elite battalion of amphibious troops, The Sea Eagles. He is known to have won considerable acclaim in the Battle of the Cut but seems to have played little part in the land campaign until the demise of The Ape. His exact age at this time is not known but can be reasonably estimated at thirty to thirty-three, the youngest officer ever to hold General rank.

For a man of such fearsome reputation, it seems odd that many contemporary descriptions of Vartek paint a surprising picture; *A more kindly soul I never met*, Entril says of him. *To win his friendship was to know brotherhood and generosity for all your days, for he never forsook a friend.* Entril's opinion may well be coloured by the fact that his subsequent fortunes were greatly improved by Vartek's patronage, but this remains a curious portrait of a man believed to have dispatched over a hundred enemies in personal combat. However, it appears Entril's admiration was far from unique, for all accounts are unanimous is recording the extraordinary loyalty and affection he enjoyed amongst his men, something Karvalev dolefully recorded in one of his last missives to escape the city: *They have their own Tavurek now. Our fate is surely sealed.*

Vartek is also unique in the ranks of notable Volarians in owning no more than one slave throughout his life, a woman captured during one of his campaigns against the northern mountain tribes. Her name has been lost but Entril describes her as:

> *. . . pale of skin and long of limb, with a pleasant aspect showing little of her savage origins. My General would allow no harshness to her, and his few private moments were always spent in her company, from which he seemed to draw considerable fortitude. Some even said he took counsel from her, but that is, of course, an absurdity.*

Vartek's first act was to pardon all soldiers condemned to the coward's punishment before embarking upon a wholesale reorganisation of the army. Ineffective commanders were dismissed and given a chance to redeem their failure via service in the ranks. The fact that most chose to do so is a measure of the opprobrium Volarian society affords to military disgrace. Under-strength battalions were merged and placed under the control of officers promoted on merit alone. Hence, former commanders found themselves taking orders from their sergeants. Entril in particular profited from the changes in winning promotion to the post of General's Eye, a highly influential role which saw him take charge of the army's intelligence apparatus and enjoy first place in the ranks of Vartek's advisors.

Vartek's most important changes, however, were tactical in nature. The naval blockade was strengthened yet further as some Kethian ships still continued to slip past the cordon. The siege lines were placed under sole control of the army's chief of engineers and new engines were shipped in from Volaria. Vartek also forbade any further frontal assaults, Volarian offensive action now consisting of digging thirty yards of trench a day whilst their ballista discouraged interference from Kethian archers. *Every siege is an epic tale*, Vartek said to Entril as they toured the entrenchments, *and this has been but the opening verse.*

For six long months the Volarians dug away at the loose red soil of the Eskethian plane, weaving a network of trenches around the low rise on which the city sat. In modern times the Volarians are strict in their control of foreign visitors, forbidding them to venture from the confines of their port of arrival unless under close escort, and then only with special permission from a Council-man. Due to such constraints My Emperor will, I'm sure, forgive my failure to undertake a personal inspection of the ruins of Old Kethia. However, I was able to pay a Volarian of some artistic skill to provide sketches of the site, duly appended for your perusal. My Emperor will no doubt perceive the fact that the siege lines remain visible today as shallow depressions in the earth, deepening into gullies where they meet the now vanished walls, for it was here that Vartek's patience bore fruit.

The Volarian engineers eschewed the traditional approach to siegecraft, whereby the engines would cast stones at the walls until a breach of sufficient width had been achieved, in favour of undermining their foundations. Unwilling to risk an assault at a single point, Vartek ordered the construction of four such tunnels, two in the south and two in the north. This necessitated extending the siege by another two months, engineers and slaves working to exhaustion as they chipped away at the foundations, replacing ancient stone with timber and close-packed bundles of oil-soaked cotton.

The great attack came on a day normally reserved to commemorate the final demise of the legendary warrior-maiden Livella. The Volarians continue to celebrate this day under its modern guise of a late summer festival of typically bloody spectacles and sword races. In antiquity, however, it was an uncharacteristic day of peace where all men would name each other brothers and all women sisters. Throughout their dreadful history, no Volarian had ever fought a battle on Livella's Day, a fact Vartek no doubt hoped would count in his favour.

Entril relates how, come the midnight hour, the general had the camp-followers and slaves caper about and raise their voices in song, giving all appearance of a festival in full swing. Meanwhile, the assault battalions gathered in silence to the north and south and the engineers crept through the tunnels with torches in hand. Entril provides the following account of the subsequent assault:

> *Vartek took his place at the head of The Sea Eagles who had threatened mutiny if not permitted to attack at the general's side. The engineers could be seen running from the tunnels as plumes of black smoke were now rising. Then, with a guttural roar, flame vomited from the tunnel mouths and a great tremor shifted the earth beneath our feet. Every man drew breath, eyes locked on the walls as countless prayers ascended to the gods. For a second it seemed all had been in vain, for the walls stood, as whole and unmoving as ever. But then the gods saw fit to answer us, two great breaches, each twenty feet wide, appearing in an instant of tumbled stone and rising dust. My General won his name that night, the Spear-point, for he charged the breach with such speed The Sea Eagles had to sprint to keep up. A great cry arose as the remaining battalions surged forward, fierce and hungry, for who now could doubt victory would be won this night? Surely the city, and all its spoils, would be ours come the dawn.*

It appears likely the Volarians were expecting the conclusion of this siege to conform to prior experience; a furious final battle to eliminate the remaining defenders followed by an extended period of loot, rapine, and wholesale slaughter. If so, it was an expectation quickly dispelled, for on clearing the breaches, Vartek's men found no Kethians waiting to sell their lives in a valiant last stand. Instead they found only more walls.

Tavurek has not been idle, Entril wrote to his wife the next day, a weary bitterness evident in his words. *Whilst we tunnelled he built, thick walls confront our men at every turn. These are more a maze than a barrier, their course winding and their height varied. Men become confused when attempting to navigate them, and when an assault is made at one point it is invariably overlooked by another. The Kethian archers have grown skilled with ceaseless practice and their slingers are surely descended from the Dermos. Today I saw a man take a lead shot through the eye from over forty paces.*

This 'Battle of the Maze,' as it became known, seems to have dragged on for several days, the Volarians achieving some breakthroughs at considerable cost only to find another set of walls confronting them a few streets on. As General's Eye, Entril had the task of attempting to find Tavurek amongst the chaos of continuing battle, compiling numerous reports, each one seemingly more outlandish than the other:

> *He leaped into our ranks, sliced the heads from four men then turned to mist before we could cut him down . . . He moved from rooftop to rooftop, leaping farther than any man could and loosing arrows at us in mid-flight . . . I saw him turn our own sergeant against us, just reached out and touched him, and this man began hacking down soldiers he had served with for years . . .*

On the fourth day Vartek seems to have suffered an uncharacteristic loss of military ardour, perhaps due to the growing butcher's bill—Entril estimates Volarian losses to date at some three thousand men—or simple fatigue. In any case, he ordered a halt to further attacks and retired to his tent with only his slave woman for company. There is a certain discomfort in Entril's tone as he tells of *raised voices in the General's tent, the woman heard to be pleading with him, both angry and tearful. 'You know what must be done here. You know what commands that thing. Falter now and watch the world burn!'*

Whether the words of a mere slave had any effect on Vartek is a matter of conjecture, but it appears he emerged from his tent the following morning with a renewed spirit. Fresh troops were sent into the maze, attacking any identified weak spots, all battalion commanders being ordered to maintain pressure without pause. Vartek himself then mustered the surviving Sea Eagles and took to ship along with some five thousand men, *every vessel so laden with troops the waves threatened to swamp the rails* according to Entril. As battle raged in the city, Vartek sailed out to rendezvous with the blockading Volarian fleet, calling all ships into close order and launching an immediate attack on the Kethian harbour. It appears Tavurek may have anticipated such a move for, on clearing the harbour wall, the oncoming ships found themselves assailed by continuous volleys of fire arrows and missiles launched from newly constructed trebuchet and mangonels. *Smoke choked every breath*, one Volarian sea captain wrote in his log shortly after. *The ships became so closely packed the masts were like a forest, bobbing in the swell as the fire raged.*

Undaunted, Vartek led The Sea Eagles across the decks of the massed fleet and onto the quayside where they were met by the well-ordered ranks of the Kethian regular army. It is clear a furious and bloody encounter then ensued, Vartek in the thick of it as always. Although outnumbered, Vartek's Eagles managed to hold the quay long enough for reinforcing Volarian troops to clamber across the smoke-shrouded decks and join the battle. By nightfall the docks were firmly in Volarian hands and a steady stream of reinforcements was being conveyed to the city by sea. Kethia's fate was sealed, although, as Entril testifies, her people showed scant awareness of the fact:

> *The entire city is raised against us. The old, the young, the infirm, all stirred to inhuman efforts by some unnatural means. Children leap at us from windows and doorways; skinny, ragged wretches, screaming hate as they stab, scratch, and bite, often urged on by their mothers who display little hesitation in joining them in death. I saw an old man cast pots filled with lamp oil at an advancing company, then set himself alight before leaping into their midst. Streets are battlegrounds and houses fortresses. In one case it cost an elite battalion fifty men to conquer one merchant's house, counting only twenty bodies among the rubble, none of them soldiers. There is truly something vile at work in this city.*

It took another five days, street by street and house by house, until the centre was reached. The unnamed building where the Kethians once chose their kings had become a stout fortress, ringed with barricades, the gaps between the mighty columns filled with brick and the roof crowded with archers and slingers. The more florid Volarian accounts have Vartek pause at this point to deliver a rousing and eloquent speech to his exhausted troops, full of passionate invective on the inherent superiority of Volarian society and the well-deserved fate of the Kethians. There are various versions of the speech, none of which I have chosen to include for the simple reason that, according to Entril and other contemporary accounts, Vartek never spoke a single word of it. Instead, he reordered his ranks to fully encircle the building, ensured all wounded were conveyed to the healers, saw to the distribution of food and water, then called up the siege engines to clear the archers from the roof and blast holes in the Kethian barricades.

When it came time for the final assault, naturally Vartek was the first through the breach, although he can hardly have been expecting the spectacle that confronted him, as later described by Entril:

> *We found only death. They lay entwined—men, women, and children—their faces serene, a single deep cut on every throat. We counted over four thousand and every one dead by their own hand, and willingly, smiling as their blood seeped away. This was the only occasion on which I saw my General truly enraged. He tore through the Kethian temple, his voice echoing as he called for Tavurek to face him, a challenge met only by the laughter of a madman. We found him on his throne, laughing and free of fear, his great axe cast aside and his hands empty. My General picked up the axe and tossed it at the feet of this mad king, commanding him to pick it up, do some honour to his people with a courageous end. But Tavurek only laughed harder. My General stepped closer to him, drawing his sword back, and I heard him ask, 'What are you?'*
>
> *The king's laughter faded slowly and he shrugged before replying, 'I am . . . very patient. And this has all been highly diverting.'*

My General killed him then, a single thrust to the heart, a far greater mercy than he deserved.

Of the Kethian population, only some three thousand survived the siege and all seem to have been rendered mad by the experience. In accordance with custom, the menfolk were executed and the women and children sold into slavery, although it seems unlikely a maddened slave would fetch more than the most meagre price. Karvalev's fate is not recorded, though some have sought to ascribe the later writings of an Atethian scholar to him as evidence that he survived the city's fall. These works do display a notable stylistic similarity to Karvalev, but their subject matter—a treatise on the most effective methods of growing cabbages, for example—seems far too mundane to have occupied such a mind.

Entril's letters cease at the conclusion of the Kethian campaign, but he is known to have stayed at Vartek's side for much of his subsequent career. They fought together in over twenty separate campaigns as Volaria consolidated its gains and the Forging Age drew to a close. Entril achieved Council-man status shortly before his death, having founded a dynasty which continues to occupy a council seat to this day.

Vartek refused a seat on the council, offered in spite of the fact that he still owned but one slave, and retired to a coastal villa near Varral. He is known to have fathered several children, all being declared free at time of birth by special decree of the council. He died at the age of sixty-nine, his will ordering the mother of his children be freed upon his death and all his property be rendered to her care. His four sons all entered the army but none ever ascended to the same heights of renown, for what son could ever hope to escape such a shadow? The Vartek dynasty was not fated to last, the name disappearing from the records during the Great Cleansing, presumably the result of an unfortunate religious adherence. However, some scholars have contended his descendants were among the exiles who fled to the damp land in the north, so it is possible his blood still lingers in some illiterate and unwashed vessel.

Kethia is now but a ruin on a hill overlooking a thriving port built by those who ruined her, adding further insult by stealing her name: New Kethia. It is said that when the city fell the Volarians salted the earth so nothing would ever again grow on such hated ground. However, My Emperor will note the illustrations provided by my Volarian hireling show copious weeds sprouting among the weathered stone, so this may well be another mythic aspect to a tale already rich in improbabilities.

I remain, Sire, your most humble and loyal servant,

Lord Verniers Alishe Someren

Author's Note

It's common for readers to have their favourites amongst a cast of characters. Whilst Vaelin surely remains my most appreciated character, Sollis, his principal mentor and Sword Master at the House of the Sixth Order, also features prominently in the mail I receive from readers. I conceived of Sollis as a cross-between the ultimate PE teacher and the ultimate Drill Sergeant. He is certainly cruel at times, never sparing with the cane, whilst being relentlessly critical and intolerant of failure. He's also fiercely intelligent, faultlessly brave, unwavering in his commitment to the values of his Order and, on rare occasions, shows glimmers of compassion. His extensive career as a Brother of the Sixth Order is hinted at in *Blood Song* and in *Many Are the Dead* I wanted to give readers an insight into the importance of his role in prior events. Here we find him already a veteran Brother at a point about ten years before the opening chapter of *Blood Song*. The story also provided an opportunity for me to indulge me love of the 'last stand against hopeless odds' narrative that lies at the heart of many of my favourite films, most particularly James Cameron's *Aliens*, Howard Hawks' *Rio Bravo* and its 1970s re-imagining by John Carpenter, *Assault on Precinct 13*.

Many are the Dead

– a Raven's Shadow Novella –

Many are the dead
Who stand in witness
To our crimes.
– Seordah Poem, Author Unknown

CHAPTER ONE

The boy stood frozen, eyes wide and wet, his sword hanging limp and useless from his hand as the Lonak warrior came for him. The lad's bleached features lacked any real expression, as if the impending certainty of his own death had somehow slipped beneath his notice. Sollis had seen this many times before, the face of one experiencing their first taste of real battle.

The charging Lonak and his hapless prey were a good dozen yards away. The warrior was wounded, one of Brother Smentil's arrows jutting from the tattooed flesh of his right arm. The limb flailed like a rag as he closed on the young Realm Guard, using his good arm to raise his war club high. It was a difficult distance for a knife throw, but Sollis had exhausted his arrows during the first few minutes of the skirmish.

The small, triangular bladed knife spun as it left his hand, describing a deceptively lazy arc through the air before sinking into the back of the Lonak's neck. Sollis grunted in frustration as he saw that the knife had missed the man's spine by a clear inch. Nevertheless, his charge came to an abrupt end as the knife struck home. He staggered, war club still raised as he tottered barely a yard from the frozen boy-soldier.

"Kill him!" Sollis shouted. The youth, however, seemed deaf to the call, continuing to stare with moist but empty eyes at the shuddering man before him. Sollis started forward then halted at the sound of feet scraping loose rock.

He sank to a crouch, spinning as he did so, the Order blade flickering across the wolf-pelt-covered torso of another Lonak. The man's war club whistled over Sollis's head as the star-silver edged steel cut through fur and the flesh beneath. The Lonak reeled back, sliced open from belly to shoulder, a shout of fury and pain erupting from his mouth. The wound was plainly mortal but, as was usual with his kind, the Lonak refused to surrender to death whilst there was still a chance to kill the hated Merim Her. Blood streamed from the Lonak's mouth as he sang, drawing back his club for another blow. Although the words were garbled, Sollis possessed sufficient understanding of his language to discern the cadence of a death-song.

Seeing another Lonak beyond the dying warrior's shoulder, Sollis flicked his sword across the man's throat and stepped to the side to avoid the spear thrust of his charging comrade. It was a good thrust, straight, swift and true, missing Sollis's chest by bare inches as he twisted, sword extended to skewer the second Lonak through the eye. This one was a woman, tall and lean, head shaven but for the long scalp-lock that sprouted from the base of her skull. She had no chance to give voice to the song that would carry her into the gods' embrace. Death came the instant the sword point reached her brain, although she hung on the blade twitching for a time until Sollis withdrew it.

The two Lonak collapsed against each other, forming a strange pyramidal tableau as they sank to the rocky ground, heads resting on the shoulder of the other, almost like lovers sharing a last intimate moment before slumber.

Sollis blinked and turned away, intending to resume his charge towards the boy-soldier and his assailant, expecting to find the lad lying on the slope with his head bashed in. Instead, he stood over the body of his erstwhile attacker, grunting as he tried in vain to tug his sword free of the Lonak's ribcage. His face was more animated now, colour returning to the pale immobile mask and tears streaking his cheeks. Apart from the boy's grunts a familiar post-battle quiet had descended on the canyon.

Glancing around Sollis saw his brothers descending the western slope. There were sixty besides himself, less than half the number of the war band they had just despatched, but the shock of their attack had done much to even the odds. Distracted by their slaughter of the Realm Guard, the Lonak had neglected to guard their rear.

As they descended into the canyon the brothers paused to finish off those Lonak who had not yet succumbed to their wounds. It was a long-ingrained tradition of the Sixth Order not to show mercy to these people, as the only reward was a knife in the back as soon as they recovered sufficiently to attempt an escape. A few Realm Guard survivors stood around clutching wounds or staring in shock at the remnants of their regiment. Over three hundred cavalry had trooped into this narrow canyon just a quarter-hour before. Sollis reckoned less than a third still lived. Most of their horses had survived the ambush, however; the Lonak were always keen to get their hands on Realm-bred stock.

"You," he said, advancing towards the boy who was still engaged in a struggle to free his sword from the fallen warrior. "Who's in charge of this farce?"

The young Realm Guard gaped at him in blank incomprehension, causing Sollis to wonder if his mind might have been unhinged by the recent carnage. Then the boy blinked and raised a hand from his sword hilt, pointing a finger at the base of the canyon. Sollis felt a small pulse of admiration for the way the youth managed keep the tremble from his hand.

"There, sir," he said, his voice coloured by the burr of those raised on the south Asraelin shore. He was a long way from home. "Lord Marshal Al Septa."

"I'm a brother not a sir," Sollis corrected, following the boy's finger to a pile of bodies in the centre of the canyon. At least a dozen Realm Guard had fallen there, covered by a small forest of the hawk-fletched arrows favoured by the Lonak. The pile of corpses twitched slightly but Sollis's experienced eye told him none of these men still held on to life.

"Spared himself the disgrace of a trial before the king, at least," he muttered. "This mad jaunt north of the pass was his idea, I suppose?"

"The Wolf Men destroyed three villages before fleeing back to the mountains," the boy said, a defensive note colouring his tone. "Killing all the folk they could find, and they weren't quick about it. Lord Al Septa was driven by a desire for justice. He was a good man."

"Well." Sollis pushed the boy aside and took hold of his sword. "All he managed to do was drive most of you to an early communion with the Departed. Good men can be fools too." He gripped the sword with both hands, putting his boot on the dead man's chest as he dragged the blade clear. A wet sucking sound rose as it came free, followed by a brief fountain of blood and a nostril stinging stench as the man's lungs let go of his last breath.

"Always better to go for the belly or the throat, if you can," Sollis said, returning the sword to the boy. "Less chance of it getting stuck."

"Faith! How old are you, lad?"

Sollis turned to find Brother Oskin approaching, his weathered features drawn into a squint as he surveyed the boy-soldier. Red Ears, his ever present Cumbraelin hunting hound, trotted from his side to snuffle at the Lonak corpse, her long tongue flicking out to lap at the blood leaking from its wound. Oskin allowed the beast a few more licks before nudging her away with a jab of his boot. It had been thanks to Red Ears' nose that they tracked the Lonak war band, so it would have been churlish to deny her a small reward, although Sollis wished the beast had managed to find them soon enough to prevent this massacre.

"Fourteen," the boy replied, casting a nervous glance at the massive hound as Red Ears sauntered towards him, licking the blood from her chops. "I'll be fifteen in a month."

"The king sends children to fight the Lonak," Oskin said with a despairing shake of his head. "Your mother know where you are?"

A certain hardness crept into the lad's gaze as he replied in a low mutter, "No. She's dead."

Oskin gave a soft sigh before turning back to Sollis. "Smentil took a shaman alive, thought you might want to talk to him. Best be quick if you do, I doubt he'll last long."

Sollis nodded and moved off, issuing orders over his shoulder as he climbed the far slope of the canyon. "Get these horses rounded up. See if there's anything to be done for the Realm Guard wounded, and see if you can find one with any kind of rank. This lot will need a captain for the journey south."

"That I will, brother." Oskin clapped a hand on the boy's shoulder and guided him to the canyon floor where most of the Realm Guard had begun to gather. "Come on, whelp. You can point me to a sergeant, if there's any left."

"It's Jehrid," the boy said in a sullen mutter as Oskin led him away.

Sollis found Brother Smentil standing over the slumped and bleeding form of a wiry Lonak of middling years. His status as shaman was proclaimed by the swirling tattoo covering his shaven skull. The exact meanings of the various symbols with which the Lonak covered themselves were still beyond Sollis's understanding, but he knew enough to distinguish the signs of a warrior or a hunter from that of a shaman.

Gut wound, Smentil told Sollis, his hands making the signs with a flowing precision that came from years of necessary practice. The tall brother held the unenviable distinction of being the only member of the Sixth Order to be captured by the Lonak and survive the experience, albeit losing his tongue in the process. Consequently, the Order's sign-language was his primary means of communication apart from the occasional written note in a near illegible script.

Sollis angled his head as he surveyed the dying shaman, finding himself confronted by a typically hate-filled glare. He spoke as he locked eyes with Sollis, bloody spittle spilling from his lips and staining his teeth as he formed the words. "*Merim Her, fogasht ehl mentah. Shiv illahk tro dohimish.*" *Merim Her, always there are more. Like maggots on a corpse.*

"*Ver dohimishin,*" Sollis replied: *You're dying*. He sank to his haunches, speaking on in Lonak, "Do you wish a quick death?"

The shaman snarled, face quivering with the effort of meeting Sollis's gaze. "I want nothing from you."

"No raids for nearly a year," Sollis went on. "Now you lead a war band of many spears to our lands. You steal nothing, take no treasure or captives. All you do is burn and kill. Why?"

A suspicious glint crept into the shaman's eye as he narrowed his gaze. "You know why... blue-cloak," he said in a hard, pain-filled rasp.

"No," Sollis assured him with a humourless smile. "I don't. Tell me." He held the shaman's gaze, seeing no sign he might yield. Sollis was tempted to draw his dagger and start probing the man's wound, though past experience told him the Lonak were too inured to pain for such encouragement to bear fruit.

"I can take you with us," he said instead. "Back to the Pass. We have healers there. Once you are made whole I will put you in a cage and parade you through the lands you raided. Merim Her will spit upon you, cast their filth at you, and no Lonak will ever hear your story again."

The shaman's nostrils flared as he drew in a series of rapid breaths. Blood began to seep through the fingers the man had clamped over his wound and Sollis saw his eyes take on a familiar, unfocused cast. "No, blue-cloak," the shaman said, a crimson torrent now flowing from his mouth as he grinned at Sollis, speaking in harsh grunts. "I… am being called… to the Gods' embrace… where my story will live forever… in their ears."

"Tell me!" Sollis reached out to clamp a hand on the shaman's neck, gripping hard. "Why did you raid?"

"You… Because of you…" The shaman's grin broadened, allowing a slick of blood to cover Sollis's hand. "You came into the mountains… and brought that which is known only to the Mahlessa… She decreed… vengeance…"

The shaman's eyes dimmed and closed, his head lolling forward as Sollis felt his final pulse, no more than the faintest flutter against his palm.

What did he mean? Smentil's hands asked as Sollis rose, hefting his canteen to wash away the blood. Like most of the brothers Smentil had only a partial understanding of Lonak. Sollis, by contrast, had used his years at the Pass to learn as much as he could. It had been a tortuous business, reliant on rarely taken captives and the few relevant books he had gleaned from the Third Order library. Whilst Lonak prisoners almost never divulged information of any value, they were always enthusiastic in assailing their captors with all the insults they could muster, which added greatly to his vocabulary and understanding of syntax. It also meant he spoke a version of Lonak even harsher than the original.

"*Rova kha ertah Mahlessa,*" he said, flicking the pinkish water away and turning his gaze north. The sun was well past its zenith and the shadows grew long on the mountains. High on the granite slopes the stiffening wind swept snow into a clear blue sky. As always when he gazed upon these peaks there was the sense of his scrutiny being returned. Bare as they seemed, the chances of journeying through the Lonak dominion unobserved were always slender at best. Veteran brothers had a saying, 'The mountains have eyes.' *She'll learn of what happened here within days,* he thought. *What will she do then?*

"'That which is known only to the Mahlessa,'" he elaborated, turning back to Smentil. "The Dark, brother. He was talking about the Dark."

He made for the crest of the slope and began to descend to where they had tethered their horses. "Best get these guardsmen into some semblance of order," he said. "We're returning to the Pass with all speed. The Brother Commander must know of this."

CHAPTER TWO

It took a night and a day to reach the Skellan Pass. Sollis pushed his mingled company hard, maintaining a punishing pace and refusing to rest come nightfall despite the condition of the wounded Realm Guard, three of whom expired before the journey was done. He had expected some level of condemnation from their fellow guardsmen but they remained a mostly silent lot. Throughout the journey their eyes continually roved the peaks and valleys in wary trepidation, faces pale with a fear that wouldn't fade until they were far from these lands.

"They were like ghosts," Jehrid, the boy-soldier, said in response to Brother Oskin's request for an account of his regiment's demise. "Just seemed to spring out of the air. The lads think it was some Dark spell cast by their shaman."

"Dark spell, eh?" Oskin enquired with an amused snort.

"How else to explain it?" Jehrid replied, face reddening a little. "Two hundred men just appearing out of nowhere. And the way they fought…" He grimaced and shook his head. "Not natural."

"One hundred and eighteen," Sollis said. He didn't bother to turn as he steered his mount along the ridgeline which descended in a gradual slope to the sparsely grassed plain north of the Pass. "And they weren't all men. The Lonak don't need the Dark to ambush fools, boy. This is their land and they know every stone of it."

The narrow gate in the Pass's northernmost wall trundled open after the customary delay as the sentries on the parapet ensured the approaching party were not Lonak in disguise. It was a ruse their enemy hadn't attempted in decades, but the Order never forgot a hard lesson. Sollis led the company inside to wind their way through the twists and turns of the inner fortifications until they emerged into the courtyard.

"Get the wounded to the healing house," Sollis told Oskin, climbing down from the saddle. "And find room for the rest to bed down. I'll report to the Brother Commander."

After stabling his horse he made his way to the tallest of the towers which crowded the southern stretch of the Pass. "He's got company," Brother Artin advised as Sollis strode through the door. He and Sollis were the most senior brothers stationed at the Pass. Artin had responsibility for the day-to-day running of the garrison whilst Sollis oversaw forays beyond the fortifications. He felt no resentment at the disparity in their roles. Artin was a sound leader and no slouch in combat, but his stolid attachment to routine made him a better fit for commanding a fortress. Sollis, by contrast, would sometimes contrive excuses to patrol north of the Pass if he spent more than a few days within these walls.

"Urgent business, brother," he told Artin, not pausing in his stride. "Something you should hear too," he added before knocking on the door to the Brother Commander's chamber with a forcefulness he hoped fell short of causing offence. There was a brief interval before he heard a muffled, "Come in," in a tone he was relieved to find free of irritation.

"Brother Sollis." Brother Commander Arlyn sat behind his desk, greeting him with his customary faint smile, one eyebrow raised in curiosity. "Back early, I see."

"With intelligence, brother," Sollis said, his gaze immediately drawn to the room's other occupant. She sat in a chair before Brother Arlyn's desk, blonde hair shifting as she turned to regard Sollis with an open smile and inquisitive blue eyes. Apart from the occasional Lonak captive, women were a decided rarity at the Pass, though he had a sense that a woman like this would be a rarity anywhere.

"Do you know Sister Elera?" Arlyn enquired. "She arrived this morning. Come all the way from Varinshold on a mission of some import."

Sollis, realising he was staring, took note of the woman's grey robe before shifting his gaze. "I do not, brother," he said. "I bid you welcome, sister. We can always use another healer. In fact, presently there are Realm Guard requiring assistance in the courtyard."

"In a moment, sister," Arlyn said as Elera began to rise. "If they've lasted this long, I daresay they can last a little longer. Our own healers know their business in any case." His eyes took on a more serious cast as he turned back to Sollis. "You found the war band, I take it?"

"We did, brother," Sollis confirmed. "Came upon them in the midst of slaughtering a regiment of Realm Guard cavalry. Apparently, their Lord Marshal thought pursuing the Lonak into their own dominion little different from chasing after a gang of common outlaws."

"I don't envy his interview with the king," Artin commented from the doorway.

"He's dead," Sollis told him. "Fortune was merciful." He saw Sister Elera's smooth brow crease in a frown of disapproval and felt compelled to elaborate. "The king is not renowned for his indulgence of incompetence, sister."

"No," she conceded with a small shrug. Her voice was smooth and cultured, lacking any trace of the streets or the fields. "But the Faith teaches that judgment should be left to the Departed."

"Our casualties?" Brother Arlyn asked.

"None," Sollis told him. "Though Brother Hestin is complaining of a sprained wrist. We brought back ninety Realm Guard, including wounded."

"A grim toll," Arlyn observed. "But the mission can still be counted a success."

"There's something else, brother." Sollis paused to cast a wary glance at Sister Elera.

"Speak freely," Arlyn said. "As I said, our sister is here on a particular mission and I suspect your intelligence will enlighten her as to its wisdom."

"There was a Lonak shaman amongst the war band." Sollis looked over his shoulder and gestured for Artin to close the door, waiting until he had done so before continuing. "He lived long enough to tell us the raid was ordered by the Mahlessa in retribution for something we had done. He made mention of the Dark before he died."

"Mahlessa?" Sister Elera asked.

"The High Priestess of the Lonak," Arlyn explained. "The clans feud amongst each other constantly, but they all answer when the Mahlessa calls." His eyes settled on Sollis. "Whatever their faults as a people, the Lonak are even less prone to superstition than the Faithful, despite their attachment to god-worship."

"Indeed, brother," Sollis agreed. "For a shaman to make mention of it would indicate trouble in the mountains. Trouble the Mahlessa, for whatever reason, has blamed on the Order."

Arlyn pursed his lips and turned to Elera. "So you see, sister. This would appear to be a particularly ill-chosen moment to pursue your course."

Elera gave a brisk smile in response, nodding at the opened letter on Arlyn's desk. "Nevertheless, the Aspects of all six orders have chosen it. It is not for us to gainsay their authority, merely to fulfil their instructions."

Sollis saw Arlyn smother a sigh as he gestured him forward, pointing at the letter. "I think your counsel would be welcome here, brother."

Sollis duly retrieved the single page of parchment, reading it through quickly. It was set down in neat precise letters, presumably the work of a Third Order scribe, and signed by all six Aspects of the Faith. He took particular note of the fact that Aspect Andril, the aged but highly respected head of the Sixth Order, had seen fit to underline his signature, twice.

"You wish to travel into the mountains," Sollis said to Elera, frowning as he read through the letter's final paragraph. "In search of this… weed?"

"Quite so, brother," she responded, her brisk smile still in place. She reached into a pocket in her robe and extracted a small paper scroll, unfurling it to reveal a drawing. It depicted what appeared to Sollis to be an unremarkable plant, a cluster of narrow stems from which sprouted small four-petalled flowers. "Jaden's Weed, to be precise," she said. "Perhaps you've encountered it during one of your many daring northward quests."

Sollis's frown deepened at that and he saw her mouth twitch a little. "I've no memory of it," he said, glancing at the drawing again and shaking his head.

"My research indicates it can be found in a particular place," Elera said, furling the scroll. "Morvil's Reach. Do you know of it?"

Brother Artin gave a derisive snort. "Morvil's Folly we call it, sister," he said. "You want to go there?"

"It seems the best place to start," she replied, apparently unconcerned by his half-amused, half-appalled tone. "Does this present a particular difficulty?"

"Oh, not at all." Artin raised his eyebrows in mock solicitation. "Once you discount the fact that it's a good sixty miles into the mountains and smack in the middle of the lands held by the Grey Hawk Clan, the most numerous and warlike clan in the Lonak Dominion, I'd say it presents no difficulty at all."

"Brother." Arlyn spoke softly, but the single word was enough for Artin to fall silent. He crossed his arms and retreated to a corner, heavy brows bunched in disapproval.

"Brothers," Elera said, her smile now replaced by something more genuine and open. "Please do not think I am ignorant of the risks involved. I would not undertake them, nor ask others to do so, unless the matter was not both urgent and necessary."

"As the Aspects' letter states," Arlyn said. "And yet the reason for such urgency is not explained."

Elera lowered her gaze, all trace of humour leaving her features. "No word of what I am about to say is to leave this room," she said, lifting her head to regard each of them in turn, eyes hard with sincere gravity. "I require your word as servants of the Faith."

"You have it," Arlyn said. After Sollis and Artin had also voiced their assurance Elera nodded.

"Four weeks ago," she began, "a ship from the far off Volarian port of Vehrel docked in Maelinscove. Half the crew were found to be dead and most of the others stricken by sickness. Their symptoms..." She trailed off, taking a deep breath before continuing. "Their symptoms were consistent with the disease we know as the Red Hand."

She fell silent, letting the words settle. Brothers of the Sixth Order were not prone to overt expressions of emotion but even so Artin couldn't contain a soft and rarely heard obscenity whilst the Brother Commander merely closed his eyes, Sollis noticing how his long fingered hands twitched briefly before he clasped them together. His own reaction was internal, a rush of memory, mostly unwelcome and not often dwelt upon. The livid red marks that encircled his mother's neck, the tears that always rose in her eyes whenever she spoke of those terrible days. She had been only an infant when the Red Hand swept through the four fiefs. There had been no Realm then, King Janus himself just a callow youth who barely survived his own brush with the plague. In those days the four fiefs bickered and warred constantly, endless columns of soldiers trampling the crops that surrounded the border hamlet where his mother lived. Then one day they stopped.

Dead men can't march, she told him decades later. *We found hundreds littering the fields, thousands even. Your grammy and I went out to rob the dead, as was custom. Don't you look at me like that, boy! Lords and their wars do nothing but take food from the mouths of folk like us. Only fair we take something back when we can. 'Cept this time we took something best left behind.*

She went on to tell him how the hamlet had died. A poor but mostly peaceful community that had persisted in the borderlands between Asrael and Cumbrael for nigh on a century, wiped out in the course of a few days. Sollis's mother woke from her fever to find herself staring into his grandmother's empty eyes. *By the time it was over the only ones left were me, Fram the wheelwright and the gormless loon they called the pig-boy. Still, we'd just gathered the harvest so there was plenty to go around that winter.* She had laughed then, as was her wont when voicing dark humour. She rarely laughed otherwise, but then Sollis recalled her having little to laugh about.

"So it's come back," he said to Elera. "How far has it spread?"

"Fortunately, the outbreak was swiftly contained," she said. "One of King Janus's earliest acts on ascending the throne was to institute a strict protocol for dealing with any vessel found to be carrying the Red Hand. The ship was towed far out to sea and fire arrows used to burn it."

"Along with its crew, I presume?" Arlyn enquired. "Even those who had not yet succumbed."

"The King's Word may be harsh at times," she replied. "But often it has saved us from disaster, as in this case. There was a fair amount of panic in the port, of course. So the king arranged for certain rumours to be spread attributing the ship's demise to poisoning or some god-worshipper's Dark design. More concerning was the news imparted by one of the crew before he expired. It seems the Red Hand now has a firm hold in Vehrel, a port from which merchant vessels sail to all corners of the world."

"Then," Sollis said, "it's only a matter of time before another plague ship turns up at our door."

"I fear so, brother."

He nodded at the scroll in her hand. "And this weed of yours?"

"The Fifth Order has spent decades trying to develop a curative for the Red Hand, without any real success. With the advent of the current crisis I was charged by my Aspect to review all the historical accounts held by our Order. It was hoped that I might find something others had missed." She looked at the scroll, giving a tight smile. "I found this. There is a fragmentary account of a Renfaelin campaign against the Lonak. A century ago an army of knights advanced into the mountains…"

"And never marched out again," Artin said. "We know the story, sister. They were led by Baron Valeric Morvil, said to be the greatest knight of his age. It was him who built the folly now named in his honour." He shook his head in professional disdain. "Only a Renfaelin noble would think to build a castle in the mountains. I'm sure the Lonak must have found it all very amusing. The story goes they actually let him finish it before wiping out his entire command in a single night."

"That campaign was accompanied by a brother from the Third Order," Elera said. "He sent periodic reports back to Varinshold, which stopped eventually for obvious reasons. However, the final account speaks of a captured Lonak shaman using this weed to cure a knight named Jaden, a knight whose symptoms indicate he may have contracted a variant of the Red Hand."

"Variant?" Sollis asked. "There's more than one kind?"

"Diseases change over time, brother," she explained. "They grow, become more contagious, more virulent. It's what made the plague so damaging when it swept through the four fiefs. We had never encountered its like before, so had no means of fighting it. The account relates how this weed," she held up the scroll once more, "was found in close proximity to Morvil's outpost. If we can find it, we may have a chance of stopping the Red Hand should it return."

"A chance to commit suicide, more like," Artin said, holding up a hand at her scowling response. "I'm sorry, sister, but this is…"

"Our mission," Brother Commander Arlyn broke in. "As ordained by the Aspects of the Faith," he added, meeting Sollis's eyes. "Tell me truly, brother, can you get to Morvil's Reach and return safely?"

"Perhaps," Sollis said. "With a small group. No more than four. But if the Mahlessa has raised the Lonak against us…"

"Then it's possible you might also discover the cause of this current unrest." The perennially faint smile returned to Arlyn's lips. "Two bucks with one arrow. Choose your brothers and be ready to leave by morning."

…

"You know this is a hopeless mission," Artin whispered as he and Sollis stepped out into the corridor.

"And yet hope remains the heart of the Faith, brother," Sollis replied, earning a scowl in response before Artin strode off, shoulders hunched in anger. Sollis, hearing Arlyn's voice, paused for a second, glancing back to see Sister Elera in the doorway, turning to regard the Brother Commander. Sollis was struck by the cautious hesitancy of Arlyn's tone. Although a softly spoken man at most times, his voice rarely lacked certainty.

"Our… former sister," Arlyn said. "She is well?"

"Very well, brother," Elera said.

There was a short interval before Arlyn spoke again. "And the child?"

"As healthy as a new born can be." The sister let out a small laugh. "Perhaps more so."

Another, shorter pause. "Please assure her of my continued friendship and regard when you see her next."

"I shall, brother. Though, I doubt she needs any such reassurance."

The warmth in Elera's voice was coloured by a faint note of something Sollis would never have expected to be directed at Brother Arlyn: pity. Seized by an abrupt sense of transgression, Sollis turned and followed in Artin's wake. He would check on the wounded then spend the hours before sleep pondering a means of surviving his mission. A brief estimation of the odds gave them perhaps one chance in three, though with careful planning and a modicum of luck he thought he might be able to make it an even bet.

CHAPTER THREE

"The weed must be tested," Sister Elera explained. "I daresay we'll find more than a few plants that bear a similarity to the drawing. I will subject a sample to various agents to ensure it does in fact hold the healing properties we require." She patted the saddle bags on the back of her stout mare before mounting up with a smooth, accustomed grace.

"You could teach me," Sollis said.

"Oh, we certainly don't have time for that." She gave him another of her brisk smiles as she guided her mare towards the first of the inner gates. "You have your task, brother. I have mine."

"This is not a game, sister," he told her.

"Good. I detest games. Such a waste of mental effort." She halted her mare at the gate and glanced over her shoulder, her smile replaced by an impatient frown. "Are you coming?"

Sollis swallowed his anger and turned away. Dealing with someone he couldn't command was always irksome, but Sister Elera was proving a very singular trial. "Brother Lemnish," he said, addressing the youngest of the three brothers waiting with their mounts in the courtyard. "Too many hooves in this party. You'll stay behind."

Sollis saw the young brother mask his relief with a regretful shrug before leading his horse back to the stable. The man was no coward, Sollis knew, but neither was he a fool. "Mount up," he told Oskin and Smentil. Of the two, only Oskin betrayed any outward sign of trepidation and that just a hardly perceptible shake of his head before he climbed into the saddle. They were the two most experienced brothers in the Pass, both having served here for years before Sollis arrived. Risking them on this mission might rob the Order of two of its most valuable assets, but he knew there was little chance of success if he chose to leave them behind.

Vensar, Sollis's own mount, gave only a small snort as he swung himself into the saddle. He had ridden the stallion since being posted to the Pass four years before. The stallion's plains origins were evident in his name, an Eorhil word for a comet that would appear in the northern sky once a century. Sollis assumed it had been chosen for the teardrop blaze of white on the animal's forehead. Despite being bred for the hunt rather than battle, Vensar's mostly sedate nature would disappear in combat, his hooves and teeth proving deadly weapons on more than one occasion.

Red Ears loped ahead as they made their way through the outer walls and the northern gate. The hound never barked, the trait having been bred out of her bloodline generations before. Instead her signals consisted of a sudden stillness, the severity of the threat revealed by the speed at which her tail wagged. Sollis saw her crest a low rise just beyond bowshot of the gate, whereupon she came to an abrupt halt, tail swishing at a slow tempo.

"Well," Oskin said, reining his horse to a halt at the hound's side. "Seems there's something on the wind today."

"The Lonak?" Sister Elera asked.

"No. When she catches their scent her tail becomes straight as an arrow." Oskin angled his head at Red Ears and made a soft clicking sound with his tongue. The hound looked up at him, brows raised, a faint whine escaping her maw. "Something unfamiliar, looks like," Oskin mused, rubbing his grey-stubbled chin. "She doesn't like it, whatever it is."

Sollis spared the hound a brief glance before turning Vensar's nose towards the west. Without any clue as to the nature of whatever alien scent had troubled the hound's nose there seemed little point dwelling on the mystery. "We'll make for the Saw Back," he said. "Cut north once we're through the Notch."

"Forgive me, brother," Elera said as Sollis kicked Vensar into a trot. She prodded her mare to follow suit and quickly drew alongside. "But our destination is to the north-east, is it not? Your course appears to be taking us directly west."

Sollis's eyes flicked to her for an instant before he slapped his reins against Vensar's neck and the stallion accelerated into a gallop. "The mountains have eyes, sister," he heard Oskin explain to Elera. "It doesn't do to follow the compass needle too closely up here."

The Saw Back came into view as the sun neared noon. It was a twenty mile long ridge that rose from the plain to snake a northerly course into the mountains. Centuries before the Renfaelins had named it for its resemblance to the jagged bones of a boar's back, but the Lonak called it Irshak's Tail and believed it to be the remnants of their god of birth. Irshak, so the shamans taught, willingly allowed her spirit to depart her mighty body so that it would sink into the earth, giving rise to the mountains thereby gifting the Lonak a home for all eternity.

Sollis followed the line of the ridge for a mile or so until the Notch came into view. It was a narrow channel that traced a jagged course through the ridge from east to west. Despite being a perfect site for an ambush, the Lonak assiduously avoided the place and no brother had ever been attacked in its vicinity. His attempts to elicit some explanation for this from captives were always met with a scowling refusal to speak a single word on the matter. He wondered if they believed the Notch to be cursed, as if venturing near such a scar in the stone flesh of their dead god was somehow blasphemous. It was likely he would never know and had long resigned himself to the fact that gaining a true understanding of these people was probably impossible.

They dismounted before leading their horses into the Notch. Elera's mare gave voice to some disconcerted snorting as the steep granite walls closed in on either side, but the Order mounts were accustomed to this route and remained quiet. Sollis called a halt about halfway into the Notch where it opened out to create an oval large enough to provide a campsite of sorts.

"Half-moon tonight," Oskin said, gazing up at the mostly grey sky. "Looks like the cloud's inclined to linger for a bit, though."

"Light a fire," Sollis told Smentil before moving to the northern wall of the Notch and starting to climb.

"We're stopping for the night?" Sister Elera asked. "We've barely travelled more than a few miles."

Sollis ignored her and kept climbing.

"And won't a fire reveal our position to the Lonak?" she called after him.

"It's likely they already know our position," he said, not turning. "And will continue to do so as long as you keep shouting."

He ascended to the top of the granite wall and took a moment to scan both the eastern and western approaches, predictably seeing nothing of interest. Sollis faced due north and sat down, closing his eyes and slowing his breathing to allow the song of the mountains to fill his ears. Long years of training at the Order House instilled in him a deep regard for the value of utilising all senses. Today the song was a familiar refrain of swirling winds rebounding from the vast, irregular edifice of the mountains and the rustle and rasp of sparse vegetation. If a Lonak scouting party were to reveal themselves it would be with a small discordant note in the song of the mountains, just a faint series of ticks that indicated unshod hooves on loose stone. Today, however, there were no such ticks. In fact, he found the song unusually muted and it took some time before he detected anything of note.

Hawk, he thought, recognising the faint birdcall, opening his eyes to scan the sky. He found it quickly, a faint speck circling against the grey blanket of cloud. The bird's presence brought a puzzled frown to his brow. Mountain hawks would hunt for mice or rabbits in the foothills, but neither were plentiful at the Saw Back. Also, they would normally only cry out to warn off those who might encroach on their nests, but these were typically found atop the steepest cliffs. It could be trying to attract a mate, though he judged it too late in the season for that.

Sollis watched the hawk until its voice faded and it stopped circling, angling its wings to fly off towards the north. Voicing a soft grunt of frustration at a minor mystery, Sollis rose and climbed back down into the Notch. Brother Smentil had used the firewood from his saddle bags to craft a decent sized blaze, sending a tall column of grey smoke into the dimming sky.

How many? he signed as Sollis moved to unsaddle Vensar.

"None," Sollis replied. He smoothed a hand over the stallion's back before laying the saddle down and extracting a handful of oats from one of the bags. "That I could find, that is."

"Meaning none at all," Oskin said. "Unusual."

"I can't be certain. We need to assume they've spotted us."

"You were expecting the Lonak to find us?" Sister Elera asked which drew an amused glance from Smentil.

We should tie her up and put her on my horse, his hands told Sollis. *He'll make his own way back to the Pass. Any Lonak scouts will most likely leave her be if they still have us to chase after.*

Sister Elera stepped into Smentil's eyeline, face set in a hard mask as her hands moved with swift, if angry fluency. The signs she made were brief though the meaning was colourful and evidently heartfelt.

"I don't think there's any need for that kind of language, sister," Sollis said, holding the oats to Vensar's snout. The stallion let out an appreciative snort as he munched on the snack.

Elera took a slow calming breath, clasping her hands together before speaking again. "Brothers," she began in a tone of measured calm. "I realise I have not your experience in this place, nor do I possess your skills. I am, however, your sister in the Faith and Mistress of Curatives at the House of the Fifth Order. I do not request your respect, I both deserve and expect it. Our mission, as you know, is of the gravest import and I feel its chances of success will be greatly improved if you would be so good as to just answer my bloody questions when I ask them."

Smentil raised an eyebrow in Sollis's direction, receiving a nod in response. Smentil tossed some more sticks onto the fire before turning back to Elera. *If there are any watching,* he signed,

as long as this stays lit they'll believe we're still here.

"I see," Elera said. "Meaning we'll soon move on and leave it burning."

"We'll wait for darkness," Sollis said. "As long as the moon stays hidden we should be able to head north without being tracked, at least for a while."

"Very clever, brother," she replied, inclining her head a little.

"Cleverness is Brother Sollis's business, sister," Oskin said, sitting down close to the fire and wrapping his cloak about him. "The Grey Eyed Fox the Lonak call him."

"One," Sollis said, seeing his brothers exchange a glance of muted amusement. He was not a man easily baited but had always found the notion of being named by others decidedly annoying, especially his enemies. "One Lonak said that, then he died."

"They tend to do that when you feather them all over with arrows. Mark my words, sister." Oskin cast a wink in Elera's direction. "We travel with a veritable legend. A scourge of Lonak kind."

A stern rebuke came to Sollis's lips but he stilled his tongue. Oskin was a veteran brother who had earned a certain leeway not enjoyed by most of his comrades. Instead, Sollis confined himself to an irritated sigh. "It's a few hours yet until nightfall," he told the sister. "We'll be pushing hard throughout the night. Best unsaddle your horse, we can't afford for her to tire."

...

Night fell quickly in the mountains, the sun dipping behind the western peaks to leave the Notch in near-pitch darkness. The clouds had lingered in the sky meaning there was no betraying moonlight as they made their way to the western flank of the Saw

Back, the fire burning bright at their rear. The firelight faded as Sollis led them through the cramped passage, guided by touch and memory. The Notch had some side-channels which would trap or delay the unwary but he had memorised the route years before. Soon the granite walls fell away to reveal a broad, rock strewn slope stretching away into the gloom.

Sollis ordered the others to mount up and they struck out for the north, keeping to the upper edge of the slope where it met the crest of the ridge. He spurred Vensar to a steady canter, unwilling to gallop in the darkness. Even so it was a risky endeavour and even a seasoned Order mount like Vensar sometimes came close to losing his footing on the loose stone of the slope. Sister Elera's mare, lacking the same expertise, was less fortunate. Sollis heard the horse let out a shrill whinny and turned to see her sliding down the incline on her rump, forelegs extended as she attempted to stall her descent. Elera held on with valiant resolve, hauling on the reins as shingle cascaded around her.

Horse and rider came to an untidy stop some thirty yards down the slope. Sollis heard the sister give voice to a muffled curse and reined Vensar to a halt, preparing to dismount and go to her aid. He paused, however, at the sound of displaced shingle and fiercely whispered instructions. Peering into the gloom he made out the sight of Elera coaxing her mare into a standing position and slowly guiding her back up the slope. He was impressed with the sister's skill in the saddle, though her stern and embarrassed visage as she fell into line led him to believe any compliments wouldn't be welcome.

"We'll keep to a walk until dawn," he said.

"That's not necessary..." Elera began.

"A walk," Sollis cut in, kicking Vensar forward.

...

Ten miles north of the Notch the Saw Back joined the southern flank of a steep-sided mountain, its slopes becoming too sheer for horse or human. Sollis led them around the peak's western base and into a narrow valley marked by the swift stream rushing through its centre. The morning sun soon began to banish the shadows and he spurred Vensar into a gallop, following the line of the stream as it curved towards the east. He was keen to cover as many miles as possible. They were a decent remove from any sizeable Lonak settlement but he knew it was only a matter of time before a hunting party happened upon their trail. The marks left by steel shod hooves were as good as a signpost in the mountains.

They exited the valley shortly before noon, Sollis slowing the pace as they ascended the forested hills beyond. Once within the trees Oskin sent Red Ears ahead to scout the route, the hound keeping about thirty yards ahead and always staying within sight. After another hour of riding Sollis saw the hound come to a rigid halt, nose pointing off to the right. Her tail wasn't swaying this time, but nor was it straight. Instead, it maintained a steady, nervous twitch.

"She's scenting a beast not a man," Oskin said quietly, brows bunching as he scanned the surrounding trees. "Something with sharp teeth otherwise she wouldn't have stopped."

Sollis nodded to both brothers and all three dismounted, Smentil signing to Elera to follow suit and holding a finger to his lips. The brothers each unlimbered their bows and notched an arrow. Sollis signed for Smentil to stay with the sister and the horses then he and Oskin moved to Red Ears.

"What is it, old pup?" Oskin whispered, crouching at the hound's side and running a hand through the sparse fur on her shoulders.

Red Ears' nose pointed at a dense patch of woodland a dozen paces off, the pines so closely packed as to banish sunlight from the forest floor. A low growl emerged from the hound's muzzle and her lips began to curl, revealing her impressive teeth.

"Rock ape?" Sollis asked Oskin in a low murmur.

The older brother shook his head. "They don't come down from the mountains until winter." The tracker's features took on a familiar frown of concentration, nostrils flaring in unconscious imitation of his dog. "Can't be," he said in a whisper, a bemused squint creeping into his gaze. "Not this far south…"

Sollis saw them then, two small pinpoints of light in the gloom. *Eyes,* he realised. *Cat's eyes catching the light.* His finger tightened on his bowstring as two more pairs of eyes appeared on either side of the first. A grating, piercing squeal cut through the hushed forest air an instant before the cats exploded from the gloom, grey and silver fur flickering as they charged, mouths gaping wide to reveal teeth the length of daggers.

CHAPTER FOUR

Sollis only had time to half draw his bow, loosing the shaft at a range of less than a yard and sinking the broad steel-head into the cat's mouth. Then it was on him, claws reaching up to clamp onto his shoulders as it sought to stab its elongated teeth into his neck. Sollis rolled with the force of the beast's charge, letting his bow fall from his grip and kicking out with both legs. His boots slammed into the cat's ribcage, propelling it away.

Sollis came to his feet in a crouch, drawing his sword from the scabbard on his back. The cat scrabbled on the ground a few yards away, rasping and shaking its head as it sought to dislodge the arrow jutting from its mouth. Sollis surged forward, bracing the hilt of his sword against his midriff to spear the cat in the chest, blade angled so it made easy passage through the ribcage. It let out a grating, gurgling yowl as the sword point found its heart. Sollis dragged the blade free and stepped away, sparing a moment to watch the cat thrash out its death agonies before whirling to check on his companions.

Another cat was already down, pierced in the chest by two arrows whilst the third was being kept at bay by the combined efforts of Red Ears and Oskin. The pair assailed the beast from two sides, causing it to whirl at each of them in turn, lashing out with its claws as blood leaked from the wounds Oskin's sword left in its flanks. Behind him, Sollis heard the hard thrum of Smentil's bowstring. There was a rush of air and the dark shaft of an arrow appeared in the cat's haunch, causing it to let out a grating, agonised yowl. Its hind quarters became suddenly limp, though it continued to hiss and slash at its assailants until Red Ears darted forward to clamp her jaws on the beast's neck, biting hard. She shook the cat until it sagged into death, limbs twitching.

Sollis retrieved his bow, glancing over to see Smentil notching another arrow. Sister Elera was close behind, clutching the reins of their horses. There was a good deal of fear in her eyes but he detected none of the panicked twitching exhibited by one about to flee.

"Shouldn't be here," Oskin muttered, squinting as he cast his expert eye over each of the fallen cats. Now he had a clear view of them Sollis was impressed by their size, six feet from nose to tail with broad, sharp clawed paws. Then there were the teeth, curved ivory blades eight inches long. He had never seen the like, but Oskin's knowledge of the wilds was far greater than his.

"What are they?" Sollis asked him.

"Snow-daggers," Oskin said. "Least, that's what the Eorhil word for them means in Realm tongue. Never seen one south of the coastal crags."

"And yet here they are," Sollis pointed out.

"Can't rightly explain it, brother." Oskin's normally placid features darkened as he scanned the surrounding trees. "Don't know what's happening here, but it ain't natural." He moved to crouch at the side of the cat Sollis had killed, running a hand over its pelt. "Ribs are near poking through its skin. And the belly's empty. I'd say this beast hasn't had a meal in a good long while."

"Wouldn't that explain why they attacked us?" Elera asked.

"Snow-daggers are solitary beasts, sister," Oskin replied. "Don't hunt in packs, and they're clever enough to avoid the scent of man, no matter how hungry they get." He rose and nodded at Red Ears who was busy worrying at the gash she had torn in the other cat's throat. "Looks like there's no more close by, at least," he said. "She wouldn't be feeding otherwise."

"Even so," Sollis said, turning back to the horses. "I'm unwilling to linger and her meal will have to wait. Mount up. No more stops until nightfall."

...

They covered another ten miles before the sun began to fade and made camp in the lee of a large, flat topped boulder rising several feet above the treetops. The horses were tethered close by and Sollis took the first watch atop the boulder whilst the others sheltered below. There was no question of lighting a fire this deep into the Lonak dominion and they were obliged to huddle in their cloaks for warmth.

The northerly winds had grown stiff by nightfall, bringing a chill that Sollis's years in the mountains had never quite accustomed him to. Unable to pace for fear of attracting attention, he sat as he maintained his vigil, continually flexing his fingers beneath his cloak. It was never a good idea to draw a sword with a benumbed grip. He counted as he sat, one to three hundred, maintaining a steady cadence. Upon reaching his total he would close his eyes and listen to the song of the mountains for a count of one hundred. It was a trick the Master of the Wild had taught him during his time at the Order House, a means of occupying the mind without losing concentration, and it had saved his life more than once.

It was during his fifth repetition that he heard it again: the hawk's call, more distant this time but unmistakably the same, plaintive cry. His eyes snapped open, ranging across the sky in search of the bird. The cloud cover was thinner now and the half-moon bright against the black of the sky. *What manner of hawk flies at night?* he wondered, finding no trace of a winged shape anywhere. The question brought Oskin's words to mind: *ain't natural.* Sollis began to rise, intending to wake Oskin for an opinion, then paused as a faint scent reached his nostrils. *Smoke,* he thought, lowering his gaze to the surrounding landscape. He found the source quickly, a blaze atop a low hill perhaps five miles north.

Hearing a scrape of leather on stone he turned to find Sister Elera clambering up onto the boulder, gazing at the distant fire with a wary expression. "A signal fire?" she asked.

"No," Sollis said. "The Lonak don't use them. You should be resting."

She gave a sheepish shrug. "I couldn't sleep. And I smelt the smoke." She nodded at the yellow-orange smudge in the distance. "If it's not a signal, what is it?"

Sollis returned his attention to the blaze. It was large, sending a tall column of thick smoke into the night sky. It was also a good deal above the trees which meant at least it wouldn't spread. "There's a village on that hilltop," he said. "It appears to be burning."

"A battle?" she wondered. "The clans war amongst themselves, Brother Arlyn said."

"It's possible," Sollis conceded. "But I've never seen them burn a whole village before. It's not their warriors' habit to kill the young or the old, unless they're Merim Her, of course."

"Merim Her?"

"It's what they call us. It roughly translates as 'sea-scum'."

"I see. A reference to our forebear's seaborne migration all those centuries ago, I presume. It's said the Lonak and the Seordah once had dominion over all the lands that now comprise the Realm."

"Then we came and took it all away. It's hardly surprising they're still somewhat bitter."

Sollis lifted his gaze to the sky once more, resuming his search for the hawk but finding nothing. The bird's unnatural nighttime flight in close proximity to the burning village was enough of a troubling coincidence to dictate their next course, albeit one he would have preferred to avoid.

"In the morning," he said, "we will inspect what remains of that village."

"Wouldn't it be better to go around?" Elera said. "Whoever attacked it may still be in the vicinity, may they not?"

"Two bucks with one arrow," he reminded her. "You have your mission and I have mine. Please sister, get some sleep."

...

They found the first body halfway up the sloping track that led to the village. A girl, perhaps thirteen years old, lying face down with an arrow in her back. *She was running,* Smentil signed as he examined the corpse with a critical eye. *From the depth of the shaft I'd put the range at over a hundred paces. In the dark too. Quite a feat.* He crouched and reached out to run his fingers over the fletching.

"Gull feathers," Oskin observed. "Looks a good deal like one of ours."

The quill isn't flush with the shaft, Smentil signed, shaking his head. *No brother's hand made this.*

"But I'd hazard whoever did wanted the Lonak to think otherwise," Sollis concluded. He looked towards the top of the slope where a dim pall of smoke mingled with the dense morning mist. The points of the sharpened logs forming the village stockade were just visible above the crest, a long row of blackened teeth in the murk.

"Anything?" he asked Oskin, nodding at Red Ears. The hound's tail swished continually, though the direction of her nose wavered.

"Just death, I think," Oskin said. "And no small amount of it either."

Sollis and his brothers notched arrows before approaching the entrance to the village at a slow walk whilst Elera followed closely behind, leading the horses. The familiar stench of the recently dead mingled with charred wood as Sollis paused amidst the ruins of what had been the gate. The large oakwood doors that had guarded this settlement were now shattered and blackened splinters. Beyond them much of the rest of the village was shrouded in mist, but he could see the bodies of a dozen Lonak lying nearby, men and women. A variety of spears, knives and war clubs lay amongst them and their wounds told of an intense close-quarters fight. Most were only partially dressed and Sollis deduced they had been roused from sleep by the attack.

Came running to defend the gate, Smentil signed. *I'd guess it had already fallen when they got here.*

"Brother," Oskin said, nodding to another corpse just beyond the gate, a corpse clad in a blue cloak. Sollis moved quickly to examine the body, finding an unfamiliar, pale complexioned face beneath a shock of close-cropped black hair. The man had a sword of the Asraelin pattern lying close to his hand and a hatchet buried in the thin leather armour that covered his chest.

"Done up like a brother, sure enough," Oskin observed. "Not well enough to convince anyone with an experienced eye, though."

Sollis scrutinised the rest of the dead man's clothing, finding the boots and leather armour of unfamiliar design. A cursory glance at the man's hands confirmed them as rough and strong, the hands of a warrior, but of what stripe?

He looked up as Smentil tapped him on the shoulder and motioned for him to move aside. When Sollis had done so the brother knelt to draw the hatchet from the dead man's chest then unfastened his armour, pulling it aside. Using his hunting knife he sliced through the wool shirt beneath to reveal a pattern of old scars scored into the man's flesh.

Volarian, his hands said. *Slave-soldier*.

"Seen this before, brother?" Oskin asked him.

Years ago, Smentil replied. *After a fight with some Meldenean pirates. They had taken a Volarian ship and were sailing it to the Isles. Hadn't got round to throwing the bodies overboard when we hove into view.*

"Then this fellow's come a very long way." Oskin retreated a few steps, shrewd eyes scanning the village. "Another one over there." He pointed to a second blue-cloaked figure lying some twenty yards on. A closer inspection revealed the same complexion and scar pattern beneath his armour. However, the cause of his death was different, a large gaping hole in his throat Oskin judged to be the result of a bite.

"Another snow-dagger?" Sollis suggested but Oskin shook his head.

"They puncture the throat and suffocate their prey." He moved away, eyes narrowed in concentration as he surveyed the muddy ground. "This was something with different teeth, and bigger." He paused and sank to his haunches, fingers reaching out to hover over a mark. "Much bigger…" he murmured, Sollis detecting a faint note of incredulity in his tone.

"It looks like a wolf print," he said, looking over Oskin's shoulder, although the size of the track made him wonder. It was at least twice the breadth and width of any wolf's paw he had ever seen.

"That it is," Oskin agreed, rising and moving forward, eyes fixed on the ground. "Got quite the stride, this fellow." He came to a halt several yards on, nodding at an overlapping matrix of tracks. "Looks like he paused here, then…" Oskin turned, striding towards the stockade. Sollis followed him through the gap between two huts whereupon they both drew up short at the sight before them. A large ragged hole had been torn in the timbers of the stockade. It was both wide and tall enough to allow the passage of a full grown man, or something of equal size.

"Faith," Oskin whispered, staring at the jagged edges of the hole. "What could do this?"

"The splinters are all on the inside of the wall," Sollis noted.

Oskin's gaze immediately returned to the ground. "It came in this way." His finger traced a route from the stockade to the village, then back again. "Killed one of the slave-soldiers, paused for a second or two then left the same way." He shook his head in grim-faced bafflement. "Why, brother? What unearthly thing has happened here?"

"Not so much an unearthly thing, brother." Sollis peered through the hole at the misted landscape beyond. "A Dark thing."

Oskin gave a perturbed grunt and moved to survey the ground beyond the hole. "Bare rock all around. Little chance of tracking it, whatever it…"

He fell silent at the sound of shouting to their rear. Sollis and Oskin raised their bows and swiftly retraced their steps. Sister Elera came into view first, standing with her arms outstretched in the wide thoroughfare that ran through the centre of the village. Smentil stood to her right, his bow drawn and arrow aimed at something to her left, though she moved continually in an obvious attempt to frustrate his aim.

"Put that down!" she commanded, though Smentil seemed disinclined to obey.

Sollis rounded one of the huts, preparing to draw his own bow then pausing at the sight of the three figures behind Elera. An old, stick thin Lonak man stood shielding two small children, a boy and a girl. All three were glaring at Elera and Smentil with a mix of fear and defiant hatred. Upon catching sight of Sollis the old man began to mutter a death song, pulling the two children closer to his side as he did so.

"Brother," Sollis said, lowering his bow and shaking his head at Smentil. The brother slowly relaxed his bowstring as Sollis stepped past him. The trio of Lonak tensed as he approached, the children's faces bunching, though the old man held them in place and they made no attempt to flee. He straightened his back as Sollis came to a halt a few yards away, snarling a rebuke at the little boy when he let out a sob.

"Isk-reh varn kha-il dohim ser varkhim ke!" Do not blight our death with your weakness!

Sollis saw that the old man held something, a crumpled, ragged edged length of tanned goatskin, clutched tight in his bony fist. Drawing closer Sollis recognised the markings stitched into the skin: *war banner*. Slowly, he removed the arrow from his bow and returned it to his quiver, holding the weapon up and raising his other hand, fingers spread wide. "We do not bring death this day," he said in Lonak.

"Why not?" the old man enquired, lips curled. "When you brought so much last night?"

Sollis looked around at the ruined village with its blackened, roofless huts and many corpses. "We didn't do this," he said.

"Lies!" the old man spat. He raised a fist to brandish the war banner at Sollis. "Kill us and have done, but do not soil my ears with Merim Her tricks."

"These men," Sollis went on, pointing to the blue-cloaked corpse lying nearby, "they wear our garb, but they are not from our lands. We have come to end them."

Sollis saw the old man's eyes twitch then, betraying a certain sly glint as he straightened a little, saying, "Then you are too late. The Varnish Dervakhim have already ended them all."

Sollis's gaze snapped to Red Ears as she let out a soft whine. The hound's nose was pointed towards the ruined gate, tail straight and unwavering. A half-dozen figures stood amidst the ruins of the gate, features obscured by the mist but evidently Lonak judging by their weapons and garb. A slender figure stood at their head. This one carried no weapons, regarding Sollis with head titled and arms folded in apparently careful scrutiny.

"Brother," Oskin said softly, Sollis hearing his bow creak as he drew the string taut. Turning in a slow circle Sollis saw other Lonak emerging from the ruins, some with lowered spears, others drawn flat-bows. He quickly counted at least twenty with more appearing behind. *Too many,* he knew, grinding his teeth in self-reproach.

"Sister," he said to Elera. "You were right. We should have gone around."

"Thank you, brother," she replied in an admirably steady tone.

"When it starts," he went on, reaching for his quiver as the Lonak inched closer, "mount up and ride off, as fast as you can. We should be able to create enough of a distraction for you to get clear. If it appears they're about to catch you, I advise that you cut your wrists. A downward stroke works best."

"Your concern is appreciated, brother."

His fingers closed on an arrow and his gaze fixed on the closest Lonak, a stocky warrior now only twenty yards away. The man's features were set in the hard mask of imminent combat, his own bow fully drawn. There were two more behind, one with a club, the other a spear. Sollis was confident he could get two with his arrows before dispatching the third with his sword. After that…

"*Reh-isk!*" *Stop!*

Sollis's gaze swung towards the gate where the slender figure was now striding forward, arms unfolded and waving dismissively at the encroaching Lonak. At the command they came to a sudden halt, although their bows remained drawn and spears lowered. As the figure came closer Sollis saw that it was a woman. A pelt of wild-cat fur covered her torso, though her lean, muscled arms were bare, each richly decorated in tattoos. A long scalp-lock traced from the top of her head and down her back. Sollis was quick to recognise the green and red ink pattern covering most of her shaven head: *shaman*.

She came to a halt a dozen feet away, looking at each of them in turn. Sollis was struck by the lack of animosity on her face, she was even smiling a little. "Hello," she said in perfect Realm tongue, the accent every bit as smooth and cultured as Sister Elera's. Her eyes tracked over each of them again before coming to rest on Sollis, whereupon she frowned, lips pursed in apparent disappointment. "She said you would be taller."

CHAPTER FIVE

"They're called Kuritai," the shaman said, kicking the blue-cloaked corpse at her feet. "The Volarian slave-elite. Deadly but mindless."

The other Lonak had retreated after she barked out a series of harsh commands. They still maintained a perimeter around Sollis and the others, but had at least relaxed their bows and lowered their spears. From the hard, hate-filled glares on every face Sollis deduced that the only thing keeping them from a swift and merciless slaughter was the authority enjoyed by this strange woman.

"And what do they call you?" he asked her.

"Verkehla," she replied, turning to him with a smile and bowing. "Tahlessa to the Varnish Dervakhim, by the word of the Mahlessa."

Verkehla, Sollis searched his memory for the meaning. *Bloody Arrow.* "I am…" he began but she cut him off.

"Brother Sollis of the Sixth Order," she said, eyebrows raised in a mockery of awe. "The Grey Eyed Fox himself. I am truly honoured."

Sollis heard Oskin let out a soft laugh before muttering, "Told you, brother."

"Varnish Dervakhim," Sollis went on, ignoring him. "The Outcast Knives?"

"Your translation is somewhat inelegant," Verkehla replied. "I prefer 'The Banished Blades.' A tad more poetic, don't you think?"

He gestured to the surrounding Lonak. "These are all Varnish?"

"Indeed they are." Verkehla's face took on a sour expression as she surveyed her fellow Lonak. "Murderers, thieves, liars and oath-breakers. All given a chance at redemption by the Mahlessa's word. They make for fairly terrible company, I must say. I find I hate them all quite a lot." Her features bunched into a sudden, resentful snarl and she called out in Lonak, "I just told him how much I hate you, you worthless ape-fuckers!"

This caused many of the onlooking Lonak to stiffen and focus their baleful glares on the shaman instead of the four Merim Her. However, Sollis noted that although their hands tightened on their weapons, not one voice was raised against her. Every warrior suffered the insult in rigid silence.

"See?" Verkehla said. "They'd dearly love to kill me, almost as much as they'd delight in killing you. But they'll put up with pretty much anything, just for the merest chance the Mahlessa might restore them to their clans."

"I assume this is the reason why we aren't currently fighting," Sollis said, nodding again at the corpse she had named a Kuritai.

Verkehla met his gaze, smiling and saying nothing for a moment that stretched as her eyes shifted from him to Sister Elera. "You're a healer, aren't you?" she asked.

"I am," the sister replied. "Sister Elera of the Fifth Order..."

"Yes, all very nice and fine, I'm sure," Verkehla broke in. "We have wounded. Will you attend to them?"

"Of course."

The shaman turned and barked out more commands at the surrounding Lonak. "Find a dwelling that still has a roof, and gather the wounded there. The Merim Her bitch will see to them, and I don't want to hear any grumbling about it."

She fixed her gaze on Sollis once again. "Whilst your sister does her compassionate duty, you and I will share stories at the fire. I'm sure you have an interesting tale to tell."

...

"Snow-daggers, eh?" Verkehla raised an eyebrow in surprise as she chewed on a roasted rabbit. They sat together in a ruined hut, alone apart from the old man and the two children. Sollis had ordered Smentil and Oskin to stay at Elera's side, although Verkehla assured him they were in no danger. A fire blazed in the central pit that served as a focal point for all Lonak dwellings, a brace of freshly slaughtered rabbits roasting on a spit above the flames. The roof had been claimed by the blaze the night before and smoke rose through the blackened rafters into a grey sky. The children huddled at the old man's side as they sat in a corner, chewing on the meat Verkehla had tossed to them and staring at Sollis with bright, fearful eyes.

"We call them *kavim kiral*," she went on. "Shadow-cats, because they're so rarely seen, especially this far south. One of many strange occurrences recently."

"We found no sign of any other Lonak," Sollis said. "Until now. Also very strange in my experience."

Verkehla gave a small grin. "They're all at home, on the Mahlessa's order. Word came from the Mountain that no war bands or hunting parties were to venture out for a full month."

"Apart from your Banished Blades."

"Quite. They are..." She paused, frowning. "Expendable, I believe the term is."

"It is. You know our language very well."

"I had a fine education." The grin disappeared from her lips and Sollis noted a hard cast creep into her eyes. Clearly, this was an unwelcome topic of conversation.

"You said something about me being taller," Sollis said. "You were expecting us."

"Just you, actually. The other three are a complication, especially your blonde sister. I can't imagine what possessed you to bring her into the mountains."

"We have a mission. And she's hardier than she looks."

"She'll need to be." Verkehla bit the last morsel of meat from the rabbit's haunch and tossed the bone into the fire, wiping the grease from her face with the back of her hand. "The Mahlessa, in her wisdom, has foreseen your coming, oh fox of the grey eyes. As she foresaw the coming of those who would wear your garb and do murder in your name. Quite where and when was not revealed to her, and so I and my company of scum were despatched to hunt them down."

"So your mission is complete?"

"Hardly." Verkehla let out a sigh and glanced at the children, causing them to huddle closer to the old man. "Not while these two are still drawing breath, at least."

"They are important?" Sollis asked.

"Apparently. Or at least one of them is. The Mahlessa's statements regarding the visions she receives from the Gods can be… vague. Like a riddle that needs a good deal of pondering before it's solved. 'They come for the child,' she said, sadly without providing a name for said child. All she could tell me is that they live in this village, and that someone has brought the Dark into these mountains to kill them."

"Perhaps this child has already perished," Sollis suggested. "There are corpses of all ages littering this place."

Verkehla shook her head, gaze lingering on the children. "No. Whatever it is waits nearby, watches. I can feel it. We killed its slave-soldiers, but it's not done. It'll come for them. Be sure of that, brother."

"How?" He squinted at her in bafflement as her gaze swung back to him. "How can you *feel* it?"

She blinked and shifted her eyes to the fire, remaining silent for long enough to allow Sollis to conclude this was another question she wouldn't answer. Finally, she said, "You mentioned a mission. Might I enquire what it is? Since you brought a healer I don't imagine you've ventured forth with assassination in mind."

Sollis pondered the wisdom of sharing his knowledge with her, deciding it couldn't do any harm. "There's a place," he said. "We call it Morvil's Reach. We need to find something there, a plant with healing properties."

Verkehla let out a soft snort of amusement. "You came into our lands to look for a plant? The Mahlessa's riddle told of a quest of fabled proportions. I was at least hoping for buried treasure. Or perhaps a lost, Dark-imbued sword from the time of the ancients."

"Sorry to disappoint you."

She shrugged and got to her feet. "No matter. We'll go with you to the Reach. We call it *Trehl kha lahk dehvar*, incidentally."

"The hilltop of the... wrong headed man?" Sollis asked, struggling with the translation.

"The Mad Man's Stockade," she corrected, shaking her head. "You certainly have a gift for mangling our language, brother." She turned to address the old man in Lonak. "Can you still fight, or is it time to leave you out in the snow?"

"I can fight," he replied, chin jutting in pique. He raised the ragged goatskin in his hand, unfurling it to reveal the markings. "Do you not know who you behold, oh Servant of the Mountain? Do you not know this banner? I am Khela-hahk, the bloody club, the Shatterer of Skulls, last of the Stone Crushers. We who stood alone against the steel-clads at the Black River. We who laid low a *kermana* of Merim Her in a single day..."

"Never heard of you," Verkehla broke in. "And since you're still alive, I'd guess you didn't do much skull shattering last night. Find a midden to hide in, did you?"

The old man glared at her, bony jaw bunching in suppressed fury as he lowered the banner to draw the two children closer still. "They required my protection," he said.

"Are they your blood?" she asked, angling her head to survey the infants.

"I was blood-father to their mother." His fury abated a little as he lowered his gaze. "She died fighting those who wore this one's garb." He jerked his head at Sollis. "And you act as if he is not our enemy. You share stories at the fire with a Blue-cloak. What a vile, shameful thing..."

"Word from the Mountain is not to be questioned," Verkehla snapped, causing the old man to fall into an abrupt silence. "Besides," she added, turning back to Sollis with a skeptical half-grin, "according to the Mahlessa he's going to be your whelps' valiant protector."

...

They departed the village at noon, Verkehla and the Banished Blades mounting up on sturdy ponies and trotting through the ruined gate. The corpses of their fellow Lonak were left where they lay, as was the custom in the mountains. "They belong to the Gods now," Verkehla said when Sister Elera enquired about Lonak funeral customs. "They will ordain how their flesh is disposed of." Sollis noticed that the woman's arch, often cynical inflection disappeared when she spoke of the gods. Apparently, the subject of the divine was one thing she took very seriously.

"I don't think he relishes our company," Elera observed, nodding at the old man's continually scowling visage. He and his two grandchildren were mounted on spare ponies and trotted at the rear of the company alongside Sollis and his fellow Merim Her.

"Too right he doesn't, sister," Oskin agreed with a chuckle. "Nothing would make him happier than slitting our throats." He raised his voice, leaning towards the old man as he asked, "Isn't that right, you old savage?"

The old man's lips curled in anger and he spat back with a few choice insults of his own. Much of it was too fast for Sollis to catch, although he did detect the words 'horse-fucking cock-swallower'.

"Leave him be, brother," Sollis instructed. "And his name's Khela-hahk."

Oskin swung to him with a quizzical frown then shrugged as he saw Sollis's intent sincerity. "Couldn't give a rat's balls for his name, brother," Oskin muttered, spurring his horse forward. "But as you wish."

"Servants of the Faith should be beyond hatred," Elera commented to Sollis, a judgmental cast to her eyes as she regarded Oskin.

"It's easier to keep to the catechisms when you spend your life in warm rooms under a sound roof, sister," Sollis replied. "And when you haven't had to carry a dozen murdered children to the fire and speak the words for them, because their parents have also been murdered."

Her gaze swung to him, narrowing yet further. "So you hate them too?"

Sollis frowned, finding it odd that the notion of how he felt about the Lonak had never occurred to him before. "No more than I hate these mountains from which I might fall one day, or the wind that could steal the warmth of my body on a stormy night. The Lonak are simply the most dangerous threat in a place full of dangers. But," he paused to incline his head at a still glowering Khela-hahk, "regardless of how we might feel about them, they will always hate us. Even the shaman who leads this band. She might speak our language and understand our customs better than any of her kind, but she hates us too. I see it clearly."

"Then why are they helping us?"

"Perhaps they aren't." Sollis looked at the two children perched back to back on a pony. The boy, marginally the older of the two, returned Sollis's gaze with a fierce, suspicious glower, whilst the girl simply stared back in puzzled curiosity. "Perhaps," Sollis added softly, "we're helping them. But to what end I cannot say."

CHAPTER SIX

"The Mad Man's Stockade," Verkehla said. She reined her pony to a halt, pointing to a steep hill rising from the floor of a shallow valley a mile or so ahead. The stronghold of Morvil's Reach lay atop the hill, its dark, weather beaten walls more intact than Sollis had expected. Noting that the western and northern approaches were guarded by the hooked bend of a fast flowing river, Sollis concluded that whatever the failings of the unfortunate Lord Morvil, he had at least possessed an eye for a sound defensive position.

"Your people left the stones in place," he observed to Verkehla who shrugged.

"The Grey Hawks shun the place," she said. "There are old stories about the spectres of Merim Her wandering the place on dark nights, crying out to be let into the Beyond. It seems the Departed have barred entry, possibly due to the shame of their defeat."

"You know the Faith?" Elera asked her. Her tone was one of gratified surprise but Verkehla turned to her with a harsh glare.

"Far better than I would like, sister," she said, baring her teeth in a harsh mutter. Elera blanched a little but didn't look away, straightening the saddle and forming her features into a neutral mask.

"The Departed are rarely so judgmental," Sollis said, nudging Vensar forward to place him between the shaman and the healer. "Those who die in honest battle can expect a place in the Beyond."

"Honest battle?" Verkehla's expression softened into one of amused scorn as she shifted her gaze to Sollis. "There was a small settlement on this hill before your people came. What do you imagine their fate to have been? Perhaps your Departed simply refused entry to a gang of murderers and thieves."

"Getting dark," Oskin said, voice gruff with impatience. "Be best if we got ourselves within those walls and settled for the night, look for the sister's precious weed in the morning."

Sollis raised a questioning eyebrow at Verkehla who nodded and spurred her pony forward, barking a command at the Varnish Dervakhim. "Spread out and scout all approaches. I want to know about any track you find, however small."

As the Lonak fanned out she led Sollis and the others along a mostly overgrown trail that led to the stronghold's gate. He judged the height of the walls at a little over twenty feet, overlooked by a single tower. The iron braced oak doors lay in rusted ruin, revealing a small courtyard of moss-covered rock beyond. The tower rose from the centre of the courtyard, its unusually wide base indicating it had served a dual role as main keep and lookout post.

Typical Renfaelin design, Smentil signed as he surveyed the structure. *Just a good deal smaller than usual.*

"Shall we, brother?" Verkehla asked Sollis, dismounting and gesturing at the unbarred gate. She started inside without waiting for an answer. Sollis told the others to stay put and climbed down from Vensar's back, handing the reins to Smentil before following the shaman inside.

"I can't see any spectres," she commented, standing in the centre of the courtyard and scanning the narrow battlements above. "Perhaps it's a tad too early for them, eh?"

Sollis ignored the jibe, one hand on the hilt of his sword as he moved in a slow circle, eyes probing every shadowed corner of the stronghold's interior. "You walk into potential danger with no weapon," he said. "That is unwise. There could be more slave-soldiers waiting in ambush."

"There aren't," she replied with casual certainty. "We killed them all. And trust me, brother, when I say I am far from defenceless."

Despite her words Sollis insisted on a thorough inspection of the structure before allowing the others inside. He found himself impressed with the solidity of the place, the precision with which the stones had been laid and aligned told of skilled hands.

"Lord Morvil knew his business in one respect at least," he commented to his brothers later. They sat together in the base of the tower around a small fire that sent a column of smoke into the skeletal rafters above. He had pondered the wisdom of lighting a fire that would be sure to advertise their presence here. However, the Dervakhim seemed oblivious to such concerns, those not posted to the walls clustering around their own fires as they roasted meat and followed their nightly ritual of sharing stories.

"Or, more likely his masons did," Oskin replied. "Poor bastards, following their lord to this forsaken place. It's safe odds they died along with all his knights and retainers. I hope he paid them well in the meantime."

Sollis's attention was drawn to the opposite side of the fire by an unusual sound, one he realised he hadn't heard in these mountains before. The little Lonak girl was laughing, small hands over her mouth as she regarded Elera with wide, delighted eyes. "Sermahkash," the sister said, smiling in bemusement as this provoked another round of giggling from the girl. "It's her name," she said, catching sight of Sollis's quizzical frown. "At least I think so."

"Your pronunciation is a little off, sister," Sollis said. "Sumehrkas. It means Misted Dawn. The way you said it resembled the Lonak word for ape piss."

"Oh." Elera laughed and poked the girl gently in the belly. "Are you making fun of me, little one?"

The girl laughed again then fell abruptly silent as Khela-hahk uttered a curt rebuke. He and the boy sat together at another fire a few feet away, the old man beckoning to the girl with a stern frown on his wrinkled brow. She gave a sullen pout and rose from Elera's side, starting forward then halting as the sister gently took her hand. "We're only playing…" she began, offering the old warrior a reassuring smile.

"Sister," Sollis said softly, shaking his head. Elera sighed and released the girl who stomped to the other fire, slumping down with arms crossed and face set in sulky reproach.

"Don't feel too bad, sister," Oskin commented, chewing a mouthful of dried beef. "Probably just trying to win your trust so she can slit your throat when you're sleeping."

"What a fount of unsolicited opinions you are, brother," Elera observed with a thin smile.

"We know what these people are," Oskin returned evenly. "You do not and would do well to listen to experienced counsel." He jerked his head at Smentil who sat running a whetstone over the blade of his sword. "Ask our brother. They held him for ten days, visited all manner of outrages on his flesh, not to say taking his tongue into the bargain. It astonishes me he can stomach being in their company."

Smentil's whetstone emitted a harsh grind as he scraped it the length of the blade, his eyes fixing Oskin with a glare of warning. The older brother flushed a little and lowered his gaze. "Apologies, brother," he murmured.

"As ever, idle hands make for useless talk," Sollis said, adopting a brisk tone as he rose, hefting his bow and settling his sword on his back. "Brother Oskin, take your hound and scout beyond the walls. The Lonak didn't find any suspicious tracks but that doesn't mean much this deep in the mountains. Stay within bowshot of the walls. Brother Smentil will go with you. Sister." He inclined his head at Elera. "My earlier inspection revealed something I believe may be of interest to our mission, if you would care to join me."

...

Despite being cracked in places, the winding stairs that hugged the wall of the building were another testament to the soundness of the fortress's construction, remaining intact all the way to the top. Sollis guided their steps with a flaming torch as Elera followed him into the tower's gloomy upper reaches.

"For all his prejudice," she said, "Brother Oskin makes an insightful point. Smentil seems remarkably free of hatred towards our new companions."

"He was always a difficult man to read," Sollis replied. "Even in the days when he could speak. In any case, the Faith teaches us that vengeance is folly, does it not?"

"'A vindictive heart stains the Beyond,'" she agreed with a quote. "As set down in The Catechism of Truth. Perhaps Oskin should pay greater attention to its message."

Sollis resisted the impulse to impart a brief summation of the many trials Oskin had suffered since his deployment to the Pass, knowing it to be an excuse. *What is the point of Faith if it is to be abandoned in the face of adversity?* he pondered, silently resolving to speak to Brother Commander Arlyn when they returned. Perhaps it was time for Oskin to take up a master's role at the Order House where he could impart his wisdom to the next generation of novice brothers.

"In here," he said, pausing at a narrow doorway. He lowered the torch to illuminate the interior, gesturing for her to precede him.

"Hardly a grand chamber," Elera said, casting her gaze around the room which was ten feet across at its widest point. "You truly think this was where Lord Morvil held court?"

"No, but I'd hazard this is where he slept. Small as it is, it's still the largest chamber in the whole fortress." Sollis followed her inside, glancing back at the doorway before lowering his voice. "I noticed something," he said, moving to the far wall and crouching. "Something I thought it best the Lonak woman didn't see."

He pointed to a mark on the brickwork an inch from the floor. It was small but neatly chiselled into the stone, a rectangular symbol inset with two dots. "Is that..?" Elera began, leaning down and squinting at the marking.

"Far Western script," Sollis said. "I believe it means 'book'."

"You can read Far Western script, brother?"

Sollis chose not to take offence at the keen surprise in her voice. Why would a brother of the Sixth know such things, after all? "Not in its entirety, no," he admitted. "But I've had occasion to fight smugglers and pirates, some of Far Western origin. They tend to mark their hiding places with symbols such as these, believing, not without good reason, that easterners are too ignorant to recognise them as anything but a meaningless scrawl."

"So, you think Lord Morvil learned the same trick?"

"The accounts of his life are colourful, full of unlikely tales of adventures in far-off lands. Perhaps some of it was actually true."

Elera let out a small laugh, shuffling closer to run her fingers over the symbol. Sollis made a conscious effort not to notice the soft caress of her hair on his neck as she did so. "It occurs to me your knowledge and intellect might have been better employed in the Third Order," she murmured.

"I doubt it." Sollis drew the hunting knife from his belt and worked the tip of the blade into the mortar that bound the marked brick in place. "This might take some time," he said, handing her the torch. "If you would care to guard the door."

"Of course."

It took close on an hour's labour to loosen the brick, Sollis doggedly scraping away the mortar until he had sufficient room to work his fingers into the gap and lever the stone free. "The torch, sister," he said, extending his hand as he lowered himself to peer into the small space. He gave a small grunt of satisfaction as the torchlight revealed the dim gleam of a leather binding. Reaching in, he extracted a small volume, the cover and spine lacking any inscription. The leather that bound it was dry and cracked with age, flaking into powder as Sollis ran his fingers over it.

"I think this calls for gentler hands," he said, handing the book to Elera.

The sister carefully opened the book, revealing pages of yellow parchment inscribed in a flowing, elegant script. Despite the precision of the penmanship Sollis found he couldn't read a word of it. "That's not Realm Tongue," he said.

"'The Conquest of the Northern Mountains and the Subjugation of the Wolf Men'," Elera read, her finger tracing across the words inscribed at the top of the first page. "'Being a true and honest account by Baron Valeric Morvil, Knight of Renfael.'" She raised a caustic eyebrow. "Clearly a fellow not lacking in self-regard." She smiled at Sollis's puzzled frown. "It's ancient Volarian, brother. At one time all scholarly works in the four fiefs were written in this script. In fact, it remained a common practice amongst the more pretentious scholars until King Janus banned its use during the first year of his reign."

"And yet, you can read it," Sollis observed.

"My…" she began then paused, Sollis recognising the familiar expression of a servant of the Faith reminding themselves that mention of one's previous life was frowned upon. "I learned a great deal before I entered the Order," she added, returning her attention to the book. "The first few pages relate his preparations for the campaign, buying of provisions, hiring of men and so on." She thumbed ahead, grimacing in consternation. "It seems the Baron's self-regard is matched only by his verbosity. It will take several hours to fully examine this for mention of the weed."

"Very well." Sollis moved to the door. "Best find a quiet corner to do so. I'd prefer the Lonak not see you with it."

"They object to books?"

"No, they love them, or rather their Mahlessa does. When they raid the only booty they prize more than horses are books. Apparently, the Mountain provides great rewards for any warrior who comes to offer books in tribute. If they see you with that, they'll almost certainly try to take it."

Elera nodded and consigned the book to the inner folds of her robe. "Do you believe her?" she asked. "That whatever or whoever destroyed that village is still out there."

"I do. In fact, I suspect it's why we're still alive. The Mahlessa has ordered it, at least as long as the threat to her people persists."

"A threat she saw in some Dark vision?" Elera shook her head. "I find it hard to credit mere superstition for our predicament, brother."

"What is superstition to us is real to them. The Mahlessa believes, and therefore so do they, that we have a role to play in ending the evil infesting these mountains. Even should we find the weed, I doubt we'll be going anywhere until this vision has come to pass. We are expected to spring a trap, and those children downstairs are but bait."

"And therefore deserving of our protection, wouldn't you say?"

Sollis saw a glint of wary appraisal in her gaze then, as if her question were a test and she feared he might fail it. "Rest assured, sister," he said. "I'll defend them as I would any child, Realm born, Faithful or not."

She gave a tight smile, stepping forward to place a hand on his, her flesh warm despite the chill that pervaded the fortress. "I must confess to always having harboured a certain… discomfort with the need for your Order," she said. "Why should a Faith that celebrates life require servants so skilled in the ways of death? I see now, my questions were misplaced…"

She fell silent as he raised a hand, his gaze drawn upwards by a new sound, a faint and plaintive call drifting through the part destroyed roof of the tower. "What is that?" Elera asked.

"Hawk," Sollis said, handing her the torch. "Make your way back down, sister. I'll be there shortly."

The faint moonlight enabled him to navigate to the tower's roof without undue difficulty where he found Verkehla waiting, head tilted at an expectant angle. "You and the sister spent a good deal of time alone, brother," she observed. "What could you have been doing?"

"Discussing the finer points of the Catechism of Truth," Sollis replied, ascending the last few steps onto the patchy stonework that formed the tower's summit. The thick beams that supported the wall could be seen through gaps in the floor, like the exposed ribs of a massive rotting corpse. The top was ringed by a low crenellated wall which remained weathered but intact. Sollis moved to it, eyes raised to the partly clouded sky and ears alive for the hawk's call.

"So you heard it too?" Verkehla asked. "A cry in the night from a bird that never flies in darkness."

"Not just tonight," he said. "I've heard it three times now, once not long before we were attacked by the snow-daggers."

"Information you might have shared with me earlier."

Sollis glanced at her judgmental frown and gave a faint shrug. "And have you shared all your pertinent information with me?"

Her face took on an impassive aspect that told of another refusal to answer so he returned his gaze to the sky. "No sign of it," he murmured.

"It's there. Whatever commands it will make sure it keeps watch on us."

"Commands it?"

Evidently his skepticism showed in his voice for her tone

was curt when she replied, "You are quite willing to believe the ghosts of the dead gather together in some mystical, invisible realm, and yet you shun evidence of what you call the Dark when it stares you in the face."

"Your people shun it, do they not?"

"Yes, because they have the wit to recognise the danger it poses. Your people hide behind scorn or choose to blame the Dark on those who deny the Faith, a Faith that preaches peace yet is quite happy to cage heretics and hang them from a gibbet to starve. Ever had to do that, brother?"

Sollis had as yet been spared the duty of accompanying the Third Order on their Denier hunting expeditions. Even so, there were many stories from brothers who had, and they were far from edifying. "No," he said.

"But you would," she persisted. "If your Order commanded it, you would."

"The Faith requires all we have. As your Mahlessa, I'm sure, requires all of you."

She began to answer but halted as a harsh scream cut through the night air beyond the battlement, quickly followed by the shouts and snapping bowstrings that told of combat. Sollis immediately unslung his bow, notching an arrow as he moved to the wall, eyes peering into the darkness. He could see only vague shapes in the gloom below, shadowed figures whirling in a chaotic dance as the tumult of battle continued, Sollis recognising the screams now. *Rock apes!*

He spied a loping shadow beneath, long arms and shorter legs propelling across the ground faster than any man. Sollis drew his bow until the arrow's fletching brushed his ear, centring the vertical line of the arrowhead on the running ape. Before he could loose, a loud, snarling bark of challenge erupted to his right. He spun, seeing Verkehla reeling back from the wall, a fur-covered, dog-faced shape vaulting the battlement in pursuit. Drool flew from the ape's bared teeth and clawed hands reached out to dig into the woman's shoulders, its massive weight bearing her down as its jaws snapped at her throat.

CHAPTER SEVEN

Sollis's arrow took the ape just behind the head. At such close range the shaft possessed sufficient force to pierce the creature's neck all the way through. It convulsed in shock, letting out a choked, rasping howl, blood colouring the drool flowing from its mouth as it whirled to face him, too slow to avoid the sword stroke that cleaved its skull. The edge of the blade cut through flesh and bone to find the brain beneath. Sollis grunted with the effort of tugging it free before finishing the twitching animal with an expertly placed slash to open the veins in its throat.

He turned his attention to Verkehla, intending to check her wounds, but stopped at the sight of her hard, implacable features, eyes focused on something over his shoulder. Sollis ducked and rolled clear, feeling the rush of air as a claw slashed close to his head. His roll brought him to the edge of a gap in the roof. He crouched, sword held low as he regarded the second ape. This one was larger than the first with an extensive mane of fur covering its neck and shoulders, marking it out as a full grown male, possibly a pack leader. Meeting his gaze the male ape growled, sinking lower and tensing for a lunge. In such a constricted space Sollis knew he would have only one chance of a kill and decided to improve his odds, using his free hand to reach for a throwing knife. It was then that the stones beneath his feet gave way.

He arrested his fall by clamping a hand onto the edge of a roof beam, the impact jarring the sword loose from his grip, the blade whirling away into the gloom beneath his dangling feet. Seeing the ape's gaping jaws loom above, Sollis prepared to follow his sword into the depths, finding the fall preferable to the teeth. Before he could do so the ape came to an abrupt halt, jaws slackening as it shook its head, huffing in confusion. It then went into an sudden, violent spasm, head jerking back and a scream of pain escaping its maw. Sollis saw blood seeping from its eyes, nose and mouth in thick torrents. It then seemed to collapse from within, deflating like a pierced bellows as its life blood flowed out of every orifice until it was nothing more than an immobile sack of fur and bones.

Sollis watched the tide of blood wash over the roof and the part collapsed stone above, trickling down to cover the beam he clung to with both hands. Realising his grip was about to be loosened, Sollis began to haul himself up. The bloody torrent was too thick, however, and he let out a frustrated grunt as his left hand lost purchase on the beam. It flailed in the air for a second before another hand reached down to grasp his wrist. Sollis looked up to see Verkehla's face above, pale in the dim moonlight with dark stains beneath her nose and around her eyes. It appeared she had bled aplenty too.

"You're not supposed to die yet," she told him, groaning with the effort of hauling him upwards.

...

The four bodies lay in the courtyard, the features of the slain Lonak warriors marred by deep claw marks that had ripped away eyes, noses and jaws. One had clearly been overwhelmed by several attackers at once, his corpse lacking a stomach as well as a face. They had been dragged into the fortress by their fellow

Lonak whilst Oskin and Smentil stood in the gate, theirs bows cutting down a half-dozen pursuing apes. Upon descending from the tower, Sollis had conveyed the bleeding form of Verkehla to Sister Elera's care before rushing to join his brothers. However, by then the apes had retreated into the gloom. The rest of the night passed without incident, though none of the Reach's occupants managed a moment's sleep.

"Must've been near forty of the buggers, brother," Oskin said, face grim. He turned to deliver a kick to the corpse of an ape that had made it over the walls to claw a warrior to death before falling victim to a dozen or more arrows.

Closer to fifty, Smentil signed. *Approached in silence from the north. The southerly wind meant Red Ears didn't catch their scent until they were almost on us.*

"It's a miracle they only claimed four," Oskin said. "If we hadn't had these walls to retreat behind..." He trailed off and shook his head, face tense with a reluctant conclusion. "First the snow-daggers, now this. A Dark business indeed."

Sollis turned as an angry shout came from the base of the tower. "Ouch! You vicious bitch!"

"Keep your hound walking the parapet," Sollis told Oskin, making for the tower. "See if her nose has any better luck in daylight. Smentil, take position atop the tower and keep watch. I'll join you shortly."

Inside the tower he found Elera crouched at Verkehla's side. The shaman winced continually as the sister worked a needle and suture through her skin to seal the wound in her shoulder. "She's deliberately taking too long," she groused at Sollis. "I can tell. And she tortured me with some vile concoction first."

"Corr tree oil to stop it festering," Elera murmured, apparently unperturbed as she kept her attention focused on her work. Sollis assumed this was far from the first difficult patient she had treated. "And you refused redflower to dull the pain," the sister added, tying off the last stitch with a swift, practiced flourish.

"The Mahlessa has decreed we shun Merim Her drugs," Verkehla replied, teeth gritted as Elera swabbed the completed stitches with more corr tree oil. "Lest our wits become as dull as yours."

Whilst Elera fixed a bandage over the wound Verkehla let out a slow calming breath. "How many did we lose?" she asked Sollis, slipping into Lonak.

"Four. No wounded, which is strange."

"Apes rarely leave their foes alive. There's a reason my people never hunt them."

"We estimate their numbers at fifty. My brothers killed a dozen or so…"

"There'll be more," Verkehla broke in. "And not just apes. Whatever's out there isn't done with us."

Sollis stepped closer, lowering his voice a notch. "What happened up there?" he said, flicking his eyes towards the top of the tower. "I've never seen a beast, nor a man, die like that."

"It's a very big world, brother," she told him with an empty smile. "I imagine there are methods of killing beyond even your extensive experience." She paused to cast a caustic glance around the gloomy interior of the tower. When she spoke again she switched back to Realm Tongue. "The Lonak fight in the open. Castles and sieges are foreign to us. But I imagine it's something you know a great deal about."

"I know how to defend a stronghold, if that's what you mean."

"Good." She turned and called to a group of warriors waiting near the entrance, beckoning them closer. "The Blue Cloak will show you how to prepare this place," she told them in Lonak. "You will follow his word as you follow mine."

From the set, rigid faces the warriors turned on Sollis at that moment, he found himself wondering if their desire for the Mahlessa's favour was as absolute as Verkehla claimed it to be. However, none of them spoke up to protest, instead continuing to stare at him in expectant if resentful silence.

Knowing any words of conciliation would be wasted Sollis nodded and started towards the courtyard. "Follow and listen well," he told them. "We have much to do."

...

"Won't work."

The Lonak's name was Fehl-ahkim, which translated as 'man of stone', or 'builder' depending on the inflection. He was both older and taller than most of the Banished Blades, his arms thick with muscle that flexed impressively as he crossed them, eying the ruins of the gate with an expert's disdain. Before his disgrace, which apparently involved a fatal dispute with a neighbour over the ownership of a prized pony, he had been renowned for his skill in building huts and maintaining the defensive wall of his clan's stronghold.

"Rust and rot," he told Sollis, shaking his head. "Can't build with that."

"We need to close this gate," Sollis insisted.

Fehl-ahkim shot him a sour look, jaws bunching as he sighed and cast his gaze around the innards of Morvil's Reach. "There," he said, nodding at a row of roofless stone enclosures that had once been the fortress's storehouses. "Wasted stone. We could tear it down, use it to seal the portal." He moved closer to the ruins of the gate, stroking his chin in contemplation as he touched a booted toe to one of the rusted iron brackets. "Nothing around to use for mortar, but we can buttress with these. Still some strength here, despite the rust."

"Very well." Sollis unbuckled his sword belt before removing his cloak, setting them aside and starting towards the storehouses. "Then we'd best be at it."

Under Fehl-ahkim's guidance the Lonak used their knives and war clubs to chip away the old mortar binding the stones at the base of the storehouse walls. Once they were sufficiently loosened he had them fix ropes around the top of the walls to haul them down. Within a few hours they were rewarded with a decent sized pile of building materials which the builder had begun to form into a stone and iron barrier some two feet thick at the base.

"Needs to be wider at the bottom," he told Sollis. "Elst it'll topple a the first blow of a ram, or whatever other contrivance is like to be hurled at it."

The barrier had ascended to a height of three feet by the time Sollis heard the sharp, urgent call of Smentil's hunting horn from atop the tower. Looking up he saw the brother leaning over the edge of the battlement to point west before forming his hands into a series of urgent signs. Sollis couldn't make out the full meaning at this distance but the gist was clear enough: *Enemy approaching. Many.*

"Keep working," Sollis told Fehl-ahkim before gathering

up his weapons and swiftly climbing the steps to the parapet of the west-facing wall. Oskin was already there, Red Ears at his side. The hound let out a low, steady growl as she gazed at the force arrayed out of bow-shot on the far side of the river. Upon first viewing Sollis would have taken the host for a three regiment strong contingent of Realm Guard, their ranks being so neatly aligned and discipline so absolute in its lack of sound or movement. But it instantly became apparent that these were not men.

"Not just apes," Sollis murmured, echoing Verkehla as his gaze tracked along the unmoving host. A long row of snow-daggers sat still as statues next to an assemblage of equally static white pelted wolves. Smaller contingents of black bears were flanked by mountain lions and lynxes.

"How..." Oskin breathed, eyes bright with both wonder and horror. "It's impossible."

Sollis heard a similar pitch of fear and mystification in the growing murmur of disquiet from the surrounding Lonak. He caught Oskin's gaze with a hard glare and the brother abruptly straightened, offering a forced grin of apology.

"Forgive me, brother," he said. "Heard whispers of the Dark all my life. It's a strange feeling when a whisper becomes a shout."

"Quiet, you worthless goat-shaggers!" Verkehla barked, pushing her way through the throng of Banished Blades. "The Mahlessa never promised an easy path to forgiveness. So put a muzzle on that grumbling."

She came to Sollis's side, eyes narrowed as she gazed at the beasts and grunted, "Impressive," in softly spoken Realm Tongue. "It must have quite the gift."

"Who?" Sollis asked.

She pursed her lips and pointed at a solitary, two-legged figure emerging from the ranks of assembled animals. "I imagine we're about to find out."

The figure was dressed much the same as the slaughtered Kuritai they hand found back at the settlement, its cloak ripped and ragged and hair an unkempt dark mess coiling in the wind. The figure approached the western bank of the river without particular haste, coming to a halt to regard the Reach with head cocked at an angle that indicated both curiosity and amusement. After a short pause the figure bowed and opened its arms in an obvious gesture of invitation.

"A parley?" Oskin wondered.

"More likely a chance to gloat," Verkehla said, turning away with a dismissive shrug. "Ignore it. It won't attack until nightfall, and anyone who goes out there is likely to become food for its army."

"You're not curious?" Sollis asked. "Every opportunity should be taken to learn more about an enemy."

The shaman paused, rolling her eyes. "Another lesson from your years of torture at the Order House, brother?" She grinned at his annoyed frown and turned away again, waving an indifferent hand. "Go and talk with the creature if you want. I'll wager you a goatskin of wine you won't learn a thing."

...

He was obliged to clamber over Fehl-ahkim's half-finished barrier before making his way around the northern flank of the Reach to the river. As he drew closer he was able to discern more details of the figure in the ragged cloak, the most salient being that it was a woman. She watched him approach with her head still cocked at the same curious angle. Sollis detected a thin smile on her pale, hollowed features as he drew closer. He judged the woman to be of either Volarian or Realm origins from her colouring, though her starved appearance make it hard to tell for sure. However, when she spoke her accent was purely Asraelin, the inflection possessed of the sharp precision of the nobility.

"That's far enough, I think," the woman called to him once Sollis had reached the eastern bank of the river. The rushing current that separated them was loud but not so much as to muffle her voice, Sollis detecting in it a strangely juvenile note of delight. "Wouldn't want your scent to rouse my friends' baser instincts," the woman added, gesturing to the beasts at her back, all still sitting in their varied poses of statuesque immobility.

"What do you want?" Sollis asked her. He kept his hands at his sides, empty but close enough to his throwing knives for a rapid draw should he need it. He also wore his sword but had chosen to leave his bow behind. Should this parley turn ugly he would do his best to kill this woman then turn and sprint for the Reach under cover of his brothers' bows and the Lonak archers on the wall.

"I'd guess that Lonak bitch has already told you what I want," the woman said, the muscles in her emaciated face thrown into stark relief as her smile broadened. "The children you have in there," she went on, pointing at the Reach. "Give them to me."

"No," Sollis stated, voice hard and flat. He watched the woman's smile twist into a muffled laugh, eyes twinkling with what Sollis took for joyful anticipation.

"Of course you wouldn't," she said. "Even though it will certainly avail you nothing but an ugly death." She barked out a laugh, harsh and grating. "I do enjoy these rare occasions when I find one of your stripe. So desperate for the glory of self-sacrifice. So in love with the myth of their own heroism. It's always such a blissful moment when I look into their eyes at the end, watching their illusions fade, watching them cry and plead like any other dying and tormented wretch. Wouldn't you rather avoid that, brother? Give me the children and you can go back to your life of pretended courage and empty invocations to the spirits of the dead who, I assure you, are quite deaf to your entreaties."

Sollis met the woman's gaze, watching her mirth subside into an unwavering stare of deep contempt. Sollis could see a redness to her eyes now, also a thin trickle of blood coming from her nose, calling to mind Verkehla's visage the night before. The temptation to reach for his knives was strong. The distance made it a difficult throw but he was confident he could get at least one blade into her before he had to run. *Every opportunity should be taken to learn more about an enemy,* he reminded himself, suppressing the impulse.

"You have a name?" he asked instead.

"I used to," the woman replied with a shrug. "I stopped bothering to remember it a long time ago. Instead of a name, I have a purpose."

"And what is that?"

"It changes according to the place and the time. Once I warned a wealthy merchant of the necessity of poisoning his brother. Once I whispered to a queen of the treachery that surrounded her so that her court might run red with the blood of her nobles. I have persuaded generals to doom their armies and priests to damn their supplicants. And today, brother, I tell you, clearly and honestly, to hand over the children or you and everyone cowering in that pile of stones will die as slow and agonising a death as I can orchestrate. And…" She paused, tongue licking over her lips before parting to reveal teeth stained both red and yellow. "I'll reserve the worst torments for the flaxen-haired sister. Have you ever tortured a beautiful woman, brother? It's a truly addictive experience, I must say."

Don't! Sollis commanded himself, rage sending a spasm through his hands. *Every word she speaks is valuable.* "Why?" he demanded, allowing his anger to colour his tone. "What do you want of these children?"

"Oh, isn't it obvious?" The woman arched her eyebrows in mock surprise. "I want to take them far away from these barbarous mountain savages so they can be raised in a fine palace and enjoy a life of peace and comfort for all their days."

The suddenness with which all vestige of humour slipped from her face and bearing was shocking, as if a veil had been ripped away to reveal a blank, expressionless edifice, almost as still as the beasts she commanded. "Enough talk," she said, voice different now, deeper and richer in authority. Also her accent had changed; the noble inflection replaced by something that spoke of a far distant land. Sollis would have taken it for a Volarian accent but for the discordant notes that coloured every word, almost as if two tongues were speaking at once. "Give me what I want," she said, "or I promise you I will carry out every threat spoken here."

"I doubt that," Sollis replied. "Elst why call for a parley? If your powers are so great why not just come and get them? Or is there something in there that you fear?"

The woman's eyes flicked to the Reach for an instant before snapping back to Sollis. The cadaverous face took on a decided twitch, a snarl repeatedly forming and fading from the bleached and cracked lips. Sollis wondered if she were simply mad and lost for words, but knew whatever afflicted this woman went far beyond simple lunacy.

Deciding he had learned all he was going to, Sollis turned away and started back towards the Reach. "Besides," he said. "I'm reliably informed that I'm not supposed to die here."

"Prophecy?!" The word was spoken in a shrill, almost shrieking tone. Sollis kept walking, maintaining a steady gate, refusing to turn. "It's a lie, you pitiful dullard!" the woman screamed after him, the voice almost childlike in its rage and frustration. "Know well that whatever that bitch has told you is a lie! You *will* die here, brother!"

Sollis fixed his gaze on the Reach, taking a crumb of comfort from the sight of his brothers on the wall, flanked on either side by the Banished Blades, each bow notched and ready. The woman continued to rant as he walked, her varied threats descending into a scarcely comprehensible babble.

"I'll make you watch… when I rip the sister from nethers to neck… I'll fucking make you watch - "

Then silence. Sollis came to a halt as the woman's dissonant diatribe choked off, leaving only the faint groan of the mountain winds. Looking up, he saw his brothers and the Lonak lowering their bows as they exchanged baffled glances. When he turned he found himself regarding an empty river bank and he caught just a faint shadowy blur as the last of the beasts crested a hilltop and disappeared from view.

"You must have been awful persuasive, brother," Oskin called down to him, his voice coloured by an uncertain note of optimism.

"No," Sollis said, resuming his walk. "I wasn't."

CHAPTER EIGHT

The gate was sealed a good few hours before nightfall. Under Fehl-ahkim's direction the stones were piled high enough so that only a gap of a few inches remained at the top. He then used five iron buttresses to secure the barrier in place, employing bolts scavenged from the ruined original gate to affix the rusted brackets to the wall on either side.

"Will it hold?" Verkehla asked, regarding the construction with a dubious eye.

"Against charging beasts, yes," the builder replied. Sollis noted how he kept his tone carefully neutral, betraying neither respect nor disdain, though the latter shone in his eyes clearly enough.

"It had better," she told him with an empty smile. "You can stay here all night to make sure. If it falls, then so do you." She flicked a hand at a trio of Lonak warriors nearby. "You lot, stay with him."

"I'm more concerned about the walls than the gate," Sollis said quietly as they ascended to the parapet. "You saw how the apes had little difficulty in climbing all the way to the top of the tower, in silence too. They're likely to ignore the gate and simply scale the walls, overwhelm us with weight of numbers."

"I trust you're about to suggest a solution, brother," Verkehla said.

"Fire," Sollis replied. "Light torches all along the walls and cast flaming fascines over when the attack starts. If we can see them as they charge, our arrows will cut them down before they can climb up."

"I've seen a full grown ape take six arrows before it deigned to even slow its charge. And there are more than just apes among them. The Varnish have perhaps twenty arrows each. They won't last long if that thing sends all of its creatures against us at once."

Hearing a small polite cough they turned to find Sister Elera standing nearby. "I may have something that could help," she said, proffering a porcelain jar about the size of an apple.

"What is that?" Sollis asked, stepping closer as Elera removed the jar's lid. The contents appeared to be a green paste that gave off a faintly floral aroma as Sollis leaned closer to sniff it.

"Best if you don't, brother," Elera cautioned, drawing the jar back a little. "It's a mixture of nightshade and yellow-cap mushrooms, with a few other ingredients to increase the potency. I came up with it by accident last year when I was attempting to concoct a new medicine to calm a fevered heart. Instead, I produced something my novice students have taken to calling Black Eye."

"Black Eye?" Verkehla said, lips curled in suspicion as she peered at the substance.

"It has a curious effect when imbibed," Elera explained. "The white of the eye turns dark, not quite black in truth but my students tend to be overly dramatic, as the young often are."

"It's a poison," Sollis said.

"Yes. Just a small amount is sufficient to kill a grown man in seconds. I imagine a larger dose will certainly kill one of those apes, even a bear."

"Why is a Sister of the Fifth Order carrying around a jar of poison?" Verkehla enquired.

"Members of my Order often give the appearance of being defenceless," Elera replied. "It doesn't mean we are."

"Is this all you have?" Sollis asked to which Elera nodded.

"Will it be enough?" Verkehla asked him.

"If only a small dose is required, we should have enough to coat every arrowhead we possess."

"And what happens when we run out of arrows?"

"If the sister's gift can be used to coat an arrowhead it can also coat a blade. Several of your people have spears. The others will have to use their knives."

"Putting them within reach of claw and tooth."

"What battle is ever easy? Besides," Sollis met Verkehla's gaze squarely, "we have at least one other weapon within these walls, do we not?"

Her face remained impassive as she returned his stare in silence before turning and walking away, saying, "I'll have them gather in the tower so the good sister can anoint their weapons."

Sollis made sure she was out of earshot before turning back to Elera. "The book?" he asked.

She gave a somewhat sheepish wince. "Slow going I'm afraid, brother. The late Baron Morvil expended many pages on recounting his life prior to the building of the Reach. I'm compelled to the conclusion that he was either an inveterate liar or had led perhaps the most adventurous life of any soul who ever lived. I've been trying to skip ahead, find some mention of the weed but as a writer he wasn't fond of a linear narrative."

She paused to glance around before stepping closer, voice

lowered. "There was one interesting passage towards the end. It's written in a hasty scrawl, so not easily read." She closed her eyes to recite from memory, "'The Wolf Men assail us from morn to moonrise. Soon it will be over. Even in my despair I know the Departed will accept me for I was wise in constructing the artery.' Later he writes his final entry, 'I have sent away those that remain. Perhaps they will find a safe route south but I will not follow. Best I die amidst this monument to my folly than suffer the shame of my father's sight.'"

"Artery?" Sollis said with a frown.

"Old Volarian often uses bodily terms when referencing architecture," she said, voice growing quieter still. "In modern Realm Tongue the closest translation is 'tunnel'."

Sollis let out a very soft laugh. "He had his builders dig an escape route."

"It would seem so."

"Where is it?"

"I have scoured this place without success, discreetly of course. The structure has no vaults, no cellars, nowhere one might expect to find such a passage. It seems his masons were skilled in concealment."

A faint flicker of movement caught the upper corner of Sollis's eye. Looking up his gaze immediately focused on a dark winged speck circling the Reach far above. The hawk was back.

"Here," he said, moving to take Elera's hand. His finger traced a shape over her open palm as she frowned at him in bemusement. "The Far Western symbol for mine or tunnel. Can you remember it?"

Her frown turned to a smile and she nodded. "He liked to mark his hiding places," she remembered.

"Quite so." He released her hand and started down to the courtyard. "I'll tell our brothers to look out for it."

"I won't leave without the children," she said, making him pause.

Sollis turned back, seeing her flexing her fingers and regarding her open hand before meeting his gaze with a steady resolve.

"Understood, sister," he said.

...

Whilst Elera went about coating the weapons, Sollis led a dozen Banished Blades outside the walls to gather fuel for the torches and fascines. The surrounding land was rich in dense gorse bushes which he knew would take a flame and burn brightly once the leaves had been stripped from the branches. The denuded bushes were bound into thirty or so tight bundles and soaked in the greasy reduced animal fat the Lonak used for lamp oil.

As night fell Sollis distributed the warriors evenly around the walls with orders to light the fascines and cast them into the gloom at the first indication of an attack. Smentil, being the best archer, took post in the tower. Sollis ordered Oskin to the south-facing wall with orders to make for the tower and protect Sister Elera to the end in the event of the Reach's fall. Sollis placed himself above the gate on the east-facing wall, judging it the most likely avenue of attack.

He ordered the torches lit as night descended, the orange glow banishing the gloom beyond the walls to a distance of about a dozen feet. It wasn't much of a killing ground but it would have to suffice until the fascines could be lit. Sollis had hoped the moonlight might have provided some additional illumination but the elements conspired to disappoint him. Cloud remained thick in the sky, leaving the landscape beyond the torchlight an almost blank curtain.

"What makes you think they'll attack here first?" Verkehla asked as they peered into the black.

"The slope is gentler in front of the gate," Sollis replied. "And we'd hear them if they tried to ford the river in large numbers. Besides, I had a sense our enemy is keen for this to be concluded quickly. From the looks of her, I doubt she has more than a few days of life left." He cast a sidelong glance at the shaman. "What is she? Given what we face here, it seems only fair you share what you know."

Verkehla kept her gaze averted as she provided a terse reply. "Some things are known only to the Mahlessa."

"And yet, I suspect you still know more than you're willing to share. She's not human, is she? At least what resides within her cannot be called human."

"You see a great deal, brother."

"I see that the Mahlessa has placed us here to draw it out. The intention is for you to kill it, I suppose. With your… gift."

"If I can."

"And if you can't?"

"Then that thing will continue to ravage across these lands until it finds what it came for."

"Meaning the children we harbour here aren't what it came for."

Finally, she turned to him, a faint twinkle of amusement in her gaze. "Yes. Perhaps you can tell it that when it gets here."

"I do not appreciate being a Keschet piece in your Mahlessa's game."

"Her game is played as much for your people's protection as mine." The humour slipped from her face as she gave a derisive snort. "Always the way with your kind. For all your Faith's pretensions to wisdom, you see nothing beyond your own prejudices."

"That sounds like the voice of experience." He studied her face as it hardened further. "You lived amongst us, didn't you? That's how you know our tongue so well. Did the Mahlessa send you to learn our ways?"

"Send me?" She let out a harsh laugh. "No, she didn't send me. I was taken. Stolen from my clan when I was yet younger than the children we protect. The man who took me was a Renfaelin knight of great renown. Having chased a war band into the mountains to no avail he and his retainers vented their wrath on a small settlement, killing all they could find, save me. He took me south to his holdfast whereupon he presented me to his wife. They had no children of their own, you see, she having lost two daughters at birth. I was to be the gift that would heal her heart."

Verkehla broke off to laugh again, the sound softer but richer in bitterness. "And I did. I resisted at first, of course. I didn't know this place or these people with their meaningless babble. Their vast huts with rooms full of pretty, shiny things that had no apparent use. Their clothes that itched and snared your feet when you tried to run. But she..."

The shaman broke off and lowered her gaze, sorrow replacing scorn as she spoke on. "She was kind, like my blood-mother in some ways, although she never beat me. And so in time my biting, screeching and smashing of crockery diminished. Their babble became words, their clothes not so uncomfortable, and I began to see meaning in the markings they scratched on parchment. For twelve years she raised me, taught me and called me daughter, though never when there were other ears to hear. They wouldn't understand, she said. I was hidden whenever visitors came calling and the master's servants promised a death by flogging if they ever spoke of my presence in his home. Then…" She ran her fingers over her forearm. "Then one day he brought home a new hunting dog. It bit me."

She fell silent, her features bunched with unwanted memory.

"You killed it," Sollis said. "With your gift."

"Don't you mean the Dark, brother?" Her eyes blazed at him. "That's the word they spoke when they all drew away from me, terror and disgust on every face. I believe the master would have killed me then and there if she hadn't stopped him, dragged me back to the stronghold and locked me away. In the dead of night she came for me, took me to the courtyard where a horse waited. 'There is no place for you here,' said the woman who called me daughter. 'They will kill you for the Dark that infects you. You must go home.'"

"She was afraid," Sollis said. "The ability to kill with a look will stir fear in the kindest heart."

"Kill with a look." Verkehla let out an exasperated sigh, turning her gaze to the top of the battlement. "Is that what you think? See this?" She pointed to a small patch of moisture on the stone, a thimble's worth of water gleaming in the torchlight. Sollis watched as her brow creased in concentration and couldn't contain a start as the water began to alter in shape, forming a long teardrop that separated into two identical beads that blinked at him before disappearing in a cloud of vapour.

"Did you know," Verkehla asked, "that everything alive is made mostly of water? The trees, the plants, the beasts of earth and sky, you and me. We are all merely sacks of water, and it appears the Gods puts the power to command it in my hands."

She straightened, letting out a sigh rich in regret and resignation. "And so I went home. My years of comfort had made me clumsy, easily tracked once I reached the mountains. I managed to kill one of the warriors who found me before another laid me low with a club. They bound me tight and took me to the Mahlessa, as she commands be done with all those who bear a gift from the Gods. She was so old then, far older than she is now. Her body bent and twisted, but her eyes were bright with knowledge and insight. She saw all of me, all of what had been done to twist me into something that was no longer Lonak. 'You cannot be mine,' she said. 'The Merim Her have despoiled you.' And I wept. For the mother who had sent me away and the Mahlessa who now saw my worthlessness. I wept long and bitter tears until she slapped me. 'Do not whimper like them!' she said. 'Corrupted as you are, know your Mahlessa still has a use for you. The Gods would not have sent you otherwise.'"

Verkehla cast her gaze to the shrouded landscape. "And so it comes to pass. After years at the Mountain, years spent gathering this scum into the Varnish Dervakhim, years pondering the mystery of the Mahlessa's vision. Finally, I arrive here. The moment I was made for."

"Destiny is a lie," Sollis said. "Our lives are what we make of them."

"And yet here we are, brother. Just as she foretold."

Her gaze suddenly grew sharp, eyes narrowed as she peered into the gloom with predatory intensity. “It’s here,” she hissed. “It seems we are about to put prophecy to the test.”

CHAPTER NINE

Sollis had time to bark out a command to light the fascines before the first beasts appeared. Four of the monstrous cats came streaking out of the gloom to throw themselves against the walls before a single arrow could be loosed. Sharp claws found easy purchase on the stone as they hauled themselves up with dismaying speed. Sollis leapt atop the battlement, drawing and lowering his bow in the same fluid movement, centring the arrowhead on the snarling maw of the cat directly below, its jaws widening in anticipation of the kill. Sollis sent his arrow into its mouth, the poison coated steel-head sinking deep. The effect was much more rapid than he expected. The cat's convulsions began almost immediately, losing its grip on the wall as it tumbled to the ground, thrashed briefly then lay still.

"It works," he heard Verkehla say with a note of surprised approval as he notched a second arrow. Pivoting to the left he sent his next shaft into the flank of another cat as it hauled itself to the top of the wall. The poison took fractionally longer to take hold this time, but the result was identical. Glancing around he saw the other two cats lying dead in front of the gate. The Banished Blades had evidently been over enthusiastic in their response for each cat had been feathered by at least a half-dozen shafts.

"Save your arrows!" Sollis called out in Lonak, repeating an order he had given several times throughout their preparations. "One for each beast is enough!"

He ordered the fascines cast over the wall. They arced out and down, bouncing along the ground until coming to rest some twenty paces out. The mingled firelight painted the landscape in shifting shades of red and gold which made the appearance of the onrushing beast horde yet more hideous. More cats came first, snow-daggers and lynxes loping up the slope in a dense mass; behind them came the pale, wraith-like wolves with the pack of apes visible to the rear.

Sollis notched again and drew a bead on the snow-dagger at the front of the pack, but before he could loose, one of Smentil's arrows arced down from the tower to take it in the haunch. Sollis altered his aim and brought down a lynx a few yards to the left. He loosed off four more arrows in quick succession, notching and releasing with a speed and automatic precision that bespoke endless hours of practice. On either side of him the Lonak worked their bows with similar speed but less accuracy, Sollis seeing several shafts missing their mark as the horde drew ever closer. Even so, with such a wealth of targets they were less inclined to waste their arrows. Once the beasts covered the distance to the Reach it was impossible to miss and soon the ground beneath the wall became littered with the twitching corpses of cats and wolves. But many still lived, and more kept charging out of the darkness beyond the blazing fascines.

Seeing a number of wolves leap up to latch onto the wall, Sollis sank an arrow into the mass of animals below before setting aside his bow and drawing his sword. He sprinted to intercept the first wolf, the poison coated blade lancing out to skewer the beast's foreleg as it crested the battlement. It let out a strange guttural sigh as the toxin flooded its veins, Sollis seeing the truth in its name in the dark grey mist that crept into the animal's eyes at the instant of death. A pained shout drew his gaze to the right where a Lonak warrior reeled back from the wall, a trio of deep cuts on his arm. The ape that had wounded him leapt over the battlement in pursuit, claws outstretched as it sought to finish its victim, then fell dead as another Lonak sank her spear into its chest.

A quick scan of the wall revealed no more enemies for the moment, though the rising tumult of alarm from the battlement atop the gate indicated their troubles were far from over. "The bears," Verkehla said as he moved to join her, her eyes grim. Switching his gaze to the slope Sollis saw the bulk of the horde had drawn back to the fringes of the light cast by the fascines, the intervening ground blanketed in corpses. For a few seconds a curious silence settled over the scene, soon broken by the loud huffing of several large animals at the run.

Eight black bears emerged from the darkness in a tight knot, the air misted by their breath as they loped forward, a dense mass of flesh aimed straight at the gate. Sollis quickly retrieved his bow and sent an arrow into the shoulder of the leading bear. Unlike the other beasts it kept on, its loping gait slowed but not halted by the poison raging through its body. Sollis swallowed a curse and loosed again, aiming for the join between the beast's neck and torso, reasoning it to be the most likely spot for the tainted arrowhead to find a vein. The bear stumbled, back arched in pain as it let out a long final breath before collapsing to a halt.

At Verkehla's command the Banished Blades let fly with a hail of arrows, claiming another three bears. The remaining four kept on, closing the final few yards to the newly crafted barrier and throwing themselves against it with a collective roar of rage. Sollis moved back to glance down into the courtyard, seeing Fehl-ahkim and his three companions pressing their weight against the barrier as it shuddered under the impact. It was clear from the despairing expression on the builder's face that it wouldn't hold for long.

Sollis notched another arrow, one of only four remaining, and leapt up onto the battlement once more. He leaned out to draw a bead on the bears, finding they had all reared up onto their hind legs, meaning their bulk was mostly concealed by the lip of the gate's arch. He contented himself by sinking his arrow into an exposed paw then turned back, calling out to the nearest Lonak warrior, "I need a rope!"

"It's all right, brother," Verkehla said, hauling herself up to stand at his side. He stared in bafflement at the hand she held out to him. "Hold me," she said, reaching out to catch his hand in a firm grip. "I need to see them."

With that she placed her feet on the edge of the battlement and leaned out at a low angle, Sollis taking a firm hold with both hands as she focused her gaze on the bears. They had reared back a little to lunge at the barrier once more, but the assault never came. Sollis heard a low, keening groan escape the throat of one, then all, forming a kind of ghastly chorus of pain and confusion that soon choked off into a wet gargle. Glancing down he saw one stumble away from the gate to collapse a few feet away. It seemed to shrivel as it fell, the surrounding earth darkening with the fluids that leaked from every orifice. The others soon joined it in death, each one slumping down to cough out torrents of thick, dark gore until they were rendered into just a large pile of empty fur stretched over denuded bone.

Verkehla sagged and went limp, her feet slipping from the edge of the battlement. Sollis quickly hauled her back onto the parapet, drawing up short at the sight of her face. From her eyes down it had transformed into a red mask, blood flowing freely from her nose, eyes and mouth. "It's done," Sollis told her, placing a soothing hand on her forehead and finding it shockingly cold. "They're gone."

Verkehla's eyes fluttered and a faint smile played over her lips as the blood flow slowed to a trickle then stopped. "Told you..." she murmured, causing a red bubble to swell and burst on her lips. "All... just water..."

...

"Will she live?"

Elera seemed reluctant to provide an immediate answer, spending several seconds pressing her fingers to Verkehla's wrist before frowning in consternation and crouching to put an ear to her chest. "Her heart still beats," she said. "But barely." She straightened, bafflement on her face as she surveyed the unconscious woman. "This I have never seen before, brother. In truth, I don't know if there's any treatment I can offer."

"There must be something," Sollis insisted. "Some kind of medicine."

"I have stimulants that can rouse someone from a coma, if that's what this is. But she's lost so much blood, it's more likely to strain her heart yet further. I won't risk it."

Sollis stepped closer, lowering his voice. "Without her... ability, this place won't survive another attack."

"Then I suggest you find a way. I am a healer, I leave the killing to you."

Sollis drew back at the harshness of her tone, seeing the determined anger in her glare. "Forgive me, sister," he said.

Elera's ire faded into a scowl and she inclined her head in acknowledgement before turning back to Verkehla. "I suspect this state is due to her losing so much blood," she said, taking a cloth from a bowl of water and using it to wipe the drying blood from the woman's face. "It will take time for her body to make good the loss. I'll do my best to get water into her, it may help the process."

"And the matter we discussed earlier?"

She gave him a cautious glance and shook her head. "No sign of it, though I've been busy stitching wounds these past hours."

Sollis looked around at the dozen wounded Lonak in the keep, most nursing various gashes to the face and limbs. After the failed assault on the gate their enemy had tried another tactic, sending a pack of apes against the south-facing wall whilst a combined force of wolves and cats circled round to attack from the west. Fortunately, Smentil had been quick to spot the manoeuvre and Sollis had time to shift sufficient forces to contain it. Even so, the apes had managed to gain the parapet for a time, killing four Banished Blades before Oskin led a counter charge. Red Ears had been in the thick of the fighting, as evidenced by the red stain that covered her snout as she huddled beside a nearby fire. Oskin sat idly stroking her fur as he stared into the flames.

"Quite the old set-to, eh, brother?" he said with a smile as Sollis approached. "Can't remember one quite like it since the Outlaws Revolt, and that was over a decade ago. 'Course we were fighting men then. Beggared, soulless wretches the lot of them, but still men."

"You should get some rest, brother," Sollis said, sinking to his haunches and extending his hands to the fire. Now the frenzy of battle had faded the mountain chill had returned with a vengeance. He had noticed before how sensations seemed to heighten in the aftermath of combat, as if the body was reminding itself it was still alive.

"Reckon I'll get all the rest I need soon enough," Oskin replied with the faintest of chuckles.

Sollis saw it then, the paleness of his skin against the dark mask of his beard, the damp brightness to his eyes. Sollis's gaze tracked lower, seeing how his brother held his left arm tight against his chest. Reaching out he pulled Oskin's cloak aside to reveal the ragged tear in his jerkin and the bloody bandage beneath.

"I'll get our sister," he said, starting to rise.

"Leave her be," Oskin said. The soft but firm insistence in his tone made Sollis pause. He met Oskin's gaze, finding a need there, a plea for understanding. "I know a mortal wound when I see one," Oskin continued. "Big bastard of an ape caught me a good one. Took his head off for it right enough, but not before he left one of his claws inside. Too deep to be dug out. Can feel it moving about." Oskin winced, features tensing in pain. Sollis reached forward, grasping his brother's shoulder to stop him slumping into the flames. Red Ears let out a high pitched whine and nuzzled closer to her master, tail moving with frantic energy.

"Good pup," Oskin said, running a trembling hand over the hound's head. "Best I ever reared. You'll take care of her, won't you, brother?"

"I will," Sollis said. Feeling Oskin sag further he reached out to grasp both his shoulders, gently easing him onto his back.

"Dying amongst the Lonak," Oskin murmured with a bitter sigh. "My reward for a lifetime in the Order. Perhaps it's punishment for hating them so. Hate is not of the Faith after a-"

He jerked in Sollis's grip, letting out a pained shout that echoed through the keep, drawing Elera to his side. "You old fool," she said, seeing his bandage. It was soaked through with blood now, torrents of it streaming down his side. "Why didn't you come to me?"

"Leave it," Sollis said as she crouched lower to inspect the wound. "Please, sister."

She drew back, briefly meeting his gaze before looking away. "I have something that will ease his pain," she said, rising and moving to one of her saddlebags.

"Sollis," Oskin whispered, beckoning him closer. "The sign... the mark you spoke of..." His voice diminished to a croak as Sollis leaned down to put his ear to his lips. "The stables... third stall from the gate..." He fell silent, his breath playing over Sollis's cheek. Once, twice, then no more.

"Redflower with powdered green hops," Elera said, returning with a bottle in hand. "I've never met the ache it couldn't banish..." She stopped upon seeing Sollis removing the medallion of the Blind Warrior from about Oskin's neck. As Sollis pulled Oskin's cloak over his face Red Ears' whines became a plaintive howl that filled the keep, drawing the Lonak closer.

"You burn your dead, do you not?" Fehl-ahkim asked, taking in the sight of Oskin's lifeless form.

"We can't spare the fuel," Sollis said.

"Dawn is fast approaching." The builder jerked his head at his fellows who duly came forward to gather up Oskin's body. "A man who fights beside you deserves respect in death. Blue Cloak or no."

...

They piled what wood they could gather in the centre of the courtyard, a few shards from the old ruined gate and the brush wood left over from fashioning the fascines. Oskin's corpse was set atop it after which the Lonak used their scant supplies of lamp oil to douse the pyre. A warrior had relieved Smentil from his vigil atop the tower and he made his testament whilst Sollis lit the torch.

This man was my brother in the Faith, Smentil signed. *And my friend in life. Never did he falter in either regard.* He lowered his hands, turning to Sollis with an expectant nod.

Sollis chose to speak in Lonak, feeling the assembled Banished Blades deserved the courtesy for the consideration they had shown. "This man was my brother," he began. "And he taught me many things. He taught me how to follow a track across bare stone. How to read the song of the wind in the mountains. How to trust the nose of a well-bred hound. But he saved his best lesson for his dying breath: it is no good thing to die in regret, despairing of the hatred you nurtured in life."

Despite their willingness to respect Merim Her customs Sollis still saw little sign that his words engendered any additional regard amongst the Lonak. Rather, they all continued to exhibit only a stern, grudging respect. Smothering a sigh he touched the torch to the pyre, retreating a few steps as the flames took hold. They quickly enveloped Oskin's body, drawing another piteous howl from Red Ears. The hound sank to her belly and tried to crawl towards the blaze, stopping as Elera crouched to run soothing hands over her pelt.

"I know you came here to honour the word from the Mountain," Sollis went on, turning to address the Lonak. "But if the beasts come against us again in the same numbers, this place cannot be held." He exchanged a brief glance with Elera before continuing. "There is a way out, a tunnel. We can escape."

The Banished Blades shifted a little at his words, but their expressions grew puzzled rather than hopeful.

"The Mahlessa's vision is not yet complete," one said, a stocky woman with a stitched gash on her forehead. "We will not be granted restitution until it is."

Her words heralded a general murmur of agreement from the others, Sollis seeing a certain scornful disdain on several faces. He had thought that, with their shaman laid low, their commitment to this hopeless enterprise might have waned. However, it was clear they didn't need Verkehla to sustain their obedience. The Word of the Mountain was not to be questioned.

"My brother died in your defence," Sollis said, suddenly angered by their subservience to a woman they had never seen. A woman he had sometimes suspected might be some mythical creation of their shamans, an immortal illusion designed to keep them cowering to their non-existent gods. "If you all die here his sacrifice means nothing."

"It means a man who was our enemy helped us regain our honour," Fehl-ahkim replied. "It means that our clans will speak our names once more and our stories will be shared at the fire without reproach or shame." He extended a hand to the barrier he had built, gesturing to what lay beyond. "The thing that commands these beasts is not yet slain. Flee like a worthless dog if you must, blue cloak. We are the Varnish Dervakhim, soon to be redeemed in the eyes of the Gods. We stay here."

Sollis searched his mind for some argument to sway them, but knew it to be in vain. Which left him a choice: stay and die, after having been forced to watch the woman fulfil her dire promises, or find the tunnel and leave with Smentil and Elera… and the children.

"No," Fehl-ahkim stated with emphatic resolve when Sollis raised the question. "They stay with us. The creature comes for them. They stay."

"They are innocents!" Sollis exploded, advancing on the builder, his hand going to his sword. "They do not deserve to be doomed by your Mahlessa's bloody game."

Smentil came to his side whilst Red Ears turned from Oskin's pyre to join them in facing the Banished Blades, a low growl rising in her throat. Fehl-ahkim crossed his arms, whilst the Lonak at his back tensed in anticipation of combat.

"They are innocents, yes," the builder said. "But they are Lonakhim and have learned from birth to honour the word of the Mountain. If you fight us you will die and they will stay."

Sollis's hand tensed on his sword hilt. He had no doubt the Lonak was right. There were too many for him, his brother and a grieving hound to defeat. Even so, he found his anger building. Rage was a rare emotion for him. The frequent irritations of life in the Order and the excitements of combat were one thing, but rage was another. It was something he thought he had surrendered to the masters' canes in the Order House. Now he found it sparked anew. It was the children, he knew that. Their plight stirred long buried memories of hunger and cold suffered in a dozen ruined hovels, of his mother dragging him away from one burning village after another as they fled the king's wars. Then came the day she took him to the Sixth Order mission house in a border village he still couldn't name. She held him by the shoulders, speaking in clipped, uncoloured tones that didn't reflect the rare tears shining in her eyes. *I can't feed you anymore. I spoke to the brothers. They'll take care of you now.*

He met Fehl-ahkim's eyes and drew his sword, the scrape of the blade leaving the scabbard swallowed by a pain filled scream from above. Sollis's gaze snapped to the top of the tower, finding it wreathed in some kind of dark cloud. The Lonak sentry who had taken Smentil's place writhed within it, lashing out with his war club as his screams bespoke terrible torment.

Not a cloud, Sollis realised, looking closer. *Birds.*

The birds, crows, falcons and hawks moving with an unnatural unity of purpose, whirled around the struggling warrior in an ever denser spiral until he was lost from view. They continued to mob him until he tumbled over the edge of the tower, crashing to the courtyard in a bloody spectacle of flensed skin and shattered bone. Above, the birds wheeled away from the tower before sweeping down onto the battlements below, a dark stream of flashing talons and stabbing beaks lacerating the sentries on the walls.

Sollis started for the nearest steps, intending to retrieve his bow and use what arrows remained to stem the onslaught, but skidded to a halt at the sound of something very large impacting on Fehl-Ahkim's barrier. The stone and iron construct shuddered, metal bolts squealing as they were worked loose from the walls.

"Get the children!" Sollis said, taking Elera's arm and shoving her at Smentil. "Find the tunnel."

She began to ask something but her words died as Smentil dragged her towards the keep. Sollis took a firm, two-handed grip on his sword and strode to a point some twenty paces from the gate, watching the barrier shudder again as whatever sought entry pounded at it once more.

"She found more bears," Fehl-Ahkim observed, coming to his side, war club in one hand, a knife in the other. The other Banished Blades fanned out on either side, some using their flat-bows to cast arrows at the birds still assailing their comrades on the walls, most readying their weapons as they stared at the gate in tense expectation.

"I think this might be something else," Sollis replied, seeing how the stone in the centre of the barrier had begun to bulge under the repeated battering. He was surprised to find his rage had gone now, replaced by the familiar mix of anticipation and certainty that always seemed to grip him in the moments prior to combat.

"I don't know if it's of any concern to you," he told Fehl-Ahkim. "But I'm glad I didn't have to kill you."

The builder bared his teeth as he barked out a laugh and began to reply, his words forever lost as the barrier shattered and a monster charged into the Reach.

CHAPTER TEN

The barrier shattered in an explosion of stone and twisted iron, Sollis and the Lonak ducking the boulders that flew across the courtyard. The four-legged beast that charged through the gate stood at least six feet tall at the shoulder, its massive, hump-backed body covered in a thick shag of black-brown fur. Its broad, bovine features were framed by a massive pair of horns, curving out into dagger-like points from a dense mass of bone in the centre of its forehead.

"Muskox!" Sollis heard one of the Lonak snarl, the stocky woman with the spear. She darted forward, nimbly diving and rolling under one of its horns to drive her spear into the beast's flank in what was evidently a long practiced move. The muskox bellowed in range and whirled, the Lonak woman leaving her spear embedded in its flesh as she dodged back, fractionally too slow to avoid the horn point that took her in the chest.

The other spear-bearing Lonak surged forward as the muskox flung the woman's body aside. It went into a frenzy of flashing hooves and scything horns, cutting down another two Lonak despite the poisoned spear blades they repeatedly jabbed into its flesh. Sollis sprinted forward and leaned back into a crouch, sliding along the mossy surface of the courtyard to slip under the muskox's belly. The star-silver edge of his sword sliced deep, unleashing a torrent of guts and blood before Sollis slid clear. He came to his feet, watching the animal let out another bellow, pain erupting from its mouth in a gout of steam as it sank to its knees. The Banished Blades fell on it, spears stabbing in a frenzy.

A fresh scream dragged Sollis's gaze to the now open gate in time to see a Lonak brought down by a trio of apes, claws and teeth biting deep whilst a tide of wolves, cats and apes rushed into the Reach. With a shout the Banished Blades charged to meet them and for a time the courtyard became a chaos of tooth, claw, knife and spear.

Sollis ducked the slashing arm of an ape then hacked it off at the elbow, the animal falling dead a second later as the Black Eye took hold. Whirling, he saw a snow-dagger coming for him, long body stretching and contracting like a spring as it closed the distance, mouth gaping. A loud, snarling growl came from Sollis's left and a brown blur caught the edge of his vision as Red Ears sprinted to intercept the cat. The hound's jaws clamped tight onto the cat's neck before they enveloped each other in a savage thrashing, tumbling away into the confusion of the courtyard.

Sollis fought down the pang of guilt as he stopped himself running in pursuit. Despite his promise to Oskin, a swift glance around the courtyard was enough to convince him there was no hope of victory now. The last of the warriors on the wall lay twitching as a crow pecked at his eyes with methodical, precise jabs of its beak. The Banished Blades still battled on in the courtyard but it seemed to Sollis that one died with every passing heartbeat. He saw Fehl-Ahkim bring down a wolf with a blow from his war club before a snow-dagger leapt on his back, its elongated fangs sinking deep into the builder's neck. Still he tried to fight on, flailing about with his club even as blood fountained from the twin wounds. Sollis lost sight of him as a quartet of wolves closed in, masking him in a mass of red and white fur.

Tearing his gaze away he ran for the stables, hacking a hawk out of the air as it swooped low to stab its talons at his eyes. He found Smentil with bow in hand, crouched behind the bulky corpse of Vensar. The stallion had plainly been set upon by multiple beasts at once, his spine clawed and bitten through in several places and his ribs showing white amidst the mass of gore that had been his chest. Sollis took a morsel of comfort from the sight of an ape lying with its skull crushed under one of Vensar's hooves.

"At least he went down fighting," he muttered, hurdling the body and crouching at Smentil's side. "The tunnel?"

His brother jerked his head to the rear then abruptly tensed and loosed an arrow. Sollis glanced back to see a charging lynx fall dead a few yards away. Proceeding into the part demolished stable, he found Elera crouched at the base of the wall, the two children and their grandfather huddled nearby. Verkehla sat slumped and grey-faced to Elera's left, Sollis seeing with surprise that her eyes were open.

"She stuffed something foul smelling up my nose," the shaman said with a grin that was more of a grimace. She flailed a hand at him. "Help me up. We need to find..."

"We're leaving," Sollis broke in. "The Reach is about to fall."

He moved to Elera's side, seeing her using a long bladed knife to scrape away the mortar surrounding a stone marked with the Far Western symbol for tunnel. Most of the mortar was already gone and Elera grunted as she worked her fingers into the gaps, vainly trying to work the stone loose.

"Won't come out," she panted. For the first time Sollis saw fear in the gaze she turned on him, though he doubted it was for her own safety. He bent lower, trying to prise the stone free but finding it stuck fast. Hearing another twang from Smentil's bowstring he tried again, grunting with the effort and cursing when the stone failed to budge.

"Could try pushing instead of pulling," Verkehla suggested in an oddly conversational tone. Her voice had the dull, distant quality of one about to lose purchase on the world.

Sollis paused then pushed a hand against the stone. At first nothing happened but then he felt it give a fraction and pushed harder. The stone slid into the wall for several inches before coming to a halt. Sollis renewed his efforts, Elera joining her weight to the labour until whatever obstructed the stone's path was either crushed or pushed aside and it slid free of their hands. Sollis heard it tumble into some empty space beyond the wall, leaving a gap no more than a foot wide.

"Not much of a tunnel, brother," Elera observed then shrank back as the lower half of the wall collapsed. The passage beyond was cramped, perhaps four feet tall, but wide enough to allow entry.

"Brother!" Sollis called to Smentil. He cast about, finding an extinguished torch that must have fallen from the parapet above, and quickly struck a flint. "Lead them on," he said, handing the lighted torch to Smentil. His brother hesitated, doubt creasing his brow until Sollis gave him a reassuring nod. "I'll be along," he said, hoisting Verkehla over his shoulder.

Smentil crouched and started into the tunnel, Elera pushing the children ahead of her as she followed close behind. Sollis nodded to Khela-hahk who took a brief look into the gloomy passage before spitting and shaking his head.

"Would you rob me of the chance for a good death, Blue Cloak?" he said. Hefting his war club, he turned towards the courtyard then paused and tugged the aged war banner from his belt. "Here," he said, tossing it to Sollis. "If the banner never falls then neither do the Stone Crushers."

The skitter of multiple claws drew his gaze back to the courtyard and he flicked an impatient hand at Sollis. "Go!"

...

Sollis had to cradle Verkehla in his arms as he shuffled along the passage, his head making frequent, painful contact with the rough hewn roof. He kept his gaze fixed on the partly obscured glow of Smentil's torch, ignoring the soft but insistent protestations of the woman he carried.

"No," she groaned. "This is not her vision…"

Behind them the sound of the old man's final battle echoed along the tunnel. The tumult continued for far longer that Sollis expected, making him wonder if the boasts of the Shatterer of Skulls hadn't been exaggerated after all. By the time the sounds of combat came to an abrupt end Sollis could see the glimmer of morning light ahead.

The tunnel opened out onto a narrow ledge barely two yards wide. It snaked along the face of a tall granite cliff rising to at least a hundred feet above. A brief glance over the edge of the cliff revealed a sheer drop into the misted depths of a canyon far below. He could see no hope of climbing either up or down, leaving them no choice but to proceed along the ledge. Smentil led the way with Elera following, the boy and girl held tight against her side. Sollis was grateful at least that dawn had finally broken, bathing the cliff face in sunlight that was for once unobscured by cloud. Navigating this route in the dark would have been impossible.

After a distance of close to a hundred paces the ledge came to an abrupt end where it met a huge curving outcrop of rock. Where the ledge joined the outcrop lay a single, steel-clad corpse. It wore the rusted armour of a Renfaelin knight, the flesh long since faded from the bones to leave a curiously clean skull. It stared up at Sollis as he came to a halt, its bared teeth conveying a distinct sense of mockery.

"At least one of Morvil's men made it out, it seems," Elera observed.

"He was wounded," Sollis said, noting the withered remnants of an arrow lying close to the fallen knight's gorget. He set Verkehla down, the shaman groaning as he propped her against the cliff.

"There must have been others," Elera went on, glancing around at the walls of granite. "Perhaps they climbed out."

Or got tired of starving and jumped, Smentil signed. He scanned the cliff above with an expert eye before turning to Sollis with a grim shake of his head. *No handholds.*

A strange groaning sound drew Sollis's gaze back to the far end of the ledge and the small dark opening of the tunnel. It took him a moment to recognise it as the massed breath of many beasts in a confined place.

"There must be some way," Elera insisted, sinking to her knees and peering over the lip of the ledge. "If they couldn't climb up, perhaps they..." She trailed off, then a moment later voiced a soft, surprised "Oh!"

"What is it?" Sollis asked, moving to crouch at her side in the hope she might have discovered some means of navigating the cliff. Instead he found her staring at a cluster of small plants growing from a patch of moss-covered rock a few feet down. Plants with narrow stems from which sprouted four, pale white flowers.

"Jaden's Weed," Elera said, voice both sad and joyful. She reached out a hand, lowering herself further over the edge.

"I think we have more pressing concerns, sister," Sollis told her, reaching out to ease her back.

Feeling an insistent pat on his shoulder he turned, finding Smentil sinking into a crouch, bow aimed at the beasts now emerging from the tunnel. The apes came first, streaming out of the hole in a dense mass at least thirty strong, spreading out to scale the cliff above and below. They seemed immune to falling, their claws making effortless purchase on the stone. The cats came next, far fewer in number but showing similar agility. Lynx and snow-daggers seemed to bound across the rock. Of the wolves Sollis could see no sign, making him wonder if they had all perished at the hands of the Banished Blades.

Smentil's bow thrummed, Sollis seeing a large male ape slip lifeless from the cliff-face, dislodging two of his companions as he tumbled into the depths. Smentil's next shaft took down a snow-dagger, his third another ape, then his string fell silent. He gave Sollis a helpless shrug, gesturing at his empty quiver before setting the bow aside and drawing his sword. Sollis followed suit, moving to stand in front of his brother and pausing to cast an urgent glare at Elera.

"Do you have any Black Eye left?" he asked.

"A little. But what good will it..?" She fell silent as he switched his gaze to the children. They sat huddled together at the end of the ledge, faces pale though lacking in tears. It occurred to Sollis that he had seen neither of them cry during this whole sorry episode.

"I don't know why she wants them," he said. "But I know it will be a kinder end."

Elera's features seemed to drain of colour and expression as she stared back at him. In anger or grim resolve he couldn't tell. "Very well," she said in a harsh whisper, reaching for her pack.

Sollis turned back to the approaching beasts, finding the nearest ape no more than ten yards off. He was reaching for a throwing knife when the beast came to a sudden, frozen halt. The stillness quickly spread to the rest of the horde. Every ape and cat stopping to hang from the rock, breath misting the air as they stared at their prey, eyes empty of either hunger or rage.

"Such perfect soldiers they make," a voice said, echoing from the tunnel mouth. The woman emerged into the light in a crouch, straightening to move along the ledge with a somewhat unsteady gait, reminding Sollis of a drunken lush seeking to convince others of her sobriety. Her features were even more emaciated now, streaked by blood that rendered them into something from a nightmare.

She bleeds like Verkehla, Sollis realised. *These gifts extract a heavy price it seems.*

"No grumbling, no lust for loot or rapine," the woman continued as she approached. "No wayward thoughts or dreams of past lives to trouble my hold on them." She came to a halt twenty yards away. Too far for an accurate knife throw. "Would that it was always so easy."

She angled her head to survey them, baring reddened teeth in an awful smile as her gaze alighted on the children. Sollis saw her lips twitch in anticipation when her eyes tracked to Verkehla.

"Not yet dead," she said with a wistful sigh. "I thought I felt a spark still fluttering away."

To Sollis's surprise Verkehla let out a harsh, half-choked laugh. "Such a fool," she said, shaking her head as she climbed to her feet. She sagged against the stone and Smentil reached out to help her up, drawing a faint smile of gratitude. She leaned heavily against the cliff as she moved to Sollis's side, her voice dropping to a murmur. "Baroness Yanna Forvil," she said. "You'll find her in a holdfast near the north Renfaelin coast. If she still lives, I should like her to know I never blamed her, never hated her for what she did."

Sollis reached out to steady her as she swayed but she shook her head, face drawn in pain as she clawed her way along the ledge to confront the woman. "The wolf already took what you came for," she told her. Sollis took note of how she leaned against the cliff, both hands flat against the stone. "The child is far beyond your reach now."

The grin disappeared from the woman's face as her gaze, fiercely inquisitive now, switched back to the children.

"Just bait," Verkehla told her, laughing again. "And how willingly you stuck your leg into the snare. All the years you have infested this world, and still you retain no more wit than the beasts you command."

The woman let out a snarl every bit as bestial as anything uttered by one of her beasts. The horde instantly resumed its charge, apes and cats swarming across the stone.

"Water," Sollis heard Verkehla say and saw that she was smiling at him, fresh blood streaming from her nose and eyes. "It's in everything, brother. The air, the earth, even the mountains..."

He felt it then, a deep tremble in the stone beneath his boots. "Back!" he told Smentil, pushing his brother towards the far end of the ledge. A huge, thunderous crack sounded and he whirled, seeing a fissure open in the cliff where Verkehla had placed her hands. Fragments of stone flew as the crack extended along the length of the cliff, sending several beasts tumbling into the canyon. He saw the woman charging along the ledge, a short sword in her hand and murderous intent on her wasted features as she closed on Verkehla.

The torrent exploded from the fissure like an axe blade, snatching away the woman and Verkehla with a swift, savage blow. They hurtled into the depths of the canyon, Sollis hearing a final scream of enraged frustration from the woman, but not a sound from the shaman. The water gave a monstrous roar as it continued to pour from the fissure, more cracks snaking through the stone to unleash fresh torrents, sweeping the entire beast horde away in a scant few seconds. It abated after several minutes of fury, leaving them gaping at a misted cliff face shot through with a rainbow as the sun crested the eastern ridge.

Of the beasts only one remained, an ape perched high above the fissure and staring about in obvious terror and confusion. It let out a plaintive hoot as its eyes roamed the canyon, no doubt searching for vanished pack-mates. Its calls subsided when no answers came and Sollis saw it cast a curious glance in his direction before it climbed to the top of the cliff and hopped from view.

Sollis rose from the tight crouch he had adopted, looking down to check on the others. Smentil stared about in relieved amazement, as did the children. Elera's face, however, betrayed no joy at their deliverance. Instead, clutching her jar of Black Eye with such a depth of shame and guilt on her face that Sollis found it hard to look upon.

"You didn't..." he began, moving to the children, staring into their eyes for the encroaching grey mist.

"No," Elera said, voice soft with self-reproach. "I couldn't. I... I am a coward, brother."

"Nonsense." Sollis bent to grasp her elbow, helping her up. "There were no cowards here. Now, let's see about retrieving your weed."

CHAPTER ELEVEN

The ledge had been left miraculously intact by the deluge and they made an untroubled journey back to the tunnel and into the Reach. The fortress was littered with the corpses of the Banished Blades and the dozens of beasts they had slain. Of all the souls that had fought in defence of this place only one remained alive.

Red Ears sat atop the corpse of the snow-dagger she had killed, letting out a soft huff of welcome as Sollis approached to rub a hand over her bloody snout. Her pelt bore numerous scars but nothing he fancied would leave lasting injury. He glanced up at a touch from Smentil, finding him pointing to a trio of Lonak ponies near the west-facing wall. Having somehow survived the carnage, they stood shivering in distress but otherwise unharmed.

At least we won't be walking home, Smentil signed.

...

Night was falling when they drew within a mile of the Lonak settlement. Torches blazed all along on the defensive wall, indicating a continued sense of insecurity amongst the inhabitants. The torches also convinced Sollis it would be highly unwise to venture any closer.

"Are you sure they'll take them in?" Elera asked as Sollis lifted the children from the back of her pony.

"It's a Grey Hawk settlement," he said. "No clan ever turns away its own blood."

"But without parents who will care for them?"

"All Lonak are parents to the children of their clan. Their ways are not ours, sister."

"My Order has many orphanages. Places where they will be cared for, educated…"

"Also shunned and hated."

Sollis sank to his haunches in front of the children, taking the Lonak war banner from where it hung on his belt and holding it out to the boy. "If the banner never falls, neither do the Stone Crushers," he said in Lonak.

The boy looked briefly at the banner before pushing it away. "He wasn't really our blood-grandfather," he said. "Just a braggart with no living kin. He only claimed us so the Varnish wouldn't kill him for his cowardice."

He cast a scowling glare at each of them in turn, small mouth twisting as he spoke the words, "Merim Her!" The boy spat on the ground before taking hold of his sister's hand and dragging her towards the settlement. The girl looked back only once at Elera, a very small smile of what might have been gratitude on her face. Then they were lost to the gloom, two small shadows hurrying towards refuge.

…

Sollis followed as short a route as possible to the pass. He didn't know if they still enjoyed the Mahlessa's protection and was keen to escape the mountains before word spread amongst the clans that the Grey Eyed Fox now travelled their dominion virtually unprotected.

They reached the pass after three days hard riding, dismounting in front of the outer gate and setting the ponies loose. Once inside Sollis and Elera gave a fulsome account of their mission to Brother Commander Arlyn who listened in silence throughout. Sollis had expected some questions or even doubt when they came to describe what had undoubtedly been use of the Dark, but Arlyn's reaction had been only a half-raised eyebrow. When they were done he nodded, offering one of his meagre smiles.

"My thanks to you, brother and sister," he said. "Your report is duly noted."

Sollis found himself blinking in surprise. "The woman, brother," he said. "It was clear to me she acted as part of a larger design. We must warn the other Orders, pass word to the king..."

"As I said, brother," Arlyn broke in, his voice possessed of an uncharacteristically hard tone within which lay a clear command to silence. "Your report has been noted."

Arlyn used a long-fingered hand to lift a length of inscribed parchment from his desk, his tone softening to genuine sorrow. "Sadly, it seems I have grim news to share."

"The Red Hand?" Elera said. "Has it spread?"

"Not to my knowledge," Arlyn replied. "This pertains to another matter. Aspect Andril has succumbed to age and illness. Our senior brothers have called me to the Conclave. They wish me to submit myself for confirmation as Aspect of the Sixth Order."

"There can be no better choice," Sollis said.

Arlyn gave a slight incline of his head. "We shall see. It is ultimately for the Conclave to decide. In one week I shall return to Varinshold. During my absence you will be Brother Commander of the Skellan Pass."

"As you wish, brother."

"As to your remarkable story," Arlyn went on, rising and

moving to the narrow window behind his desk. "My many years in service to the Faith have left me of the opinion that such things are best left to the shadows. There will be no written account of your journey and I require that you speak no word of it to another soul without my explicit command."

He only gave a vague nod as Sollis and Elera spoke their agreement, the corners of his thin-lipped mouth turning up a little as he gazed out at the walls of the pass. "I believe I might actually miss this place."

...

"You're sure you'll be able to find it?"

"The holdfast of Baron Forvil near the north Renfaelin coast." Elera tightened a strap on her mount's saddle, one of the more placid Order mounts from the stables. "I doubt it will be hard to locate, brother."

"Thank you. I would go myself but…"

"The Faith requires that you stay here and fulfil your duties. I know." She ran a hand over her saddlebags, frowning. "Brother Oskin gave his life for a weed. A cure to a disease that may never trouble this Realm again."

"It will ease his soul in the Beyond to know that at least now we can defend against it should we need to."

"It could take years to develop a cure, and perhaps sharper minds than my own. But yes, at least now we have a chance." She turned to him, her frown deepening to sad reflection. "A battle fought. Great courage shown. All those people lost. And the tale will never be told."

"The Lonak will tell it," he assured her. "When the night grows dark and they gather at their fires. They will speak of the

Varnish Dervakhim who redeemed themselves in the eyes of the gods. And the shaman who led them and died to honour the word from the Mountain."

"And us? Do you think they'll speak of us?"

"They will." Sollis thought of the Lonak boy's final, sneering farewell. "But not well."

She laughed a little, but sobered quickly. "What was it? That *thing*?"

"I wish I had some notion, sister. Perhaps it was something that defies our understanding. But I doubt this world has seen the last of it."

She reached out to clasp his hand, her grip strong with certainty. "Something stirs, brother," she said. "Something Dark and terrible. We will be needed. All other needs, or wants, must be set aside."

She met his gaze for a brief second, her eyes a brighter shade of blue than he had seen before, and Sollis realised they were close to tears.

"Oh well," she said before he could respond. She released his hand and turned to climb into the saddle. "Best be off. Be sure to say goodbye to Brother Smentil for me, and your dog, of course."

With that she spurred her mount to a trot and rode through the southern gate. Although he tried to resist the impulse, Sollis found himself climbing the steps to the battlement. Looking to the south he spied a small grey figure amidst the heather clad slopes, riding with practised ease, keeping her gaze firmly on the trail ahead. Somehow, in a small, rarely explored corner of his heart, Sollis knew she badly wanted to turn around as much as he wanted to go after her.

Author's Note

I've loved spy stories since catching my first glimpse of Sean Connery as James Bond on television when I was too young to understand such concepts as 'self-hating alcoholic' or 'rampant misogyny.' A more nuanced appreciation for the genre came in early adolescence with the excellent TV adaptation of John Le Carre's *Tinker, Tailor, Soldier, Spy*. I found myself immediately fascinated by this cold war shadow-world where characters spoke in deliberately cryptic riddles, truth was a malleable concept and betrayal a constant threat. Later, I would discover the morally ambiguous delights of Len Deighton's Bernard Samson novels, the adrenalized action hit found in the techno-thrillers of Tom Clancy and the compelling, race-against-time adventures of Jack Bauer in *24*. It was therefore something of an inevitability that the *Raven's Shadow* books would feature a shadow-world of their own, a place of assassins, codes and secrets where nothing and no-one can be trusted. In *Blood Song* the principal representative of this world came in the form of Derla, later to re-emerge under a different name in *Tower Lord*. I had included a few sketchy details of her past and how she came to find herself recruited into the intelligence network of King Janus, but she remained something of a cypher, as befits a spy. Upon receiving an invitation to contribute a novella to *Grimdark Magazine* I had the opportunity for a more fulsome exploration of Derla's past, as well as throwing more light on how she came to meet a Cumbraelin noble with a talent for Warrior's Bluff and an excessive fondness for wine. I'm sure many will also be quick to recognise cameos from a familiar pair of bumbling thugs, a one-eyed crime lord and a certain urchin with a temper.

THE LADY OF CROWS

– a Raven's Shadow Novella –

CHAPTER ONE

"You stupid little shit!"

Frentis shrank back as Derla advanced on him, though his gaze retained the usual gleam of uncowed defiance. It was one of the things she liked about him, but not today. "If you're going to do something so utterly mad you could at least have made sure you finished the bastard!" He flinched at the cuff she delivered to the top of his head, shrinking further into the corner of the room, a sullen grimace on his lips.

"Would've done if 'is lads hadn't dragged 'im off so quick," he muttered.

"What did you expect them to do, just bloody stand there?" Derla raised her hand for another blow, this time clenching her fist.

"I think he knows he did wrong, Derl," Livera piped up in her soft, sing-song voice. "You do, dontcha Frentis?"

Derla's fist hovered as she stared down at him, watching him fail to summon enough contrition to offer more than a brief nod. But for the bright defiance in his eyes he would have been just another wretched, rag-clad pickpocket infesting the slums of Varinshold. She had always known there was a great well of anger behind those eyes, but had never thought it deep enough to compel him to such an extreme.

"My arse he does," Derla said, lowering her fist and turning away. She took a deep breath, smoothing her hands over the green satin of her bodice as she sought to calm herself. "Hunsil will have the gutters running red for this," she sighed. "And, of course, you had to come here."

"Came over the rooftops," Frentis said. "No one saw me."

"He'll know I've fenced your stuff before. Or if he doesn't, one of his lads will. How long do you think it'll be before they're knocking on our door? You can't stay here."

"Derl..." Livera came to her side, dusky hands reaching for hers. "The boy's got nowhere else." She leaned close, smelling of jasmine and honeysuckle, Derla's favourite. She knew Livera would have dabbed on a spot or two upon hearing her ascend the stairs to their rooms. "And he's always done right by us," Livera said. "Never lost money on the stuff he brought us."

"For which he was paid a fair price." Derla felt her resolve erode a little as Livera pressed her violet painted lips to her neck, letting the kiss linger.

"He's a good boy," Livera whispered, raising her lips to hover over Derla's ear. "Reminds me of my brother…"

"Your dead brother," Derla said, putting an edge on her tone that made Livera step back, her small oval face bunching with hurt. Derla's resolve almost faded completely but she clamped it in place, pulling her hands free of Livera's and turning back to Frentis. *One of us has to do the hard things.*

"You need to get out of Varinshold," she told the boy flatly, moving to the mantel above the fireplace. She opened the small chest sitting below the gilt framed mirror and extracted half-a-dozen silvers. "Get yourself to the docks," she said, holding the coins out to Frentis. "Find a ship called the *Sojourner*. The bosun's got certain… habits."

A frown creased Frentis's besmirched brow as he stared up at her. "Habits?"

"Kind've habits that'll let a boy earn his passage across the Erinean." She jangled the coins in her palm. "But he'll still expect a little something up front."

"Fuck that…" Frentis began, lips forming a sneer.

"You think you've got any other options!" Derla grabbed the scruff of the boy's rags and dragged him upright so that he stood on tiptoe. "You stuck a throwing knife in the eye of the worst shit this city has to offer. What did you think would happen next? A nice frolic through the flower beds?"

"I ain't selling my arse to no sailor! Not everybody wants to be a whore!"

There was no holding her fist this time. It caught him a hard blow on the side of the head, sending him sprawling and provoking a sob from Livera. "Derl!" she scolded her, rushing to the boy's side. Derla ignored Livera's reproachful scowl as she helped Frentis up, putting a protective arm around him and smoothing a hand over the knot of greasy hair left by Derla's fist. His eyes, she noted, remained as bright and defiant as ever.

"You don't want my help, fine," she told him, returning the silvers to the chest and closing the lid with a hard snap. "Feel free to take your troublesome arse elsewhere. Piss off to the Sixth Order, why don't you? Since you're such great friends with the Battle Lord's whelp and all."

"Never said 'e was my friend," Frentis retorted. "Just that…"

"…he gave you a knife the day he beat the merry shit out of a bunch've guardsmen at the Summertide Fair. I know." Derla gripped the mantelpiece, frowning as she sought to control an anger laced with no small amount of fear. "Come to think on it, it's not that bad a notion," she said after a moment's contemplation. "Hunsil won't think of it, not right off anyway. You being an orphan with no one to give you over to them."

"He can't go there," Livera said, holding Frentis closer. "Boy's die there."

"What d'you think he'll be doing tomorrow if he doesn't?" Derla watched Frentis's face as the notion took hold, a small flicker of determination passing across his brow.

"Why would they take me?" he asked. "Some gutter born dipper with no family to put 'im in the Faith's hands?"

"Doesn't have to be family. Just someone who can vouch for you. Who better than your knife gifting friend?"

Frentis briefly clasped Livera's hand then disentangled himself from her, getting to his feet and moving to stand in front of Derla. "That hurt," he said, rubbing his head.

"It was supposed to, you mouthy little sod."

She glanced at the window, seeing the lengthening shadows stretch over the tangle of chimney and slate. "You can stay till it gets dark. Don't use the rooftops, Hunsil's boys will be watching them by now. There's a passage through the cellar to the sewers. I suppose you still know the way to the drains that feed into the Brinewash?"

"'Course," he said with an aggrieved pout.

"Good. You'll have to swim for it, steer clear of the bridges. Once your out, stay off the road. If you're not at the Order House by morning…"

"I will be." He paused, a small grin of gratitude playing over his lips. "They'll still come looking," he said. "Hunsil's lads."

"Yes, they will. Liv, fix this boy some soup. No point sending him off to the Sixth Order with an empty belly."

CHAPTER 2

Hunsil sent Ratter and Draker, which Derla would normally have considered something of an insult but assumed his more reliable employees were otherwise engaged just now.

"Too much to expect you to wipe your feet, I see," she greeted them, casting a caustic eye at the mud Ratter's boots had left on her fine Alpiran carpet.

Ratter began to respond with a sheepish shrug, then stopped himself, fixing an unrepentant glare on his narrow, pointy nosed face instead. Draker was apparently too preoccupied with ogling Livera to respond at all, so much so that Ratter felt obliged to deliver a hard shove to the side of his companion's shaggy-haired head. "Wake up, lack-wit! We're here on business, remember?"

"Not that you could afford either of us," Livera said, not looking up from her embroidery. She sat by the window, working a needle and thread through a circle of framed silk. Her pleated skirt was long enough to conceal the daggers she had strapped to both legs. Derla's own knife was tucked into a hidden sheath at the small of her back, a curved fisherman's gutting blade useful for swiftly laying open a belly or a throat in a confined space.

"Watch your lip," Ratter said, making an effort to sound menacing. However, his threatening tone was undermined somewhat as he gave a short backward step, removing his muddy boots from the carpet. Derla had always thought him too wary a character to make a successful thug, but today his habitual nervousness had blossomed into outright fear. *Fear is bad,* she knew. *Fear makes even a coward dangerous.*

"State your business or piss off," she advised, her tone one of weary disdain. "We have appointments to keep."

"Frentis," Ratter said. "Where is he?"

"How should I know?"

"You fence for him. Everyone knows that."

"I fence for half the dippers in this city. Doesn't mean I know where they are at any given moment." She angled her head in a display of calculation. "But that also doesn't mean I can't find him, if I'm adequately compensated for my time and trouble, of course. What's he done, anyway?"

"You been asleep all day or something?" Ratter asked. "The whole quarter's in uproar."

"We had a late night," Livera said, raising her head to smile at Derla. "Didn't do much sleeping, did we Derl?"

"What's that..?" Draker said, voice husky with lust as he took an involuntary step forward. Derla could smell the cheap grog matting his beard.

"Business!" Ratter reminded Draker, applying another hard shove to his head. This time the larger man responded with a growl, rounding on his diminutive companion and crouching in readiness for a lunge.

"You two fuckheads want to fight, do it outside," Derla said.

The pair glared at each other for a second before slowly turning back to her, Draker's bearded face displaying a sulky frown, though his eyes inevitably began to stray to Livera once again.

"Hunsil lost an eye last night," Ratter said. "Frentis's doing."

"That scrawny whelp?" Derla scoffed. "Come off it."

"We was there," Ratter insisted. "He sank a throwing knife into Hunsil's eye from fifteen feet away, then went skipping off across the rooftops. I've seen less tidy jobs from lifelong cut-throats."

Tidier still if he'd actually finished it, Derla thought, putting the appropriate measure of surprise on her face as Ratter continued.

"So y'see," he said, "Hunsil won't want to hear any shit about addyquait compysashuns and such. In fact, we tell him you weren't generous with your help he's gonna send us back with different orders."

Derla said nothing, watching the increasingly bright sheen of sweat form on Ratter's balding pate. "You were there," she said. "Supposed to be guarding him, right? Didn't do a very good job, did you? 'Spect he's awful riled about that. Seems to me he's likely to be angrier at you two than me right now."

"Just tell us where he is, Derla!" Ratter started forward, teeth bared in a snarl of impending violence as Draker followed his lead, dropping into a preparatory crouch.

Derla saw Livera tense, hands stopping their work to settle into her lap and grip her skirts. Derla resisted the impulse to reach for her knife, instead arching a tired eyebrow at the two visitors and asking, "Is that really the best idea?"

There were times when a reputation born of excessive violence had its advantages. Derla's had been won after a brief but spectacularly bloody encounter with a Volarian sea captain. Having employed her services for the better part of a week the fellow then avowed a disinclination to settling his bill, employing an unwise level of incivility in the process. Although Derla hadn't been able to extract the required funds she took some comfort from the knowledge that the man would have great difficulty voicing such language in future, she having shortened his tongue by two inches.

Draker bridled at her words but Ratter, the smarter of the two by a small margin, reached out a hand to restrain him. "If you won't talk to us he'll send others who ain't so nice," he said in a rare display of honesty.

Derla gave an annoyed sigh and turned to Livera. "You knew the little bastard best, Liv. Where's he likely to be?"

"He knows the sewers better than anyone," Livera replied, smiling sweetly at Ratter. "Even you."

"They've already been scoured from end to end," he said. "Has to be somewhere else."

"He was always going on about getting enough loot together to buy a berth on a ship one day. 'Gonna sail away from this pit for good,' he said."

"The docks've been scoured too."

"Is the *Sojourner* still at anchor?" Derla asked before going on to elaborate on the bosun's proclivities. "Any berth will do if a boy's desperate enough," she added with an explanatory shrug. In fact, she had made a surreptitious trip to the docks at first light to ensure the *Sojourner* had sailed with the morning tide. By good fortune the vessel was destined for the Far West which meant she wouldn't return to Varinshold for at least a year.

"We'll check on it," Ratter said, shoving Draker towards the door.

The larger man stayed put, his gaze lingering on Livera once more. "I got some coin…" he began, reaching for a purse on his belt.

"There's not enough gold or liquor in the world," Derla told him then jerked her head at the door. Draker's face darkened but he duly shuffled after Ratter as he stepped out onto the landing. "If I were you," Derla added, "I wouldn't stick around too long. Once Hunsil's scraped this city clean looking for Frentis he'll need to sate his anger on someone. I hear there's profit to be had on the southern shore, if you don't mind getting your feet wet."

Ratter met her gaze for an instant, giving a faint nod of a grim acceptance before closing the door.

"That could've gone worse," Livera said quietly once the footsteps had faded from the staircase. Derla went to the window, watching the pair of miscreants make their way along Lofter's Walk, in the direction of the docks.

"With any luck," she said, "they'll linger long enough to tell Hunsil the ship's already sailed and flee the city as soon as they can."

"Doesn't mean he won't send someone else."

"No," Derla admitted, sinking down next to Livera and taking her hand. "Best if we stay quiet for a while, no more fencing dippers' loot until this dies down. No appointments for the next few weeks. Also, keep a bag packed in case we have to run."

"But Kwo's got another client lined up," Livera said with an aggrieved pout. "A Nilsaelin merchant who just bought a Royal warrant to trade in Varinshold." She rested her head on Derla's shoulder, brows raised and eyes wide in kittenish solicitation. "Merchants always know so much," she purred. "And think of all that loot his ships will be bringing in. Silks and porcelain, Kwo said. He's a big fish, Derl, be a shame not to land him. And

Hunsil's likely to pay well for knowledge like that. Make him less peeved, maybe."

"I sometimes think I taught you too well," Derla muttered. "When?"

"Next Oprian."

"Is this merchant a civilised sort or another of Kwo Sha's deviants?"

Livera's slim shoulders moved in a shrug. "A man of simple tastes, apparently. Easily pleased."

"Alright." Derla squeezed her hand. "But I'll hire Gallis to keep tabs, just in case this fellow's not so simple. And make sure to take your knife."

CHAPTER 3

Derla spent Oprian evening at her studies. Aspect Dendrish's *Rise of the Merchant Kings* had been recommended to her by one of her clients, a Master of Histories from the Third Order who agreed to provide tutelage in return for a reduced hourly rate. After wading through a hundred pages of overblown prose long on narrative and short on analysis, Derla concluded her client had been somewhat biased in his opinion of his Aspect's work. Still, the volume contained some useful statistical tables on the growth of Far Western trade since the days of the Red Hand which she spent a contented hour or two transcribing into her own notes. Besides Livera, economics had been Derla's principal passion for the past several years and their rooms were increasingly filled with her reference library. It was all greatly amusing for Livera. "What use does a whore have for all these words and numbers?" she had asked shortly after moving in.

"The mind stays healthy longer than the body," Derla told her. "And I've got no intention of living out my elder years in penury."

She became so engrossed in her transcription that she failed to notice the hour until the faint tolling of the Midnight Bell beyond the window. Whilst their shared occupation invariably involved late hours Livera was usually capable of satisfying her clients and returning home well before the bell. Derla returned to her work for a spell but soon found herself pacing the room, nerves fraying with every prolonged second. After an hour in which Livera had signally failed to reappear Derla strapped her knife around her waist, pulled on her cloak and went out into the street.

She tried the Red Anchor first, a small but orderly drinking hole she knew Gallis favoured for a nightcap or two on the rare occasions he had money in his pocket. She found it only half full of patrons too insensible to even make the effort of a cat call. There was no sign of Gallis and the barkeep denied seeing him all night.

"Probably off climbing some rich bugger's wall," he said with a shrug, before leaning closer and adding, "Don't suppose you're working tonight, Derl? Been awful dull in the evenings since One Eye went on the rampage."

One Eye. She supposed the name was inevitable. In the days since Frentis's disappearance Hunsil had embarked on the kind of purge not seen in the Varinshold underworld for years. Rumour had it well over a dozen bodies had been consigned to the depths of the harbour, most of them slain by Hunsil himself, who made a point of wielding the knife in front of the victims' kin. It was also rumoured that he forced them to look into his empty eye socket at the final moment, commanding that they cough up any knowledge of Frentis as the ghost of his eye now had the power to see lies. Such was the fear engendered by One Eye's rampage that criminal activity had died down to almost nothing. Whores and thieves stayed home and went hungry rather than attract the notice of their new king, which is what Hunsil's purge had made him now.

Derla ignored the barkeep's offer and slid a couple of coppers across the bar. "Gallis shows up, send someone to tell me," she said before turning and walking out.

Gallis kept an attic above a tanner's shop on Skinner's Row. Rents were cheap here due to the smell and Derla was obliged to shield her nose with a scented handkerchief as she pounded on the tanner's door. "Ain't been back all day," the bleary-eyed and evidently peeved proprietor reported. "And I got no time for pestering doxies…"

He was an old man and lacked the strength push the door closed as Derla stepped forward to brace her shoulder against it. "And I'm in no mood to suffer insult, you old fuck," she informed him quietly, bringing her knife up, quick and neat, pressing the tip of the blade to his nose. "Gallis comes back tell him Derla's looking and he'd better not delay in finding me." She kept the knife pressed into the warty mass of the tanner's nose until he gave a very slow nod.

She spent another fruitless hour touring any haunt where Gallis or Livera might have gone, finding nothing. Eventually she forced herself to turn for home as the first glimmerings of dawn broke over the rooftops. Upon rounding the corner into Lofter's Walk she came to an abrupt halt.

Little Dot waited on her doorstep. Although a woman of nearly twenty years Dot stood a hair over three feet tall. Her miniature features, usually so bright and cheerful, were set in a mask of grim sympathy. "My sister sent me," she said as Derla forced herself to take a forward step, a hard ball of dread forming in her stomach. Dot's sister, Big Dot, was both healer and mortician for much of the Varinshold criminal fraternity.

Derla managed a few more steps before coming to a halt, taking a second to steady her suddenly dizzy head as she stood staring down at Little Dot. The small woman clasped her hands together, blinking tears. She had always liked Livera, but then, so did everyone.

"She dead?" Derla asked, surprised by the calm she heard in her own voice.

"I'm so sorry, Derl…"

"Gallis?"

"Bashed up but still breathing." Dot stepped forward, reaching out to take Derla's hand. "C'mon," she said and Derla allowed herself to be tugged along in numb silence. "Arrangements need to be made."

CHAPTER 4

Big Dot was of a markedly less sensitive disposition than her sister, standing with her meaty arms crossed over her chest and heavy jawed features impassive as Derla looked down at Livera's body. It was, Derla knew, the accustomed detachment of the veteran physician, learned thanks to years of watching grieving souls weep over murdered kin, or lovers. But Derla didn't weep.

Dot had cleaned Livera's corpse, wiping the blood from her skin and washing it from her dark curls. She had also dressed her in a plain cotton shift before laying her out on the table in her vault-like cellar that served as a mortuary. A cloth was draped over Livera's neck, presumably to spare Derla the sight of the bruising. Big Dot had also sewn Livera's lips together with near invisible catgut stitches to remove the death grimace. Derla felt a small flutter of gratitude for this, but it faded almost as soon as it rose in her breast.

We both died tonight, she decided, eyes tracking over Livera's empty form. She felt no inclination to touch her, feel the cold, lifeless chill of her skin. *She's not there anymore.*

"How many times?" she asked Big Dot, raising her gaze from the corpse.

The woman took a moment to reply, heavy brows creasing a little. Clearly it wasn't a typical question. "Times?"

"You said she was strangled then stabbed. How many times?"

Big Dot blinked and exchanged a glance with her sister

who sat perched on a stool by the door. "Just tell her, Dot," Little Dot said softly.

"Counted fifty wounds altogether," Big Dot said, adopting a brisk professional tone. "All in the chest and stomach."

"Was she raped?"

More blinking, another glance at her sister. "There was… damage to her nethers," Big Dot said finally. "Lack of blood means it happened after death."

"Strangled her, stabbed her then fucked her corpse," Derla mused. "Man who does that doesn't just do it once."

"Haven't seen one like this before," Big Dot said. "Been years since the Hacker was about, and we settled with him right and proper."

Derla remembered the Hacker well, a deserter from the Realm Guard some said had been driven mad by one battle too many. He'd hidden himself in the Southern Quarter and embarked upon a month-long rampage that left every whore in the city fearful of venturing out in darkness. The madman had eventually been cornered by a mob near the docks who, after a thorough beating, handed him over to a select group of aggrieved ladies. Derla still recalled the fellow's screams and they didn't trouble her sleep one whit.

"I'd wager there have been others like this in Nilsael," she told Big Dot. "Where was she found?"

"The back yard of the Black Boar," Little Dot said.

Hunsil's place, Derla thought. *Where no one will be surprised to find another body come the morning.* It was a decent enough ruse but she saw through it instantly. One Eye had no need to trouble himself with such an elaborate trap when all he had to do was send his lads to break down their door in the small hours of the morning.

She allowed herself a final look at Livera's face, seeing only a flaccid, bleached facsimile of the woman she loved. "Where's Gallis?" she said, turning away.

"Down the hall," Little Dot said, hopping down from her stool. "I'll show you."

"Derla," Big Dot said, making her pause at the door. "What do you want done?" she asked, gesturing at the corpse. "I know a discreet Brother from the Second Order who'd be willing to say the words and give her to the fire."

"She held to the Alpiran gods," Derla said. "They entomb their dead. Find somewhere… deep and hidden for her. I'll take care of any expense."

…

Gallis perched his muscular form on the edge of the bed, arms resting on his knees and his head slumped forward. Big Dot had shaved his normally thick black hair down to the scalp to get at the three cuts on his head. They were small but deep, the stitches dark spidery clusters amidst the grey stubble. Derla knew the pattern well enough. *Three rapid blows from a cosh. More than one attacker.*

"Can you talk?" she asked him.

Gallis's head slumped lower still at the sound of her voice, his long-fingered, climber's hands bunching into fists. "Yeh," he said in a gruff mutter, the voice possessing a tension that told of lingering pain.

"I think another dose is in order," Little Dot said, moving to the earthenware jug and cup on a nearby table. She poured a measure of dark liquid into the cup and held it out to Gallis. It was, Derla knew, one of her more potent pain remedies, Redflower infused with various herbs to alleviate the soporific effect. Big Dot set the bones and stitched the cuts whilst Little Dot mixed the medicine, much of it more efficacious than anything the Fifth Order could provide.

"Don't wannit," Gallis said, waving her away.

"It'll clear your head," Dot insisted, reaching out to clasp one of his hands which he snatched away.

"Just drink it," Derla told him. "You're no use to me with an addled brain."

Gallis looked up at her for the first time, red, moist eyes shining with what Derla discerned to be guilt rather than fear. After a second he blinked and took the cup from Dot, downing the contents in hard, punishing gulps that left him retching.

"Leave us for bit, would you Dot?" Derla said. She waited for the healer to leave then closed the door behind her, turning back to Gallis. He continued to cough for a few moments then gave a heavy sigh, darting a look at Derla.

"You want blood you can have it," he said.

"Not yours," she replied, moving to sit on the small stool next to the bed.

"I messed up, Derl," Gallis went on, still avoiding her gaze. "Didn't do what you paid me for…"

Derla slapped him, the blow swift and hard, leaving a red patch on his cheek and bringing some life back to his eyes. "We have work to do," she said. "When it's done go and chuck yourself in the Brinewash for all I care. Until then, you owe me a debt and I expect payment. Understand?"

He met her gaze, holding it this time. "Whatever you need."

"I need you to tell me what happened."

"Got jumped is what happened. Picked up Livera as promised and escorted her to the place Kwo Sha said, rooms above the old pottery on Raddler's Lane. Client wanted discretion, Livera said. They jumped us at the corner. Three of them, and they knew what they were doing. I fought, Derl. I did. Managed to get my knife in my hand, pretty sure I scarred one good on the face. But..." His hand went to the stitched scars on his scalp. "Three to one is bad odds. I didn't come to until the small hours, and she was gone. I looked, but..." He trailed off, letting his gaze drop.

"You scarred one on the face," Derla said. "Did you get a good look?"

"They wore scarves. Caught a glimpse of the one I cut, though. He'd be hard to miss, got him from here to here." Gallis traced a finger from the bridge of the nose down to his chin.

Derla sat in silence for a time, mind churning over the various possibilities, though it was an effort to prevent it straying back to the sight of Livera's empty, stitch-mouth face. *Ambushed before they got to the place. Means the client was waiting somewhere else.*

"We need a crew," she said, getting to her feet. "Reliable folk who don't balk at the wet stuff."

"Hiring help ain't too easy just now," Gallis said. "One Eye's calmed down a bit, but not much."

"Offer two golds each for a few nights work. Double it to four if you have to."

Gallis's brow creased in a doubtful frown. "I know you do well for y'self, Derl. But that's a lotta coin."

Coin can't be spent by a dead woman. "Vouch for me," she said. "Make sure they know I'm good for it." She moved to the door. "Bring them to my place tonight. We have a call to make on Kwo Sha."

CHAPTER 5

Kwo Sha claimed to be a bastard born to the favourite concubine of some Far Western merchant king. His mother, having fallen pregnant thanks to a forbidden tryst with a minor courtier, had fled the palace to raise him in a secret mountain hideaway. Kwo was fond of recalling his early years in the mountains where he received the fruits of his mother's excellent education in languages and mathematics. However, the merchant king's reach was long and his desire for vengeance implacable. As his soldiers drew ever nearer Kwo Sha's mother grew resigned to her own fate. At best she would be permitted to commit suicide and at worst subjected to an inventive form of torture involving a thousand scorpions and a bed of rusty nails. However, her love for her son was fierce and she contrived to spirit him to the coast and thence onto a vessel which would carry him far away to a small, damp land beyond the vengeance of the Merchant King. Abandoned as a boy on the Varinshold dockside, Kwo Sha had been forced to make his own way. Thanks to his mother's tutelage he quickly carved out a place in the spice trade and in time became something akin to a minor merchant king himself. His success was ostensibly rooted in the lucrative contracts he arranged with ships plying the spice routes to Alpira and beyond. However, his true source of wealth lay in his role as intermediary between those at the top of Varinshold society who wished to make use of the various services only those at the bottom could offer.

"Tell me something, Kwo," Derla said, poking a toe through the detritus littering the floor of the trader's shop, "is any of it true?"

Kwo Sha looked up at her from amidst a pile of shattered glass and pottery. Blood leaked from his rapidly swelling nose, staining the fine silks he wore. At her instruction Gallis and the others had kept the beating brief, but possessed of sufficient bone breaking force to leave no doubt as to their intent tonight. Kwo Sha had been wise in employing a trio of bodyguards, but unwise in not employing more. They lay about the ruined shop in various states of bloodied unconsciousness as Derla's new employees helped themselves to whatever trinkets or stock took their fancy. There were five besides Gallis, all willing to work for just one gold apiece, another mark of Livera's popularity.

"Your fascinating life story, I mean to say," Derla said, moving to crouch at Kwo Sha's side. She smiled, angling her head and raising an eyebrow. "It's not, is it? Your mother wasn't some tragic heroine saving her darling little bastard from the evil king. Most likely she was a sea-whore who dumped you on the orphanage steps before climbing back on whatever bilge-tub brought her here. I'm guessing you never even knew her. It's your accent, y'see? Pure Varinshold under all the soft vowels and occasional memorised phrases spoken in a language you don't really know. I'm right, aren't I?"

She reached behind her back and drew her knife, Kwo Sha's eyes widening considerably at the sight of the curved gutting blade. "Your mother was a whore," Derla said, placing the edge of the blade against his cheek, "just like me, and Livera."

He tried to speak, producing a bubbling froth of blood and

spit instead. Derla let him sputter on until he achieved a modicum of articulation. "I didn't… know."

"How unusually ignorant of you." Derla turned the blade a little, pressing the edge into the flesh of his face, just enough for a small line of blood to colour the steel.

"The client…" Kwo Sha spoke in a rapid, wet babble. "Wanted an Alpiran girl… Sweet natured he said. He was new to the city. I couldn't know his habits…"

"You're a surprisingly poor liar, Kwo." She turned the blade, more blood welling on the edge. "He had help. Locals who knew the best place to dump her. Where'd he find them, if not thanks to you?"

"He had his own people…" Kwo Sha choked off into a pained squeal as Derla added pressure to the blade. "Meldeneans," he went on quickly. "Pirates by the look of them. They know this city as well as any local."

Derla glanced over at Gallis, standing close by with his bloodied cudgel at the ready. "Could be," he said with a shrug. "But pirates would've been more likely to finish me off. Meldeneans ain't known for their merciful customs."

"Killing you would've left them with another body to deal with," she said. "And I'd guess they were in a hurry."

Derla returned her gaze to Kwo Sha, watching the relief flood his eyes as she lifted the knife from his cheek, then flood back in again as she pressed it to his throat. "I know discretion is the foundation stone of your business," she told him, "so I would like to propose a transaction of such profitability as to overcome your admirable scruples. Tell me the client's name and where I can find him and I won't pull your tongue out through the hole

I'm about to carve in your throat."

...

"Nice place," Gallis commented, a small glimmer of greed lighting his gaze as he surveyed the mansion. Derla supposed it was too much to ask for him to forgo his thief's instincts for one night. She had to admit it was an impressive house, standing three stories high with numerous windows of glass rather than shutters. It lay just to the north of where the Brinewash deepened and curved back on itself for a short stretch, creating a teardrop-shaped bulge where many of the city's merchants made their homes. The depth and course of the river insulated these worthies from Varinshold's less desirable precincts whilst remaining within a reasonable carriage ride of the docks.

They had crossed the river just after the tenth bell tolled, making use of a somewhat leaky boat procured by a bargeman of Gallis's acquaintance. Once ashore they hid themselves in the deep shadows of the house's exterior wall, Gallis peering through the railings to gauge the best way in.

"Plenty of pickings to be had in a house like that," he went on, Derla detecting an obvious question in his tone.

"Get me where I need to be," she said, "then the place is yours."

"Kwo said he's got a wife and two daughters."

Derla met his gaze, seeing another, weightier question there. "Not my concern," she said, "or yours," she added, raising her voice to address their five compatriots. "Tie them up and gag them. That's all."

"And the pirates?"

"That's your score to settle. Just don't be too quick about it."

"Right then." He settled the coiled rope over his shoulder and reached up to grasp the railings, pausing for a second before hauling himself up. "You know you should've killed Kwo, right?" he asked Derla.

She ignored the question and gave an impatient flick of her hand. *Get on with it.* Gallis pulled on a leather mask that covered the upper side of his face, flashed her a brief grin and leapt, gripping the top of the railings and vaulting over in an effortless display of his art. He landed softly, took a second to scan the surrounding flower beds then made a beckoning gesture to the rest of the crew. They duly clambered over the railings to crouch at Gallis's side whereupon he led them towards the house in a straight sprint across the lawn. Derla lost sight of them as they rounded the mansion's north facing wall. Now she could only wait.

Her eyes flicked from one dim window to another, ears alive for the sound of alarm as the seconds stretched to minutes. She knew Gallis would be climbing the rear of the house, searching for an unsecured window or other useful entry point. Once inside he would toss the rope to his crew and the night's business would begin in earnest. She found her hands trembling a little as the minutes dragged by, and frowned in puzzlement at the sweat dampening her palms. Since viewing Livera's corpse she had felt little save an unwavering sense of purpose, yet now the fear chose to make itself known.

Is it fear? she wondered, smoothing her palms over her skirt. *Or anticipation?*

The signal came a short while later, a single oil lamp flaring to life in one of the front facing windows, unnerving in its suddenness as she hadn't detected a single sound during her vigil.

Derla rose from her hiding place and made her way to the front gate. It stood closed but unlocked, one of several misjudgements made by the mansion's owner.

Gallis opened the front door with a florid bow, stepping aside to allow her entry to a marble floored lobby from which a curving staircase ascended to the first floor. Four people lay on the floor, servants by their dress, each with their hands bound behind their backs and gags securely wedged in their mouths. Gallis's crew stood behind them, a few already sporting silver candlesticks and sundry other valuables.

"Where's your mask?" Gallis asked, casting a wary glance at the servants who stared up at Derla with bright, wet eyes.

"Won't be needing one," she said.

Gallis muttered a curse and ordered the servants to close their eyes. "Keep 'em shut tight, y'arse licking fuckers," he growled. "Else I'll forget how nice I'm s'posed to be tonight."

Derla moved to the foot of the staircase where a body lay sprawled across the lower steps. He was a tall, broad shouldered fellow with a face that might have been handsome but for the fresh scar running from his nose to his chin. Blood leaked from the numerous stab wounds visible through his torn shirt.

"Too quick for my liking," Gallis said, coming to her side. "Still, it was rightly satisfying." He hesitated. "We didn't get 'em all. The other two pirates ran for the cellar. Got one as he was climbing up the coal chute, the other's gone though."

"The wife and daughters?" Derla asked.

"Trussed up in one of the bedrooms, like you said. The merchant's in his study, up the stairs on the left."

"You and the others had better grab what you can and take

yourselves off. It's a fair bet the pirate will bring the Guard, or run off to tell someone who will."

"Reckon we've got a half hour or so before they show up. I don't mind waiting."

"I mind." Derla started up the stairs then paused and untied the purse from her belt, tossing it to him. "Payment. Make sure everyone gets their share."

He looked at the purse in his hand, heavy with double the coin she had promised. When he looked up at her once more his gaze was dark with understanding. "Ain't no use nor point to you dyin' tonight," he said.

"I died already." She turned away and resumed her ascent. "Might as well make it official."

...

"You should have been more careful," Derla told the merchant, setting her heavily stained knife down on his desk. "And more honest in your dealings with Kwo Sha. Had you told him your true purpose I'm sure he would have kept you supplied with suitable victims for years, and you and I would never have crossed paths."

She moved away, tracing a gore-covered finger over the well stocked bookshelves in his library. Some volumes were clearly for show, the classics every Realm subject of appreciable wealth felt obliged to keep in their home. They were easily distinguished by the uncreased spines and perfect lettering, whilst others showed signs of frequent reading. She paused at one particular tome, a thick book with the title 'Legends and Myths of the Alpiran Empire' embossed in faded gold letters on the spine.

"Ahh," she said, plucking the book from the shelf. "Lord Al Avern's much acclaimed first foray into the scholarly realm,

I believe. Clearly you're a man of some taste, sir."

She opened the book, leafing through the pages which, she found, had been defaced by numerous notations in a spidery, almost unreadable script. Words were underlined and passages encircled, the margins crammed with dense scribblings which made little sense to Derla, although the words 'beauty' and 'blood' appeared with the greatest frequency. Keeping hold of the book she moved to sit in the chair positioned opposite the merchant's desk, turning page after page decorated with feverishly inscribed gibberish. Eventually she paused at the title page to the final chapter; 'The Paths of Revenna'. Here the scribblings became so intense they obscured much of the text, the jagged hand-wrought letters overlapping and entwining in an indecipherable melange, although she noted that the word 'DARK' was now most often repeated.

"Alpiran legends, Alpiran victims," she mused, regarding the merchant over the top of the book. "And an obsession with the Dark. What a curiously mad bastard you are."

Derla closed the book and tossed it aside, reclining in her seat to stare into the empty eye sockets of the man behind the desk. "Did you talk to her first?" she asked him. "I'm sure you would have found her conversation fascinating. She knew many an old legend from her homeland, though to her they weren't legends and she'd get awful huffy if I ever suggested otherwise. 'The histories of the gods are not to be made light of,' she'd tell me. Livera tended to laugh off most things in life, except any suggestion of insult to her gods even though they'd never been especially kind to her. Father run off after her mother died bringing her brother into the world and him taken by the fever before reaching his tenth year. She never told me the truth of why she left the empire, the story would change. First it was to escape a vicious pimp, then she claimed she made the mistake of marrying a client and stowed away on a ship to the Realm to escape him. Not because he was a bad man, just boring. She could never abide boredom."

Derla felt something on her cheeks, a new wetness beyond the sticky spray left by the merchant's opened veins. "Oh, how embarrassing," she said, touching a finger to the tears. "You'll have to forgive me, sir. Surely I am not fit for such fine company."

Her gaze slipped from the merchant's ravaged eyes to his bare chest, punctured by forty eight precisely placed stab wounds. Derla had always been good with numbers and her occupation gave her a reasonable understanding of anatomy, so it hadn't been too difficult to keep him alive for the last two blows. Given the man's beastly habits Derla had expected more of him, some measure of malevolent defiance at least, or perhaps an insight into his evidently diseased mind. But he had acted as any other man might upon finding himself tied to a chair to be slowly tormented to death by a vengeful whore. Even after she stabbed out his eyes he lingered for a while, gibbering slurred pleas to spare his family until, finally, his head slumped to his chest and he left the world with a small, almost wistful sigh. Derla's numbness had lingered throughout it all, her heart maintaining a steady rhythm, untroubled by either enjoyment or pity. Except now it was done there were tears.

A loud thud echoed from downstairs, quickly followed by two more and the sound of splintering wood. Derla got to her feet, her gaze shifting to the knife lying on the desk. If she had it in hand when the Guard entered the room it would save a lot of tedious rigmarole.

No, the voice whispered in her mind as she reached for the knife. It was Livera's voice, as clear and real as if she stood at her shoulder. Derla froze, an icy chill vying with joy in her breast.

"You're not here," Derla groaned in grim realisation. "There are no whispers on the wind. I just wanted to hear your voice once more. You died. I died."

No, Livera's voice told her, rich in the sweet kindness that had killed her. *You didn't.*

Derla found herself withdrawing her hand, letting it fall to her side. She turned as the first Guardsman burst into the room, a bearded sergeant with a drawn sword who drew up in shock at the sight that greeted him.

"Took you fuckers long enough to get here," Derla told him, putting her hands on her hips.

CHAPTER 6

The man had to stoop a little in order to enter her cell, being so tall. He was old, the wrinkles on his face and the grey shining in his hair and beard told her that, but he stood with the straight-backed surety of a much younger man and Derla could see an intelligence in his eyes that no amount of years could dim.

The gaoler's lamp caught the ermine hem of the old man's cloak as he stood regarding her in wordless scrutiny for a time. It was the first true light Derla had seen in over a week. She was somewhere deep, she knew that. Also somewhere far from the Vaults into which she had expected to be cast to wait out the days until her hearing before the magistrate and inevitable hanging. Instead a few hours detention at the City Guardhouse had ended with a bag being thrown over her head. There had been lots of shoving, a carriage ride, then more shoving as she tripped her way down numerous steps before the bag had been unceremoniously torn away, affording her the brief sight of the cell door slamming closed. Since then all had been darkness save for the brief glimmer of lantern-light once a day when her gaoler pushed bread and water through a slot in the base of the door.

Derla surmised this was all intended to drive her to madness; leave the vile torturess to scream and wail in the dark for the rest of her days. But she didn't go mad. She waited, for some small instinct told her there was more to this torment than punishment. And so it proved.

She sat with her back to the wall and knees drawn up, returning the old man's scrutiny until he said, "Is this how you greet your king?"

She saw it then, as he angled his head to reveal a prominent nose and strong jaw. It was a profile she knew well, having been stamped onto every coin she had earned over the past ten years.

Derla got to her feet and dropped into a deep curtsy, keeping her head lowered until he spoke again, "Alright. Give me that." She looked up to see him taking the lantern from the gaoler. "Close the door. I'll knock when you're needed."

The gaoler hesitated, his brutish features hardening as he glanced at Derla. "They say this one's awful vicious, Highness. . . ."

"I'll knock when you're needed," the king said, softly but precisely. The gaoler didn't so much retreat as vanish, the door slamming shut and leaving a loud echo.

"Any notion of where you are?" the king asked Derla as the echo faded.

Derla began to give a subservient head-bob but stopped at the king's exclamation. "Ach! Enough of that. Speak plainly, woman."

"This is not the Vaults," Derla said, finding she had to swallow to get the words out. Days in the silent dark made speech feel strange in her mouth, her voice sounding far too calm and detached to be real.

"No, it is not," the king agreed. "Then where else could it be? The Blackhold perhaps?"

"Only Deniers and those who pretend to know the Dark end up in the Blackhold. And I am neither. Besides, the carriage that brought me here passed along Mendings Way before crossing the bridge south of Watcher's Bend."

"How could you possibly know that?"

"The cobbles are smoother the closer you get to the Northern Quarter and that particular bridge has the highest arch in the city."

She saw a small flicker of emotion pass across the king's face, too quick to judge his feelings but she fancied it was either amusement or satisfaction. "Very astute of you. Therefore I consider it will be an easy matter for you to deduce your current whereabouts."

Derla had in fact considered then discounted this possibility, the notion being so absurd. Now, it seemed her judgement had been all too accurate. "The palace," she said. "I'm in the palace."

"About thirty feet below the wine stores actually, but close enough."

The king came closer, holding out the lantern to fully illuminate Derla's face, his eyes narrowing in an appraisal that she knew had nothing to do with lust.

"Do you know how much the man you killed was worth?" he asked.

"A great deal of money I imagine."

"Worth is not always measured in wealth. I do not mean the gold he piled up, or the ships and houses he accrued. I mean his worth to this Realm. In particular, his worth to me."

"What worth would a just king find in so perverted and murderous a soul?"

"None." The king's teeth gleamed yellow in the lantern's glow as he drew back his lips in a smile. "I, however, found a great deal of worth in him. I am frequently unjust in my governance of this Realm, but any injustice is the product of necessity. I didn't know of the merchant's peculiar tastes, and had I known he would most likely be dead by my order rather than your hand, but," the king's smile had gone now and his face was a mask of intent sincerity, "only after I had ensured someone of equal worth could take his place. You should understand this about your king if our association is to continue."

"Continue?" Derla asked. Having presumed herself dead the prospect of deliverance was felt strange, adding an unexpected energy to her pulse and sweat to her hands. She tried to hide it by folding her arms but knew the old man had seen it.

He smiled again, with a semblance of kindness this time, before moving back, the lantern's glow shrinking. Derla resisted the lure of the light. She suspected he wouldn't be impressed if she were to follow him doglike about her cell.

"You identified and killed the merchant in a matter of hours," the king said, "despite the efforts he made to obscure his trail. Such an achievement is evidence of a considerable set of skills, not to mention a singularity of purpose. Both traits I can make use of."

The lantern shrank into a glowing ball at the far end of her cell, illuminating the door. The king raised a hand to knock, then stopped. Derla couldn't make out his face now, but knew he had turned his scrutiny upon her once more.

"Just one other thing," he said. "Your accomplices."

"I have no accomplices," she replied. "I was called to the merchant's house to provide my particular brand of services. He tried to strangle me then produced a knife, avowing his intention to have his way with my corpse. I killed him in defence of my own life. Everything that was done was done by my own hand and no other."

"Yes. So you told the City Guard. However, the merchant's servants say otherwise, as do his family. Their testimony indicates your visit was driven by a desire for personal retribution."

"Liars, seeking to explain away their own cowardice and shameful complicity in his crimes."

"If I am to find a use for your skills, there can be no one to gainsay the story we must weave to explain your release. Without the names of your friends, I may as well just leave you here."

Derla's face was fixed on the king's hand, the bony fist poised an inch or two from the door. When she spoke, the words scraped over her throat like a blacksmith's file. "I had no accomplices."

A soft sigh in the darkness, then two sharp raps of his fist on the door. "Loyalty," the king said as the gaoler worked the key in the lock. "Also a useful trait."

He raised the lantern and stood aside, gesturing at the open door. "Come along, my good woman. There is something I would like to show you."

...

"Who was she?"

The body hung in the gibbet, a slumped tangle of skin and bone wrapped in mildewed rags. The crows were at it, one pecking at the tattered flesh of the corpse's feet whilst another worried its beak in the dead woman's vacant eye socket.

"As mad and wretched a soul as you are ever likely to meet," the king told Derla. "She killed her children, some delusion regarding denier beliefs. Apparently she was fully convinced that once dead they would rise again imbued with all manner of Dark gifts. She managed to hang herself before they could administer justice, but the Fourth Order still felt obliged to string her up in the cage. Appearances sake, I suppose. It is my belief that her passing was in fact a mercy, for herself and the Realm."

"And her connection to me?" Derla asked, quickly adding "Highness," as the king raised an eyebrow. He had led her, accompanied by two palace guards, to the parapet above the north gate where the bodies decayed in their iron cages leaking a thick stench of corruption into the misted morning air. The hour was early, the sun only just beginning to crest the rooftops and there were no eyes to witness their visit save the guards at the gate who were conscientious in averting their gaze.

"She is you," the king explained. "Or rather, she is the inheritor of your crime. Having killed her children she then paid a visit to the merchant's house. Apparently, her ritual required the blood of a rich man."

Derla watched the crow withdraw its beak from the eye socket. It angled its head at her for a moment, black eyes flashing white as it blinked, gave a brief squawk and returned to its meal.

"Inquisitive creature, the crow," the king observed. "Curiosity is the principal trait of all scavengers, coupled with keen eyesight and remarkable patience. Tell me, what does your inquisitive nature tell you at this very moment?"

"She was a Denier so her crimes lay outside the scope of Crown law," Derla said. "She would have been judged by the Fourth Order. The details of their judgements are never revealed."

"Quite so. As you have no doubt discerned, the Fourth Order and I have our little arrangements. What a clever crow you are."

Derla removed her gaze from the feasting scavenger and

afforded the king another curtsy. "Thank you, Highness."

"It was a trifling issue really. The merchant's family and servants were another matter." Derla kept her features impassive as the king's gaze lingered on her, searching, she assumed, for any sign of concern. "Don't worry, they're alive," he went on. "Although shipping the entire household off to the Northern Reaches wasn't an inexpensive exercise. The merchant's wife has been allotted a generous pension, on the understanding that it will disappear the moment she ever again makes mention of her husband's ugly demise."

"Did she know, Highness?" Derla asked. "About his… habits."

"I expect so, wives always see more than you want them to." He grinned a little, reading the dark shade that had crept into Derla's gaze. "Wishing you'd killed her too now, aren't you?"

The crow squawked again, flapping its wings in warning as its companion began to clamber up the cage.

"My wishes are now for you to ordain, Highness," Derla said.

His grin broadened into a laugh and he turned away, beckoning another man forward. He was of trim build and an inch or two shorter than average, his features lean but otherwise bland. His clothes were similarly nondescript, reasonably well tailored but lacking anything that might draw the eye. For Derla, the most significant thing about him was that she had failed to make any note of his presence until now.

"Allow me to introduce you to Master Alveric," the king said as the bland-faced man bowed to him. "He'll be your tutor for the next few weeks. Skilled as you are, the mere fact of your capture indicates you have a great deal yet to learn. You'll find him a kindly teacher, for the most part, with many a clever trick to impart. I call him my Lord of Foxes. You, however," the king's gaze switched between Derla and the now squabbling crows on the gibbet, "will be my Lady of Crows. You do know how to play Warrior's Bluff, I assume?"

The Lady of Crows was one of the cards forming the Noble Suit found in the standard Asraelin card deck. The more superstitious souls amongst the gambling fraternity tended to regard it as an ill luck card, the kind that would turn up in a winning hand only for the victor to keel over stone dead a moment later.

"I know the game very well, Highness," Derla said.

The king gave Master Alveric a slightly smug glance before moving back from the parapet. "I'll leave you to get better acquainted," he said. "It's unlikely we'll meet more than once a year from now on. But rest assured, any instruction you receive from my Lord of Foxes is to be regarded as a Royal command."

Derla curtsied as he walked away with a brisk step, his two guards hurrying in his wake.

Master Alveric stood regarding Derla in silence for a second, a faint animosity discernible behind his otherwise placid gaze. *Not his idea to recruit me,* she realised.

"Go home," Alveric said abruptly. "Resume your normal routine, re-establish your standing amongst the criminal element." With that he turned to go.

"King Janus said you would be my tutor," Derla said.

Alveric paused to offer her the briefest glance. "Your education has already begun," he told her before turning and walking away once more, Derla hearing him add in a low mutter, "the first lesson being the value of following instructions."

CHAPTER 7

"Put it on."

Derla eyed the garment set out on the table. It was a dress, finely crafted from silk and lace with a red and black skirt and bodice to match. Fine as the dress was her attention was mostly occupied by the sheathed dagger that sat beside it. "Will it fit?" she asked. "My dimensions are a little out of the ordinary. You may have noticed." She favoured Master Alveric with a smile and arched eyebrow.

"It will fit perfectly," he said without any discernible change of expression. "Put it on."

Derla sighed and glanced around the unadorned dining room. She had woken this morning to find a note had been pushed under her door sometime during the night. On it the location of this house had been printed in small, neat letters. It was a plain free standing, two-storey dwelling positioned halfway along Hawker's Street, the kind of place a man might buy when he's done well for himself, but not so well as to secure a residence in the Northern Quarter proper. Alveric had answered the door after the first knock and led her wordlessly to this room where the dagger and the dress were waiting.

"You expect me to strip in front of you?" she asked Alveric.

"I do," he replied, as tonelessly as before.

"Despite my occupation I do retain some notions of modesty, you know."

"No." A certain hardness crept into Alveric's voice then, his eyes locking with hers. "You do not, because the king requires it. As he requires you to put on this dress."

She swallowed a tart reply and turned away, hands moving to the laces on her bodice. She forced herself to undress without any obvious haste, unwilling to allow him the notion that she might be flustered. "I usually insist on payment up front," she said, turning to face him, a hand on her hip. She had expected some sort of advance, an attempt to extort services from her or face a return to the unlit cell beneath the palace.

"A small mole on your right upper thigh," he said. "A deep crescent shaped scar on your shoulder. Distinguishing marks that will enable me to identify your corpse should it be discovered without a head." He nodded once again at the dress. "Put it on."

He hadn't been lying about the fit. The dress had evidently been made for her, without benefit of a measuring string. It was in fact the most well tailored garment she could remember wearing. It was also remarkably light and she couldn't contain a small laugh of appreciation as she strolled from one end of the room to the other. A garb that, to all appearances, should have rendered her clumsy and short of breath in fact allowed for remarkable comfort and ease of movement.

"Quite a gift, Master Alveric," she said with a curtsy. "My thanks, sir."

He ignored her and moved to her discarded clothes which now lay neatly folded on the table. A moment's rummaging and his hand emerged holding her curved gutting knife. "This is effective," he said, setting the weapon aside. "But too messy. Precision," he lifted the sheathed dagger from the table and tossed it to her, "will be your watchword from now on."

Derla's hand explored the dagger's plain, redwood handle for a moment. Like the dress, it fitted her perfectly. Drawing the knife she found it had a six inch blade with an edge that seemed to cut the light as it caught it. "Very nice," she said, hefting the weapon. "Feels a little light though."

"Lightness equates to speed," Alveric said. "And speed is more important than strength." With that, he punched her in the stomach.

The blow was hard enough to make her stagger, grunting in pain, but not so hard as to be incapacitating. Derla's reaction was swift, street-honed instincts making her lash out at Alveric's eyes with the dagger. He made no move to evade or block the blow and it was his calm, narrow gaze as the blade flashed closer that made her stop. The tip of the dagger hovered next to his left eye, twitching as she struggled to contain her anger.

"You do like your tests, don't you?" she asked, stepping back and returning the blade to its sheath.

"The people you will be set against," Alveric replied, "will test you far more than I ever will. This is not a game and we are not engaged in chasing phantoms. The threats to the Crown and the Realm are real and manifold." He ran his gaze over her once more, nodding in slight satisfaction. "A good fit. More dresses will be delivered to you tomorrow. You will find each has several concealed pockets for weapons or messages. Familiarise yourself with them and report here after the midday bell for more instruction."

...

"Eyes."

"Blue."

"Hair."

"Light Brown."

"Accent."

"North Asraelin with a touch of the Renfaelin border country."

"Rings."

Derla hesitated, her mind racing to recall every detail of the man she had been instructed to observe. *He wore gloves,* she remembered. *Thick gloves, the kind worn by a cavalryman.* So no rings. She began to reply then stopped as her memory dredged up an additional detail, something she hadn't been aware of her eyes capturing at the time.

"A thin band on the small finger of his right hand," she said. "Silver or steel. Worn over his gloves."

Alveric looked at her across the table. Derla had been reporting to this house every seven days for the past six weeks and in that time she hadn't seen another occupant besides Alveric. She would knock on the front door, he would admit her and she would be led to the dining room. The first two weeks had been taken up with his particular brand of instruction, usually involving a brief but bruising round of hand-to-hand combat in which she invariably came off worst. It had quickly become apparent to her that Alveric was a far more dangerous individual than she could ever hope to be. She could fight, she knew that, but she also knew herself to be a brawler at heart. The streets had taught her the value of combining aggression with a certain lack of restraint. Alveric was a craftsman in comparison, countering her every clumsy move with a fluid grace and economy of movement that left her in no doubt as to her own skills. She did improve, however, learning his more obvious tricks and even managing to dodge a blow or two. But it was only when she managed to wrestle herself free of a chokehold that he called a halt to this phase of her instruction.

"Your first assignment," he said, handing her a rolled up piece of parchment. Derla unfurled it to find it held a few lines of script set down in the same neat hand as the note that had been pushed under her door; 'Forty to fifty years old. Bearded. Wears shoes of red leather. The Sea Horse Inn.'

"Follow and report," Alveric told her. "Do not be seen."

So she followed the man with the red leather shoes and reported on his movements. The next week she followed a plump washer woman employed at a nobleman's mansion. This week the young Realm Guard cavalryman with the steel or silver ring. With every new assignment the amount of information she was expected to provide increased and it was a continual marvel to her that her mind managed to accumulate so much detail. But then, the knowledge that Alveric might tell the king that her usefulness had in fact proven illusory was a persistent and effective spur to enhanced efforts.

"His companion at dinner?" Alveric enquired.

"A sailor, garbed as a South Cumbraelin but his accent was poor. I'd guess Meldenean."

"Guess?"

Derla swallowed a sigh. Alveric was irksomely insistent on a formal and uncoloured report, free of what he termed 'ill-informed conjecture'. "It is my belief," Derla said, "that the subject's dinner companion was a Meldenean attempting to disguise his origins with his garb and a false accent."

"Their conversation?"

"Ribald talk of the best whores and taverns to be found in the city. However, I have never heard the names of the whores they mentioned. Also, one of the taverns they spoke of burnt down two years ago."

Alveric's gaze grew ever so slightly more intent, his trim frame inching forward in his seat. "And what did you conclude from this?" he asked. Derla had yet to see this man exhibit any obvious emotion but knew anticipation when she saw it. *He's hoping for a wrong answer,* she realised.

"They were speaking in code." She reached into her bodice, plucking a thin paper scroll from between her breasts and laying it on the table. "A verbatim account of their conversation," she said, managing to keep the self-satisfied tone from her voice. "Which I believe will assist in deciphering said code."

Alveric's eyes flicked to the paper before he reclined, making no move to pick it up. "What do you know of a ship called the *Margentis*?" he asked instead. Derla had become accustomed to such abrupt changes in subject. Every time she completed a task he would offer no thanks, or any indication as to the quality of her work, and simply issue a new set of instructions. She suspected she would never know what use might be made of the information.

"It's a Meldenean freighter," she said. "Works the Redflower trade from Volaria. The captain's never been openly linked to piracy but he's known to bring stolen cargo here once a year to fence on behalf of his fellow captains from the Isles." Derla hesitated, but only for a second. The information she was about to reveal was dangerous, but she no longer harboured any doubts as to which king presented the most potent threat in this city. "A man named Hunsil has a monopoly over all pirate goods landed in Varinshold, although he's better known as One Eye these days. There's always a celebration of sorts when the *Margentis* arrives, the most prominent members of the criminal element gather aboard ship to whore and drink, apart from Hunsil himself who's rarely seen outside his den these days."

"Whoring and drinking," Alveric said. "What about gambling?"

Derla recalled the smug expression on the king's face that morning atop the gatehouse when he asked if she knew how to play Warrior's Bluff. *So, this is what he spared me for,* she surmised.

"Dice and such," she replied. "But there's only one game that matters. The Invitational. The best gamblers in the Realm will be invited to take part in a game of Warrior's Bluff. It's always the richest game of the year, each player is required to have at least five hundred golds in their purse before sitting down. None can leave the table until they lose every coin or win the game."

"You have attended this celebration in the past?"

"Just once, some years ago. It wasn't to my professional tastes. I prefer a more civilised and less inebriated clientele."

"There is a man, a recent arrival in the city who has nevertheless rapidly acquired a reputation for skill at cards. It is believed he will soon receive an invitation to join the game aboard the *Margentis*. You will make his acquaintance, win his trust and accompany him to the ship when the time comes."

Derla frowned. This was the first time she had been instructed to make herself known to a subject. "As you wish. Where do I find him?"

"Most nights at the House of Blue Orchids. I trust you're familiar with the establishment."

"It's a Redflower palace and whorehouse, not one of the nice ones. I'll need ten silvers to pay off the owner before she'll let me in. A matter of courtesy, you see."

"Keep a tabulated list of any expenses incurred. It will be paid in full at the conclusion of your task."

"My task being to simply keep this card sharp company?"

"His presence in this city is the result of a royal command, although he is officially a favoured guest of the king and may enjoy all the freedoms afforded any other Realm subject. It is important that this fiction continue. Your task is to ensure that his recreational pursuits don't see him floating in the harbour with his throat slit."

Alveric leaned forward once more, meeting her gaze and speaking in a soft, flat tone that left an unwelcome chill in Derla's breast. "Rest assured," the Lord of Foxes told her, "that whatever favour you enjoy with the king will disappear should any harm come to this man. Your continued survival is now entirely dependent on his."

Derla nodded, managing to contain the growing list of questions crowding her head, except one. "Might I know his name?"

"His name is Sentes Mustor, Heir to the Fief-Lordship of Cumbrael. He'll be easy to find by virtue of his accent and the fact that he's invariably by far the drunkest soul at any gathering."

CHAPTER 8

"Cowards I call you!" Sentes Mustor rose to strike a pose rich in theatrical disdain as the last of his opponents slunk away from the card table. An untidy pile of coins lay beside the Cumbraelin's overturned cards which, Derla was surprised to see, displayed a poor hand; the Blind Blacksmith being the most high-valued card and the five others all drawn from the lesser suits. In all, the hand's value amounted to less than half that of Mustor's final adversary, and yet this overly vocal drunk had managed to bluff his way to victory. The entire game had lasted barely two hours, something of a record in Derla's experience.

"Is there no one in this den of vice with the stomach to face me?" the Cumbraelin demanded, sweeping his wine cup from the table, raising it high and spilling a portion of the contents in the process. Beyond the glow of the lantern suspended above the table the shadows stirred with a few grumbles and muttered insults, but none of the Blue Orchid's patrons rose to the taunt. Instead, the clientele preferred to return their attentions to their paid companions or overpriced drinks.

Sentes Mustor maintained his pose for a few seconds, his expression of resolute challenge slowly subsiding into resigned chagrin. "Clearly, I've milked this particular teat dry," he sighed, sinking back into his seat. He took several long gulps from his wine cup before setting it down and embarking upon a clumsy attempt to assemble his winnings into some semblance of order, muttering, "My brother always said true skill was more a burden than a blessing."

"'The measure of a man lies in how he profits from his labour.'" Mustor looked up as Derla stepped into the light, his brows raised in surprise and, she was gratified to see, no small measure of carnal interest. "'The humble woodcutter who spends his earnings on food for the needy,'" Derla went on, "'is to be valued more than the man who carves the finest statue and fritters his wealth on vice.'"

"What an unexpected delight," Mustor said, getting unsteadily to his feet, "to meet an Asraelin lady educated in the Ten Books." He bowed, one arm across his midriff and the other extended to the side in what she assumed was the Cumbraelin courtly fashion. "Lord Sentes Mustor, my lady. At your service."

She responded with a curtsy. "A pleasure, my lord. So," she moved to his side, leaning close to collect the cards, lingering a second to allow him to catch the scent of her perfume before circling the table to retrieve the others. "Shall we play?"

"You are fond of cards then, my lady?"

"I play fairly well, so I'm told." Derla took the seat two chairs away from his, a decently enticing remove that allowed the lamplight to play over her cleavage to good effect. She met his gaze and gave a small smile as she shuffled the cards, her hands working the deck with unconscious precision.

"Fairly well won't do, I'm afraid," Mustor advised with a regretful wince. "Not against me. And I shouldn't wish to alienate so charming a companion. Why don't we have a drink instead?" He waved his wine cup and a serving girl duly arrived bearing a fresh bottle and another cup for Derla.

"Are you new to this house, perhaps?" Mustor asked Derla as the girl poured the wine. "I feel certain I would have recalled seeing you here before."

"I am not employed in this establishment," Derla replied, fanning the cards on the baize. "I merely came to play and will consider myself sorely aggrieved should you deny me, my lord."

Mustor's eyes narrowed a little as he raised his cup to his nose, though the smile lingered on his lips. "A pale red from the Mentari vineyards," he said, sniffing. "One of the south facing slopes. Three years old. It rained more than usual that summer." He took a sip and pursed his lips, shrugging. "Passable, but Lord Mentari should really stick to the whites. Too much sand in his soil for a decent red. I'll have to write him an advisory letter one of these days."

He set the cup down and turned to the serving girl. "I think my new adversary would appreciate something more full-bodied, my dear. Bring us the Umblin Valley Red, if you please. Now then." He turned back to Derla, clasping his hands together. "What shall we say for the opening bet? Does two silvers seem fair?"

Derla met his gaze again, fixing it with a half-smile. "I regret that I neglected to bring any coin tonight, my lord."

An extra line or two appeared in Mustor's already creased brow as he gave a small huff of annoyance. "Charming as you are, I do not play for mere amusement. A game with nothing at risk is a dull affair indeed."

"Oh," Derla said, sweeping the cards and dealing out two hands with practised ease, "I'm sure we can think of something worth playing for."

...

"Sorry," Mustor groaned, breath hot and laboured against her neck as he subsided atop her. "Too much wine. If only the Umblin vintages weren't so confoundedly tempting."

"I think you more than demonstrated your fortitude, my lord," Derla said as he rolled off her. His frame was a curious mix of bony and flabby, a substantial paunch married to spindly arms and legs, and yet he had proven more accomplished a bedmate than most of her clients, if somewhat lacking in stamina.

"How kind you are," he said in a sleepy murmur. "I hope it's not extra."

"You won the bet," she reminded him, shifting to lay her head on his chest. "Everything's on the house tonight."

He played a hand through her hair, fingers tracing gently through the thick auburn curls. "You shared these rooms with someone until recently," he said. "How long since they left?"

Derla stiffened, all artifice suddenly draining from her as she withdrew from him and turned away. She sat on the edge of the bed, frozen and staring into the dark until she felt his hand on her back. "I apologise," he said. "Clearly I have overstepped."

"You see a great deal, my lord," she said.

"Life as a drunk has a few advantages. Being continually underestimated is one of them." He pressed a kiss to her shoulder before climbing free of the bed and reaching for his clothes. "I should go. The palace guards get a mite prissy with me if I don't stumble back before daybreak."

"Palace?" she asked. Before now she had assumed he had a house of his own somewhere in the city.

"Oh yes," he replied, pulling his shirt on. "I am a guest of his Highness King Janus Al Nieren. I even have a courtly title, Minister of Cumbraelin Affairs. Fortunately it doesn't involve a great deal of work beyond signing the occasional document I'm not even required to read."

He managed to don his trews after a protracted struggle then perched on the bed, attempting to pull on one of his shoes without much success. "Allow me," Derla said, kneeling to manoeuvre the shoe in place before tying up the laces.

Mustor watched her, unshaven features suddenly sagging into a morose grimace. "In truth, I'm no more a guest than a dog is a guest in his master's kennel."

Derla reached for the other shoe. "Then why stay?"

His face gave a brief twitch of amusement. "Your question implies a choice in the matter, my dear. And I assure you, I have none. What hostage would choose to stay in his prison? Although," Mustor smiled as he reached out to caress her hair once more, "I find I grow increasingly fond of the distractions to be found in this particular prison."

"Hostage?" Derla finished tying the shoe and rose to retrieve his cloak.

"Oh yes." Mustor rose to a reasonably steady stance and turned so she could fasten the cloak about his shoulders. "The king imagines having me in his clutches is surety against any mischief my father might get up to. A surprising misjudgement for a man of such renowned insight." He turned, leaning close to kiss her, more fulsomely this time, then shifted to whisper in her ear. "Between us, he chose the wrong son." He gave a conspiratorial wink then started towards the door.

"You're always welcome here, my lord," Derla said. "Pleasing distractions are my business, after all."

He paused and turned back, eyebrow raised at a knowing angle. "And I can assume the next appointment won't be free?"

"It depends."

She watched him ponder for a second, hand hesitant on the door latch. "On what, might I enquire?"

"Cards," she said. "You play better than anyone I know, and I know many a card player."

"You wish me to teach you?"

"If you're so minded. Although, I find I learn best through simple observation."

She saw his brow furrow once more, eyes narrowing in calculation. She could see the depth of his intelligence in that frown, it was one she had often seen on her father's face. *Drunk or not, he's far from stupid.* "The *Margentis*," Mustor said finally, grinning a little. "Heard about my invitation, did you? Keen to get yourself aboard? For what, may I ask? I find it hard to believe you're short of custom."

"I am not. But I do have a keen eye for fresh opportunities. Besides the Invitational there are numerous other games played aboard the *Margentis*, games frequented by inebriated outlaws likely to underestimate a whore, as many underestimate a drunk."

Mustor thought for a moment and shrugged. "Oh, why not? It'll be amusing if nothing else. Though, I'm told they're a rowdy lot, the kind that might not take well to having their purses emptied by a woman, or anyone else for that matter."

"Your concern is touching." She moved to him, planted a kiss on his cheek and opened the door to usher him out. "But I have a sense my reputation will protect me."

"Reputation?" he asked, lingering at the top of the stairs. "For what?"

"Merely a spot of torture along the way, my lord. Best not keep the palace guards waiting."

CHAPTER 9

The *Margentis* lay at anchor a good distance beyond the outer mole of Varinshold harbour, presumably as surety against the night's festivities attracting any unwanted attention from the City Guard. She was one of the largest ships Derla had seen, broad in the beam with three tall masts and a wide, curving hull. The freighter reminded her of a toad squatting atop a lily pad in the way she rose from the surrounding cluster of boats. The dozens of small craft that had conveyed a host of senior Varinshold criminality from the docks were all tethered together, forming an undulating walkway across which Derla and her lordly companion were obliged to navigate in order to reach the ship.

"I've always regarded sea travel as an unnatural pursuit," Mustor griped as he made a clumsy leap from one bobbing deck to another. "If the World Father wanted us to traverse the oceans he would surely have given us fins."

"Not much farther now, my lord," Derla said, glancing up at the ship's hull. The portholes were all open and brightly lit from within, casting forth a discordant chorus of raucous merriment. "It appears we've arrived somewhat late to this gathering."

"A certain lack of punctuality is expected of the noble class, dearest Derla. It's one of the tricks we use to maintain the illusion of innate superiority. My father kept my mother and the entirety of Cumbraelin nobility waiting for several hours on his wedding day. Although, rumour has it the delay could be blamed on a dalliance with a maid in the mansion house cellar, not to mention the fact that he detested the very sight of his bride, of course."

Derla allowed a reluctant smile to play over his lips. She had been in his company most nights over the preceding two weeks, during which time Mustor's facility for indiscretion had been one of his more endearing traits. She found herself harbouring a slight resentment at his ability to make her like him; it chafed on her professional instincts, both as a spy and a whore. *He's a client and a subject of the King's scrutiny,* she reminded herself, not for the first time. *Nothing more.*

After several minutes of precarious navigation they came to a steep gangway ascending from the deck of a large boat lashed to the ship's hull. Mustor was not the most physically able of men and spent a long moment gasping for breath after they stepped on to the upper deck.

"Lord Sentes Mustor and companion," Derla introduced them to a pair of scowling Meldenean guards as Mustor leaned heavily on the rail, too winded to speak. "We're expected."

"He is," one of the Meldeneans replied, a hand resting on the hilt of his sabre as he jerked his chin at Mustor. "You aren't."

"Mistress Derla..." Mustor began, wheezing as he straightened to address the guard in lofty tones, "is here at my invitation. If her presence is unacceptable we shall adjourn forthwith." He turned back to the gangplank, gesturing for Derla to follow.

"Alright," the Meldenean growled. "Your whore can stay." He turned and nodded at the stairwell leading to the hold. A heavy glow emanated from the hatch along with the sound of many voices raised in inebriated jocularity. "Better get y'self seated, m'lord," the Meldenean said, offering Mustor a humourless grin.

"The Invitational was s'posed to start and hour ago and your opponents aren't the most patient of folk."

The hold was thick with noise and the mingled scent of five-leaf and spilled ale. Men grouped together to play dice or cards whilst others nuzzled the giggling, barely dressed women in their laps or dragged them into a secluded alcove for more fulsome entertainment. Derla recognised various outlaw luminaries amongst the throng, along with their more senior lieutenants. She drew a few nods of recognition as she and Mustor made their way aft, though most of the assembly were too drunk or lost in the varied delights on offer to afford her much attention. However, there was one exception, picked out of the crowd thanks to her recently honed observational skills. He was a slender fellow with long hair, leaning against a barrel and regarding her with a steady gaze as he puffed from a long-stemmed pipe. A pipe, Derla saw, that had no smoke rising from the bowl. She knew him only as the Stitcher, due to his rumoured habit of stitching closed the wounds of those he tortured so they wouldn't bleed to death too quickly. *One Eye's man,* she recalled, allowing her gaze to slip over the slender man's face without obvious sign of recognition. *Not drunk and puffing an empty pipe.*

Her gaze found two more of One Eye's crew in the crowd as she continued to follow Mustor forward, a stocky man known for his skills with the cudgel and a woman of far more worrying abilities. She was small and slight with a deceptively sweet countenance. Derla had never learned her true name but she had earned plenty of others in recent years, the most notorious of which was Lady Venom. She possessed a similar talent to Little Dot. But, whereas the diminutive healer's skills were directed towards preserving life, Lady Venom's were skewed very much to the opposite.

Like the Stitcher, neither the cudgel expert or Lady Venom showed any signs of intoxication, keeping to the shadows and taking no part in games or carnality. *He must have sent them to oversee the festivities,* she decided, although it wasn't their typical role. Keeping watch on gatherings like this was a task usually reserved for low-status thugs like Ratter and Draker, but, as she had expected, those two had vanished from the city soon after Frentis's as yet unexplained disappearance. *Perhaps he's short-handed.* The notion afforded only a small crumb of comfort and she found she had to resist the impulse to place a reassuring hand on the knife concealed at the small of her back.

After much jostling they came to the wide oval table where the Invitational would take place. A burly Meldenean sat at the table with three other men. He was marked out as the captain of the *Margentis* by the red scarf on his head, which added a tinge of fury to his countenance as he growled "Where the fuck've you been?" at Mustor.

"'Where the fuck've you been, *my lord?*' if you don't mind," Mustor replied in a brisk but affable tone as he took a seat to the captain's left. "I do prefer a civil tone when at table."

This drew a laugh from two of the others and another growl from the captain. "No lords on this ship or at this table," he said. "Here there's just the cards and the luck the gods allow us."

"Luck," Mustor repeated, raising an eyebrow. "What a quaint notion of this game you have, good sir." He smiled at the captain's deepening glower, spreading his hands. "Shall we be about it?"

The captain gave another growl, wordless this time, then turned to beckon a short, neatly attired man from the shadows. "Wentel," the Meldenean said and the short man gave a respectful nod to the players. "Our dealer for tonight. He's renowned in Varinshold and beyond as an honest pair of hands. Any who find him unacceptable, speak now and state your reasons."

"I've had the pleasure of sitting at Master Wentel's table before," Mustor said. "And I find him more than acceptable."

The man seated on Mustor's left was of dark complexion and clad in silks that marked him out as an Alpiran from the western provinces of the empire. He bared a wall of gold-inlaid teeth in a smile and inclined his head at Wentel, speaking in softly accented Realm Tongue, "I too know this man as both skilled and honest. Acceptable."

The man on the Alpiran's left was large, unshaven and seemed to have been wearing the same clothes for at least a week, judging by the multiple wine and food stains besmirching the fabric, and his somewhat ripe aroma. He spared Wentel a brief glance, large shoulders moving a shrug as he muttered, "Acceptable," in an gruff Nilsaelin accent.

Derla couldn't see the face of the final player who sat directly opposite Mustor. He reclined in his chair, features lost in the shadow beyond the reach of the lantern hanging from the beams above. Derla noted that he was of athletic build with a pair of broad, strong hands resting on the table. She saw two points of light glimmer in the shadow that masked the man's face and realised he had blinked, but the two glimmers didn't match. One was small and bright whilst the other was duller, as if the lamplight caught something other than an eye. She managed to conceal a start as the familiar voice came from the shadows, a voice she had heard only a few times, but had hoped to never hear again.

"Unacceptable," said Hunsil, king of the Varinshold criminal class, now better known as One Eye. He lifted one of his broad hands and pointed a finger across the table, a finger aimed straight at Derla. "I want her."

CHAPTER 10

"The Cumbraelin's doxy?" the captain scoffed as One Eye's finger continued to point at Derla. "I think not."

Silence reigned at the table for a full minute during which the scorn slowly faded from the captain's brow. The moment ended when Master Wentel, now noticeably more pale of face, turned about and walked swiftly into the shadows.

"Are there, ahem, any objections?" the captain enquired, voice suddenly hoarse and sweat staining his headscarf.

None of the other players said a word, although Mustor turned to afford Derla a puzzled frown. She laid a hand on his shoulder, leaning close to nuzzle his ear. "Don't drink anything," she whispered, squeezing his shoulder hard to emphasise the point before moving to take the dealer's chair to the right of the captain. "Standard rules?" she asked, reaching for the deck.

"Asraelin No-blind," the captain said. "Minimum bet one gold per hand, fold or not."

Derla fanned the deck before giving it a rapid but thorough shuffle. The cards were all brand new, the ink fresh and the colours vibrant. She could see no obvious marks amid the spiral patterns on the back of each card, nor any subtle changes in dimensions which might afford a dishonest player an advantage.

"As per the rules of Asraelin No-blind," she said, cards flying across the table as she dealt, six cards to each player, "all folded hands and exchanged cards to be shown. Coins in the pot if you please, good sirs."

She watched each player toss a single gold coin into the centre of the table before checking their hand. Their experience was evident in the care with which they kept any expression from their faces, apart from the captain who bit down a curse and flipped his cards over with a distinct lack of grace. *Owes his invitation to his captaincy of this vessel,* Derla decided, responding to the man's suspicious glare with a placid smile before turning her attention to the other players. Mustor exchanged two cards from his hand, the Candle and the Poisoned Cup, both low value cards typically discarded at this stage of the game. The gold-toothed Alpiran exchanged three similarly poor cards and the ill-smelling Nilsaelin one.

Derla watched One Eye's finger tap out a slow drumbeat. After a moment he shifted in his seat, leaning forward so that the lamplight revealed his face. He had been handsome before, possessed of well drawn features Derla had felt were wasted on a man of his profession. Now any pleasing aspect was completely overshadowed by the scar that bisected his left eyelid and the smooth orb of carved jet that filled the socket. He angled his head at her, the edges of his mouth curling in something that approximated a sympathetic smile.

"I heard about your recent troubles," he said, voice soft with sincerity. "A bad business to be sure. What was her name?"

"Livera," Derla replied.

"Yes, Livera. Alpiran, as I recall. Very comely to the eye, was she not?" He reclined a little, the upper half of his face lost to shadow once more, speaking on without waiting for a response, "Beauty can be dangerous. Still, I'm given to understand the matter was swiftly resolved, by your own dainty hand no less."

"Sadly, the miscreant was taken from me. By a madwoman, so I'm told."

One Eye's lips parted to release a fractional laugh. "Of course he was." He tapped the table with his thumb, indicating he didn't wish to exchange any cards.

"Lord Mustor," Derla turned to her left, "your bet, if you please."

"Two golds." Mustor tossed the coins into the pot. Derla noted how his puzzlement had transformed into one of his contemplative frowns, presumably as he pondered One Eye's words. *Seeing me clearly for the first time,* she thought. *I wonder if he likes the view so much now.*

The Alpiran folded, turning his cards over with a careful lack of expression, followed immediately by the Nilsaelin, leaving Mustor and One Eye to contest the pot.

"Stick." One Eye placed both hands flat on the table, leaning forward to cast a questioning glance at Mustor. The Cumbraelin's eyes continued to linger on Derla for a moment before he switched his gaze to his opponent. He could raise the bet and force One Eye to either match it or fold. Either option might be taken as an insult by this singular king. It occurred to Derla for the first time that Mustor might not fully understand who One Eye was. It seemed impossible that his forays into the seedier corners of Varinshold had left him ignorant of the name, but did he truly understand the danger this man posed?

Mustor lowered his gaze to the revealed cards, brows bunching. Derla knew this to be for show; drunk or sober, this man could calculate even the most complex odds in a matter of seconds. "Call me a poor sport, good sir," he said, offering One Eye an apologetic smile as he added another two golds to the pot. "But I believe a raise is in order."

One Eye retreated fully into shadow once more, turning his cards over to reveal a hand with a collective value of less than twelve points. "Fold," he said. "You intimated to the good captain that luck was not a factor here. However, there was an equal chance that I held three of the Noble Suit, was there not?"

"Actually, no." Mustor flipped his cards; the Queen of Roses, the Prince of Snakes and the Lord of Blades plus three low value cards from the minor suits.

A moment's silence as the two mismatched glimmers blinked in the gloom. "How pleased I am to find your reputation isn't exaggerated, my lord," One Eye said, raising a hand and clicking his fingers. "Wine, I think."

A trio of serving women appeared out of the shadows bearing bottles and goblets. From the swiftness of their arrival it was clear they had been awaiting this summons. "A Cumbraelin vintage, naturally," One Eye said as the women set a goblet down beside each player. "A subject on which I hear you're something of an expert, Lord Mustor."

"I've always felt a man should embrace his passions wholeheartedly," Mustor said, nodding his thanks at the woman filling his goblet. When she set the bottle down and disappeared back into the gloom he kept his hands clasped together, making no move to drink it. The other players were not so restrained, the Alpiran taking a small but appreciative sip whilst the Nilsaelin and the captain indulged in a generous gulp or two. *Well,* thought Derla as she strove to keep the dismay from her face, *at least the game will be shorter than expected.*

"A fine and commendable attitude," One Eye told Mustor, lifting his own goblet. "And what is your wholehearted opinion of this offering, might I ask?"

Derla's gaze locked with Mustor's and she gave a near imperceptible shake of her head. He forced a smile and began to reply, then stopped as he saw something beyond Derla's shoulder. She didn't need to turn to see what it was, for she saw it beyond his shoulder, a slender blade gleaming in the shadows, one of several. Beside her the Meldenean captain gave a short cough.

"A moment, if you will," Mustor said, lifting the goblet and raising it to his nose. "Levlin Vale," he said after a prolonged sniff during which both the Alpiran and the Nilsaelin had also begun to cough. "From south-western Cumbrael. A lovely stretch of country, I should say." He sniffed again then winced as the captain coughed once more, louder this time. The Meldenean put his hand to his mouth and Derla saw a pinkish froth on his fingertips.

"This is a ten year old vintage," Mustor went on, "the grapes picked when their ripeness was peaking. A difficult thing to judge, so I'd say this comes from Lord Ester's holdings. Now, there's a man who knows his trade."

"All correct so far," One Eye conceded, sniffing his own goblet. "And the taste, my lord? Tell me, what secrets can you divine from the taste?"

The captain, who had been staring at his pink-stained fingers, abruptly convulsed, doubling over with such force his forehead collided with the table.

"Excuse me a moment," One Eye told Mustor, turning to the

now violently retching Meldenean. "By the way, Captain Alrath, I believe it's time we ended our association. Your decision to raise prices yet again was truly unfortunate. For you and your crew, not to mention your guests."

The captain reared back, face crimson and eyes bulging as blood flowed thick from his shuddering lips. Beside Mustor the Alpiran surged to his feet, blood-stained gold teeth bared in a grimace as he drew a thin-bladed knife from the folds of his silks. Something flickered in the darkness behind him and he arched his back, the knife dropping from spasming fingers as an inch of steel erupted from his throat. The odorous Nilsaelin slumped forward, twitching as a crimson torrent streamed from his nose and mouth.

"Your pardon, sir," Mustor said, setting his goblet down with a poise Derla would have thought beyond him. "But I suspect the taste may be somewhat bitter."

CHAPTER 11

One Eye laughed, a strangely melodious sound, rich in genuine humour. "Oh well," he said, laughter fading as he rose to his feet. "Trust a drunkard to spoil my fun."

Captain Alrath roared, his reddened features devoid of all reason as he launched himself at One Eye, hands latching onto his throat. Derla rolled free of her seat as the table went over, scattering coins and cards. She sank to all fours, scurrying away, glancing back just long enough to see the captain bear One Eye to the deck, furious gibberish spouting from his mouth along with a bloody torrent as he tried to throttle his murderer. A flurry of blades flashed out of the gloom and the captain stiffened, blood pouring from the numerous wounds in his back, but still he held on, repeatedly slamming One Eye's head to the boards. Derla tore her gaze away and crawled on.

From the sound of it the entire ship was in uproar, filled with a nightmarish cacophony of men and women screaming in pain or terror, clashing blades and splintered furniture all punctuated by the occasional snap and thud of a loosed crossbow bolt. It was dreadfully clear to her that One Eye intended no witnesses to escape the night's events.

She covered only a few yards before a hand reached down to snare the laces on the rear of her bodice, holding her in place. "Kwo Sha sends his regards," a male voice informed her, the tone heavy with anticipation.

Derla wasted no time by looking up at her assailant, jerking her head aside as the knife came down, leaving a small cut on her ear before sinking into the deck boards. She twisted her neck and clamped her teeth on the hand holding the knife, biting deep into the flesh behind the thumb. Blood flooded her mouth as the assailant voiced a high-pitched curse. She felt the grip loosen on her bodice and opened her mouth, releasing the hand and drawing her own knife from the small of her back. She lashed out at the attacker's legs but he was quick, dancing clear so that the blade caught only an inch of boot leather.

Derla rose to a crouch, raising her gaze to find the Stitcher staring down at her, clutching his maimed hand to his chest, thin face white with pain and fury. "Was just going to bleed you," he hissed. "Now I think I'll fuck you to de-"

The bottle exploded against the side of the Stitcher's head in a dark blossom of wine and shattered glass. Despite appearances, Mustor had a strong arm and the outlaw dropped like a stone, lying senseless and still on the deck save for the occasional twitch. But he wasn't still enough for Derla's liking.

"My thanks, my lord," she said, sinking her knife into the base of the Stitcher's skull, drawing it clear and wiping the blade on his jerkin. "I think it's time we left, don't you? You'd best keep hold of that," she added, nodding to the jagged neck of the bottle still clutched in Mustor's hand.

She led him towards the stern of the ship, skipping over the dead and dying and dodging around the frenzied knots of combat. In the gloom it was hard to make out the various factions; Meldeneans and unaffiliated outlaws fought each other in their drunken confusion whilst One Eye's sober minions killed indiscriminately. Derla saw a man drag a bare-chested whore from her hiding place and forced herself to turn away when he pulled the woman's head back by the hair, laying his dirk against her exposed neck. Mustor, it transpired, had more chivalrous instincts. He lunged forward, jabbing his broken bottle into the man's eyes and sending him screaming to his knees. The whore gaped up at her saviour for a few seconds then scrambled to her feet and fled into the shadows, yelping like a startled dog.

"Come on!" Derla grabbed Mustor's hand and dragged him away. "No more heroics, if you don't mind. I need to get you out of here unharmed."

"On whose orders?" he asked. "You are here at someone's instruction, I assume."

"A question you are more than capable of answering for yourself, I'm sure."

Derla saw a figure loom up before them, dim light catching a short vertical gleam from the constricted arms of a steel crossbow. She shoved Mustor against the bulkhead, displaced air caressing her cheek as the crossbow bolt buried itself in a beam two inches away. She whirled and charged the crossbow man. He had another bolt between his teeth and the stock braced against his midriff as he drew back the string. His eyes widened at the speed of her attack and he dropped the crossbow, reaching for the hatchet in his belt just as Derla's knife slashed across his throat. She left him drowning in his own blood and beckoned urgently to Mustor.

"Here," she said, moving to an open porthole. Leaning out to survey the surrounding waters she was relieved to find the encroaching cluster of boats undisturbed. "It's a fair drop, but better than the alternative."

Mustor glanced at the porthole, staying still as he turned to her with a dark, distrustful gaze. "Who was Livera?" he demanded. "Is she the reason you latched yourself onto me?"

"Do you want to fucking die here, you stupid drunken bastard?"

He retreated a step at her shouting fury, blinking at the spittle landing on his face. "No," he said, wiping a finger across an eyelid. "I suppose I don't."

"Good." She stepped back, nodding at the porthole. "After you, my lord."

He grimaced and clambered into the opening where he hesitated. "That is quite the fall..."

Derla's foot slammed into Mustor's posterior with sufficient force to send him on his way. She quickly clambered through the opening, launching herself clear with a hard shove of her legs. She had the ill luck to descend at the join between two boats, scraping her ankle on the timbers before plummeting into the sea. She sank quickly as the water soaked her dress. Light as it was the additional weight was still enough to drag her down. Derla fought the water's pull, arms and legs flailing as she struggled to the surface, managing to get an arm clear before the water reasserted its grip. A hand caught hers just before it slipped back, gripping tight and pulling hard.

Derla's head came free of the water and she found herself face-to-face with Mustor. "I trust they're paying you well for all this," he said, reaching down to grip her beneath the shoulders and haul her into the boat.

Derla allowed herself only a moment for the requisite gasping and retching before struggling to her feet. "There," she said, pointing to the boat they had left at the edge of the cluster a dozen yards away. They covered the intervening distance in a series of stumbling, frantic leaps, Derla taking hold of the oars whilst Mustor cast off the lines. She pulled hard, Mustor angling the tiller to aim the prow at the twinkling lamplight of the Varinshold quayside. They managed only a few yards before a hail of crossbow bolts descended into the surrounding water like steel rain.

"It's a little rude to leave without at least thanking your host, don't you think?" a voice called from the ship.

Derla lowered the oars, her gaze quickly finding One Eye standing on the rail of the *Margentis's* upper deck. A dozen men were arrayed on either side of him, all armed with crossbows. One Eye held something in his hand, something large and round that leaked dark fluid over the flanks of the *Margentis* as he swung it back and forth. "Captain Alrath is mightily offended, I must say." He raised the severed head level with his own, leaning close as if listening to a conspiratorial whisper. "Really?" he asked, turning back to Derla and Mustor with brows raised in regretful surprise. "Seems a harsh punishment to me, but you are the captain."

He tossed Alrath's head away, raising a dull thud as it landed somewhere amongst the encroaching boats. One Eye reached for a rope and launched himself from the rail, swinging out wide before letting go. He performed a perfect somersault then landed on a boat at the edge of the cluster, accepting their non-existent applause with a modest bow. "Thank you. I have learned a great deal of new tricks recently, and find I can't resist showing off."

He straightened, all humour slipping from his blood-spattered face as he regarded them, features twitching a little. *He didn't just lose an eye,* Derla realised. *He also lost his mind.*

"If you kill this man," she said, voice as steady as she could make it, pointing at Mustor, "King Janus will tear the quarter apart to find you. His torturers will ensure your death lasts for days."

One Eye smiled, though she noticed his twitch become momentarily more agitated. "At this moment there is only one king that need concern you," he said in a strange voice that jarred on the ear. It sounded to her like a mix of accents all spoken at once. Surely another symptom of his madness. "Kwo Sha has paid me well for your death," One Eye continued. "I was going to fulfil the contract later in the month, but fortunately you saw fit to make yourself so readily available on the very night I had arranged my coronation. As for him." One Eye turned to Mustor, his face twitching with fresh energy. "He has to die…" One Eye's voice trailed off and the twitch abruptly faded. When he spoke again the curious mix of accents was gone. "Not sure why exactly… But he does." He turned and began to raise a hand to the crossbowmen on the ship.

"Frentis," Derla said.

One Eye froze, then slowly lowered his hand. When he turned back to her his entire face seemed to be twitching, the flesh bunching and lips curling almost as if it was trying to turn itself into something else. "Frentis," he said, in his usual voice, slurred somewhat by the constant curl of his lips.

"I know where he went," Derla said. She gripped the oars, raising the handles so the blades dipped into the water.

"That buys *your* life," One Eye said, spittle now leaking from his lips. "Not his," he added, the mangled tones returning as he jerked his head at Mustor. His body had begun to shudder now. It looked to Derla as if he were trying to contain something, perhaps clamp down on his madness long enough to learn what she knew.

"Both of us," Derla said, giving a slow pull on the oars, drawing the boat away from the ship. "Or you may as well tell your men to loose those bolts, because if this man dies tonight I'll cut my own throat before I'll tell you a thing." Another pull on the oars, One Eye's shuddering form receding further.

"Self-sacrifice is not in a whore's nature," he said in his mangled voice.

"I already died," Derla called back. She pulled the oars again, harder this time.

"Where?" One Eye demanded, his normal tones now fully reasserted. Also, the shudder had disappeared from his body. "Tell me where. You know you can't hide in this city. Not from me."

Derla gave a full-strength pull on the oars, the boat slipping smoothly through the placid harbour waters. They weren't quite clear of the reach of the crossbows yet, but few archers could be sure of hitting the mark at such range.

"The Sixth Order!" she called back, her voice breaking and an unexpected wetness blurring her vision. She dragged air into her lungs and shouted it out, "He's with the Sixth Order! Good luck getting to him there, you mad fucker!"

She started rowing again, with furious energy now, pulling hard until the *Margentis* had shrunk back to a toad-like lump and One Eye was just a speck. She kept at it, chest, arms and legs burning from the effort, breath coming in ragged sobs.

"I think you can stop now," Mustor said, reaching out to grip her shoulders. "We're clear."

Derla dragged the oars through the rowlocks, letting them fall from her hands. She sagged, borne down by exhaustion and a sick, fiery ball burning in her stomach. Guilt was an unfamiliar emotion.

"You asked who Livera was," she said in a murmur after the sobs had finally ended. "She was the woman I loved. I suspect the only soul in this world I'll ever love. She died, and so did I. The king took me into his service and… and I thought I might live again, carry the gift of her life with me like the catechisms say. But now… Now I have betrayed her."

"You saved my life." Mustor's hand cupped her chin, raising her face. He smiled, thumbing away her tears. "Albeit at the king's order. But that does not dim my gratitude. Nor will it ever, Derla. Whatever service you require of me, I'll give it, to the end of my days. I swear it by the Ten Books and the Father's love."

Derla sniffed, nodding and gently pushing his hand away. "We both appear to have become uncharacteristically devotional tonight, my lord," she said, reaching for the oars and angling the boat towards an open stretch of quay. The dockside was loud with the familiar chorus of drink, argument and lust that wouldn't fade until the smallest hours of the morning. She felt it to be as good a welcome as she deserved.

"Do you know," Mustor said, working his lips together, a frown of realisation creasing his forehead. "I believe it's been more than a full day since I had a drink."

"An impressive achievement."

"Yes, but one never to be repeated if I have any say in the matter. I happen to know a wine seller with an establishment close to the docks. He's been promising me something special for some time now. You're welcome to join me."

"Sadly I must decline, my lord. I have a report to make." She turned her gaze to the dim bulk of the *Margentis*, hearing the faint overlapping splashes of many bodies being consigned to the water. *With one more to come.* "And then," she added in a whisper, "there's a spice merchant with whom I am keen to renew my acquaintance."

"Another time then."

Derla and Mustor shared a faint smile as they sat in the boat. She wasn't sure if this was the ending or the beginning of something. It seemed entirely possible that Alveric might one day hand her a note ordering this man's death. *More likely, he'll hand someone else a note ordering mine.* The notion stirred a flutter of fear in her breast, a fear she found herself holding to with sudden fierceness. She fed it with the horrors she had witnessed, this night and before, the sight of Livera's bleached, vacant face and the empty eyes of the man who had killed her. The fear blossomed, burning with a heat that banished her guilt and brought a laugh to her lips.

So I didn't die after all, she thought. *You have to be alive to know fear.*

Author's Note

Sollis returns! In fact, for me he returned in "Many Are the Dead" since I wrote *The Lord Collector* three years before. However, *The Lord Collector* is placed last in this collection because, along with *The Lady of Crows*, it falls within the timeline of *Blood Song*. For those who like to nit-pick such things, Sollis's sojourn to the south-Asraelin coast takes place about four years subsequent to the narrative described in *The Lady of Crows* and shortly after Vaelin's Test of the Sword in *Blood Song*, the event which marks the beginning of a prolonged estrangement. This novella also gave me the chance to explore a character who had a bit-part in *Tower Lord* and a slightly expanded role in *Queen of Fire*, namely Jehrid Al Bera, Tower Lord of the Southern Shore. Although never a major character, I had peppered his story with a few details that made him a fellow with an interesting backstory, one I didn't know at the time but wanted to find out later. The main source of inspiration for the setting derives from 16-17th century Britain when excise duties were high and smuggling rife. This was particularly true on the southern coast where customs officials regularly fought deadly skirmishes with ruthless, heavily armed gangs who were not above luring ships onto the rocks to harvest their cargo. It's a period most famously evoked in Daphne du Maurier's *Jamaica Inn* and the poem "A Smuggler's Song" by Rudyard Kipling:

Five and twenty ponies,
Trotting through the dark -
Brandy for the Parson, 'Baccy for the Clerk.
Them that asks no questions isn't told a lie -
Watch the wall my darling while the Gentlemen go by!

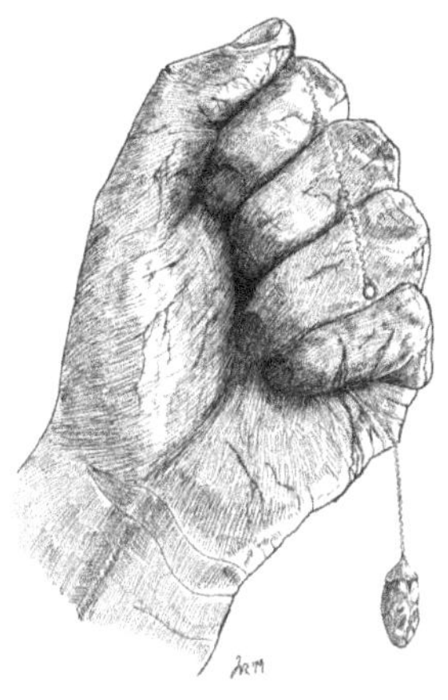

THE LORD COLLECTOR

– a Raven's Shadow Novella –

"Where are they, Varesh?"

Varesh Baldir was a tall man, somewhere past his fortieth year, thickset with a copious unkempt beard that partly concealed the weathered features common to those who eked a a living from the shore. His heavy brows furrowed as he stared at Jehrid, eyes lit mostly with hate and fury, but also betraying a momentary flicker of fear.

"We counted near two score corpses on the beach after you lured that freighter to its death," Jehrid continued, sensing a fractional advantage. "I know the code as well as you. Blood pays for blood."

Varesh took a deep breath, closing his eyes and turning his face out towards the sea, hate and fear fading as his brow softened under the salted wind. After a moment he opened his eyes and turned back to Jehrid, mouth set in a hard, unyielding line, and his tattooed fists bunched, jangling the manacles on his meaty wrists.

Silence is the only law, Jehrid thought. First rule of the smuggler's code, drilled into him over many an unhappy year. *This is a waste of time.*

He sighed and moved closer to Nawen's Maw, an unnaturally regular bore-hole through the rocky overhang on which they stood. Varesh's chain traced from his manacles to an iron brace set into the top of a stone resembling an upended pear, a wide rounded top narrowing to a flat base. It had been carved from the pale red sandstone that proliferated on the southern Asraelin shore and made the buildings here so distinctive. One of Jehrid's first acts upon assuming his role had been to hire a mason to fashion the stones, insisting they be at least twice the weight of a man and shaped so as to allow them to be easily tipped into the maw. When complete, he had his men arrange them in a tidy row atop the overhang; a clear statement of intent. He had begun with twenty, now only five remained, soon to become four.

Jehrid rested a boot on the stone, glancing down at the waves crashing on the rocks far below. The terns had already begun to gather, wings folding back as they plunged into the swell, eager for the fresh pickings below. This shore had ever been kind to scavengers. The diving birds were the only sign of the six men he had already consigned to the Maw, Varesh's kin; : four cousins, a brother and a nephew. Last of the Stone Teeth, a brotherhood of smugglers and wreckers that had plagued this shore for more than three generations. Before kicking each boulder into the Maw Jehrid had asked Varesh the same question, and each time the leader of the Stone Teeth had stood silent and watched his kin dragged to their deaths. Varesh's only child, a daughter of notoriously vicious temper, had fallen to a crossbow bolt when Jehrid led his company into the smuggler's den, a narrow crack in the maze of cliffs east of South Tower, crammed with sundry spoils looted from the Alpiran freighter they had enticed onto the rocks a month before. One of Varesh's cousins had allowed wine to loosen his tongue upon visiting a brothel in town the previous night, and Jehrid had always found whores to be excellent informants.

"My mother once told me a story of how the Maw got its name," he told Varesh in a reflective tone. "Would you like to hear it?"

"Your mother was a poxed bitch," Varesh told him, voice quivering with rage. "Who whelped a traitor."

"It's not natural, you see," Jehrid went on, his tone unchanged. "Nawen, or Na Wen to give him his correct name, was captain and only survivor of a wrecked ship from the Far West. A lonely old fishwife took him in, though he was quite mad by all accounts. Every day he would come here and chip away at the cliff with hammer and chisel. Every day for twelve years until he had carved a perfect circular hole through this overhang. And when he was done… well, I assume you can guess what he did next."

Jehrid stiffened his leg, tilting the stone towards the maw. "No-one knows why he did it, for who can divine the mind of a madman? But my mother was wise, and judged it an act of revenge, a desire to leave the mark of man on the shore that wrecked his ship and killed his crew."

He gave Varesh a final questioning glance. "Life in the King's king's mines isn't much," he said. "But it is life. I know the Stone Teeth allied with the Red Breakers to wreck that ship. Things must have come to a desperate pass to forge an alliance between hated enemies. Settle some old scores, Varesh. Tell me where their den is."

Varesh spat on the rocks at Jehrid's feet and straightened his back. "If I find your mother in the Beyond..."

Jehrid kicked the stone, sending it tumbling into the maw, the chain rattling over rock as it snapped taught. Varesh had time for only the briefest shout as he was drawn into the hole, bones cracking as he rebounded from the sides, followed by a despairing wail as he plummeted towards the crashing waves.

"Make a note for the Royal Dispatches," Jehrid said, turning to his Sergeant of Excise, a squat Nilsaelin recruited as much for his facility with letters as his skill with a crossbow. "Varesh Baldir, leader of the gang known as the Stone Teeth, executed this day with six of his cohorts. Execution carried out under the King's Word by Jehrid Al Bera, Lord Collector of the King's Excise. Append a list of the contraband we recovered, and be sure the men know I'll check it against stores."

The sergeant gave a brisk nod, wisely keeping silent. Like most of those recruited to the Lord Collector's service, he had quickly gained an appreciation for Jehrid's intolerance of even the most petty theft. "You are paid twice the wage of the Realm Guard for a reason," he had told their assembled ranks the morning he flogged a former Varinshold City Guard for helping himself to a single vial of redflower. "Greed will not be tolerated."

"Rider coming, my lord," another Excise Man called, pointing to the north. The rider wore the uniform of a South Guard, a youthful recruit as many were these days. The new Tower Lord had been punctilious in enforcing the King's order that his command be purged of the lazy and corrupt, though it left him in sore need of guardsmen.

"Tower Lord's compliments, Lord Al Bera," the young guardsman said, reining in and bowing low in the saddle. "He requests your presence with all urgency."

"Another wreck?" Jehrid asked him.

"No, my lord." The guardsman straightened and gave a wary smile. "We have… visitors."

…

Tower Lord Nohrin Al Modral greeted Jehrid with an affable nod as he entered the chamber, but failed to rise from his plain, high-backed chair. Although they were technically of equal rank Jehrid took no offence at the absence of an honorary greeting. He had known this man as captain and, later, Lord Marshal throughout his years in the Realm Guard and was well acquainted with his former commander's disdain for useless ceremony. Also, Al Modral was only two years shy of seventy and his legs not so sturdy these days.

The plainness of his chair, and the mostly bare audience chamber where he received visitors, were a stark contrast to the previous incumbent. Former Tower Lord Al Serahl had maintained a richly decorated chamber and greeted visitors perched atop a tall, throne-like chair, so tall in fact he required a ladder to ascend it. He had been a small man, narrow of face with a prominent nose, and Jehrid recalled seeing a resemblance to a suspicious parrot the day he and Lord Al Modral had walked in six months before, unannounced and bearing a warrant of arrest adorned with the King's seal. The full company of Realm Guard at their back had discouraged any unwise intervention from those South Guard present, despite the pleas of the unfortunate Al Serahl who screamed himself quite hoarse before tumbling from his lofty perch in a tangle of robes fashioned from the finest Alpiran silks. When Jehrid led him to the gallows, his clothing had been much more modest.

"It seems we have occasion to celebrate, Lord Collector," the Tower Lord said, gesturing at the three figures standing before him. "The Faith sees fit to lend aid to our cause."

Jehrid went to one knee before the Tower Lord before rising to survey the visitors. The tallest wore a sword on his back and the dark blue cloak of the Sixth Order, returning Jehrid's scrutiny with impassive pale eyes. His closely cropped hair was flecked with grey gray at the temples, and his features had the leanness typical of the Faith's deadly servants. Jehrid knew him from a best forgotten foray into Lonak territory, though he entertained no illusions the brother would remember the boy-soldier who stood staring in blank amazement as he cut down three Lonak warriors in as many seconds.

"Brother Sollis, is it not?" Jehrid greeted the pale-eyed man with a bow. *Deadliest blade in the Sixth Order,* he pondered as Sollis inclined his head. *Come south to battle smugglers. Does the King think so poorly of our efforts he begs aid from the Order?*

"This is Brother Lucin and Sister Cresia," Sollis said in a dry rasp, nodding at his two companions, both wearing the dun-coloured robes of the Second Order. Brother Lucin was a thin, balding man somewhere past his fiftieth year. It seemed to Jehrid that his apparently serene expression was somewhat forced, his features tensed as if holding a mask in place. Sister Cresia seemed to be little more than sixteen years old, honey blonde hair tied back from youthful features, her slight form concealed within robes worn with evident discomfort. Unlike Lucin, she felt no need for a false air of serenity, returning Jehrid's gaze with a barely suppressed scowl.

Second Order, Jehrid mused inwardly. *What use have we for missionaries here?*

"Our visitors come on a special errand, Lord Al Bera," the Tower Lord went on. "Regarding the Alpiran vessel wrecked last month. I was explaining you had the matter well in hand. You have finished with the Stone Teeth, have you not?"

"As of this morning, my lord," Jehrid replied. "Though the Red Breakers remain elusive. Perhaps another week of investigation will root them out. My agents are busy, promise of rich reward always stirs them to greater efforts."

"A week is too long," Brother Sollis stated. "With luck, our assistance will assuage any delays."

"The help of the Sixth Order is always welcome, brother," Jehrid replied before casting a pointed glance at the two missionaries. "However, I confess myself at a loss as to the aid offered by your companions. No offensce, good brother and sister, but the hearts of the Red Breakers will not open to the Faith, regardless of how many catechisms you cast at their ears."

Sister Cresia's half-scowl twisted into a smirk, her voice betraying a faint note of contempt as she looked down, muttering, "Got more than catechisms to throw at them."

Brother Lucin gave her a sharp glance, saying nothing, but the severity of his gaze was sufficient to make her lower her head further, sullenness replacing contempt. "My apologies, my lord," Lucin said to Jehrid. "My pupil is barely a week into her first foray beyond the walls of our house and knows little of the world, or, it seems, common courtesy." He glared again at Cresia who kept her head lowered, though Jehrid saw her hands were now clasped tight together, quivering a little.

This girl's no more a missionary than I am, Jehrid thought. *What do they want here?*

"The ranks of my Order are filled with varied talents," Brother Lucin went on. "The missions test our bodies as well as our Faith. I myself was a hunter before I felt the call to don these robes."

No you weren't, Jehrid surmised from the briefest glance at the brother's spindly arms and lined but unweathered features. *I doubt you spend one more minute out of doors than you have to.* However, he merely nodded as the brother continued, "Sometimes my brothers in the Sixth have occasion to call on my tracking skills, when their own talents are otherwise occupied."

"We need to see the wreck," Sollis said.

"There'll barely be anything left," Jehrid told him. "A month of tides will have cleansed the shore of timber, and the sands of tracks."

"Even so," Sollis said, meeting his gaze, pale eyes unblinking.

Jehrid had been a soldier for twenty of his thirty-three years. He had fought Lonak, outlaws, heretics and, though he preferred not the dwell on it, Meldeneans, and knew himself to be the equal or superior of most men he was likely to meet in combat. But this one was different, for he had never forgotten seeing him fight. Nevertheless, he had ever been a slave to his temper and resentful of those who sought to stir fear in his breast, a long dulled sensation, summoning ugly boyhood memories, and unwise notions.

"May I ask," he grated, turning to face Sollis squarely, "what interest you have in this particular wreck?"

Sollis angled his head slightly, expression unchanged apart from a narrowing of his eyes. Jehrid felt his temper quicken yet further at the knowledge of being assessed and, no doubt, found wanting. Fortunately, the Tower Lord intervened before he could give voice to any anger.

"It seems there was a passenger aboard," Lord Al Modral groaned, levering himself out of his chair with difficulty, hand trembling on the heavy staff he was obliged to carry these days. Jehrid knew better than to offer assistance, the old man retained a surfeit of pride and had a temper of his own. "A passenger of some importance, eh brother?"

"Quite so, my lord," Sollis replied, blinking before switching his gaze to the Tower Lord. "One King Janus is keen to recover."

"Every soul on that ship perished on the rocks or drowned in the surf," Jehrid said. "The Alpiran merchants in town saw to the bodies and did what they could to glean names from their belongings."

"The passenger we seek was not among them," Lucin stated in an emphatic tone Jehrid found near as aggravating as Sollis's appraising gaze.

"They're all dead," Jehrid repeated. "You come here on a fool's errand…"

Lord Al Modral's heavy staff thumped onto the flagstones. The old man's legs might be failing but his arm remained strong. The echo birthed by his staff resounded through the chamber for some seconds before he spoke again, "Brothers, and sister, the Lord Collector will be more than happy to escort you to the wreck and render any and all assistance required. Please leave us whilst we discuss other matters."

After the trio had made their exit the Tower Lord moved to the stained glass window set into the chamber's south facing wall. The window was the only vestige of the deposed Lord Al Serahl's love of expensive ornamentation, conceived to celebrate a battle, and an atrocity, he had taken no direct part in. It was a floor-to-ceiling wonder of expert craftsmanship, lead and glass of various hues rendered into an ascending narrative. At the bottom many ships sailed from a harbour, marked as South Tower by the lance-like structure rising above the docks. The middle panes depicted a vicious sea battle that failed to conform to Jehrid's memory. Most of the Meldenean fleet had been absent that day and the pirates hadn't been able to muster even a third of the ships ascribed to them here. Unlike the sea battle, the window's upper panes were entirely in keeping with Jehrid's memory: a city… burning. The late afternoon sun was clear of cloud today and painted the scene across the chamber floor in vivid detail, leaving Jehrid unable to escape its dreadful spectacle, and the memories it provoked.

"More than ten years on," Lord Al Modral said, nodding at the window. "But it seems like yesterday sometimes. Then there are days when it's just a dim memory, like a fragment from a nightmare you can't quite shake."

"Indeed, my lord," Jehrid said, keeping his gaze lowered. He hated the window and had in fact petitioned for its destruction. The Tower Lord, however, had far too much respect for the arts to allow it.

"Before... this," Al Modral waved his staff at the burning city. "I recall a captain less inclined to anger."

"Ten years is a long time, my lord," Jehrid replied, resisting the impulse to close his eyes. Whoever had crafted the window had somehow managed to capture the exact shade of flame that had consumed the Meldenean capital, though, fortunately, there was no art that could recreate the screams.

"Nevertheless," Al Modral went on. "I think the King would prefer his Lord Collector keep a clear and level head during this mission."

Jehrid blinked, forcing himself to focus on the Tower Lord. "Of course, my lord."

"They arrived unannounced, bearing missives from the Aspects of the Second and Sixth Orders, but no royal warrant. Curious, don't you think? Given that they come on royal business."

"Certainly, my lord. Sufficiently curious to require them to wait whilst we seek clarification from court."

Al Modral shook his head. "Life as a Lord Marshal taught me many lessons, Jehrid. Lessons you would do well to learn if, as is my fervent wish, you are to succeed me one day in holding this Tower. Today's lesson is twofold. First, the folly of obstructing the

Orders, the Sixth in particular. Second, the value of information. I should like to know the identity of this passenger they seek, and the nature of their business on this shore."

Never reckoned him a schemer, Jehrid thought. *But the king gave him the Tower for a reason.* "I'll see to it, my lord."

"Good." The Tower Lord placed a hand on his shoulder as they turned and moved back to the chair, the old man more willing to accept aid now there were no witnesses. "And, if this passenger is still alive we know full well who holds them. With the Faith's help, mayhap you'll finally find what drew you back to this shore."

He settled back onto his chair with a sigh, his hand slipping from Jehrid's shoulder like a limp rag. "Do you think it'll be sweet when you finally taste it, my fierce and implacable friend?" he asked. "They say vengeance can be bitter."

"It could be wormwood and I'd still drink until my belly bursts." Jehrid stepped back, dropping to one knee before rising to deliver an impeccable salute. "By your leave, my lord."

...

Shelter Bay was a misnamed, rocky notch in the shoreline some thirty miles west of South Tower. It was formed of a hundred yards of beach flanked by tall bluffs. At high tide the sea became a fury of roaring breakers, churned up by the plentiful rocks lurking beneath the surface. They only became visible at low tide, a dark maze of jagged reefs making this such a favoured spot for the wrecking gangs.

They had set out from South Tower the previous evening, Jehrid riding with twenty of his most trusted men. Brother Sollis rode with the two missionaries and a dozen brothers from the

Sixth Order. They had camped in the dunes overnight before proceeding to the bay where, contrary to Jehrid's expectations, the tides had contrived to spare some vestige of the Alpiran vessel.

She had been named as the *Selennah* by the Alpiran merchants who came to lay claim to whatever cargo Jehrid might recover, an archaic term but within his grasp of Alpiran: *Voyager.* An old ship, but large and well captained, though not well enough to resist the lure of the wreckers' false lights. Jehrid assumed a junior mate must have had the watch when they neared the shore. A veteran sailor would have known better. Three of her arched beams rose from the waves like the bared ribs of some scavenged beast, all that remained of a freighter that had sailed the Erinean and beyond for three decades.

"And you found no survivors at all?" Sister Cresia asked, eyeing the wreck with little sign of the sullen frown she had worn throughout the journey.

"The sea is ever an efficient assassin, sister," Jehrid told her. "Though there were a few with their throats cut, fingers hacked off. Wreckers don't like to leave witnesses behind, or their jewellery."

Her features gave a twitch of mingled disgust and anger which Jehrid found himself liking her for. *Some sense of justice behind the scowl, it seems.*

"Best if we three proceed alone," Brother Lucin said, climbing down from his horse with a discomforted wince. "My... skills work best without distraction."

"The sand is bare, as I said it would be," Jehrid pointed out as Sister Cresia and Brother Sollis followed Lucin to the beach. The balding brother merely waved and kept labouring through the dunes. Jehrid watched the three of them approach the shoreline. For a time Lucin walked back and forth with Sollis and Cresia in tow, pausing occasionally to point at something on the sand before stroking his chin in apparent contemplation. Jehrid had never been one for plays, but he knew a performance when he saw one. *Tracker my arse.*

After some further mummery, Lucin came to a halt, turning his gaze out to sea. He stood still for some time, back straight and arms loose at his sides, seemingly uncaring of the waves lapping around his feet and dampening the hem of his robe. Abruptly, Lucin jerked as if in pain, clasping himself tight and doubling over. Sister Cresia came to his side in evident concern but he waved her away. Even from this distance Jehrid could see his hand was trembling.

"What is this, my lord?" the Sergeant of Excise murmured at his side, swarthy features bunched in suspicion.

"King's business!" Jehrid snapped, though in a low voice. "Still your tongue."

He watched Lucin say something to Brother Sollis before slumping with a weary shake of his head, kept upright only by Sister Cresia who came to his side. Jehrid saw Lucin wipe at his nose before turning and raising a hand, now free of any tremble and pointing firmly west. It was too far away to tell for sure, but Jehrid could have sworn the brother's hand was stained with blood.

...

They followed the coast until the sky began to dim, Brother Lucin riding in front with Sollis at his side. Jehrid found it odd that Lucin barely glanced at the ground as he led them in apparent pursuit of the wreckers' trail. He had no guess as to where the brother was leading them; this stretch of coast was mostly bare of the caves or inlets beloved by smugglers, distinguished by tall cliffs and narrow stretches of shingle where only the most skilled or foolish sailor would seek to ground a boat.

Lucin and Sollis eventually came to a halt after ascending a steep rise over twenty miles from Shelter Bay. Jehrid trotted his mount closer as Lucin indicated a point a few miles ahead, a narrow channel cutting into the shore where waves broke on a series of tall sandstone columns, each shaped and honed by centuries of tides and wind so that they resembled a line of jagged swords.

"There," Lucin said.

"The Blades?" Jehrid asked, unable to keep the scorn from his voice. "You think the Red Breakers are sheltering in the Blades?"

"You know this place?" Sollis asked.

"Everyone raised on the southern shore knows this place, and they know to avoid it. It's completely unnavigable, even at low tide."

"The channel leads to a waterfall, does it not?" Sollis pressed.

"It does. Pretty enough place but the walls are too steep and damp to climb, and free of caves, which is why it's of no use to the Breakers."

He saw the brothers exchange a glance before Sollis gave a small nod. "Not caves," Lucin said. There was a wariness to his voice, conveying the sense of a secret shared only through dire necessity. "Tunnels, built many years ago."

"By who's hand?" Jehrid asked.

"The Orders have a long history, my lord," Lucin replied. "And there are builders in our ranks as well as trackers."

"That farce you played on the beach," Jehrid grunted with a laugh. "Why not simply tell me of these tunnels back in South Tower?"

"We needed to be certain. And now ask for your discretion."

Jehrid glanced again at the Blades, the silent monolithic swords rising from ceaseless white fury. He recalled his first sight of them one frigid morning years ago, shivering at the rail as a large man pulled him into a warm hug and reeled off a list of foolhardy sailors who had ventured too close to this channel, among them his great uncle, dashed to ruin during a desperate gamble at evading the Lord's bounty-men. "That's how they kept law in those days," the large man had told him. "Put a bounty on our heads and set the scum of the fief on our tail. We fought a war to win this shore, boy, though you'll not find it in any history. Now we have a king, things are more civilizsed, but blood always pays for blood."

"What's in there?" Jehrid asked Lucin.

"Something that will remain hidden," Sollis stated before the tracker could answer. "With your assistance, for which the Faith will ever be grateful."

Jehrid had never been particularly scrupulous in his observance, but he had been raised in the Faith and the myriad dangers of a soldier's life had often found him holding to it with fierce conviction. Also, he had an obligation to honour Lord Al Modral's desire for information. "You know of a way in?" he asked Lucin.

...

Wary of lookouts, Jehrid insisted they approach on foot and in darkness. This scarcely troubled the Brothers of the Sixth, who moved with an unnerving silence and sureness of foot, or his

own men, well accustomed to finding their way across darkened country. Brother Lucin and his pupil, however, were not so attuned to stealth.

"Quiet!" Jehrid hissed at Sister Cresia as her foot contrived to find a rabbit hole, provoking a frustrated yelp. He saw her eyes gleam in the dark as she rounded on him, no doubt ready to deliver a retort, but a nudge from Brother Lucin was enough to still her voice.

Jehrid could hear the waterfall now, a low, steady rumble drifting across through the small copse of trees where they lay. The narrow but fast flowing river that fed the waterfall gurgled past fifty yards to their left, a clear track to their goal, but guarded. They were only the dimmest shapes in the gloom, wisely denying themselves a fire but well wrapped against the chill, four in two pairs on either side of the river, each hefting a crossbow and moving in tight circles, one never straying from the sight of the other.

"Easy targets," Sollis whispered at Jehrid's side, his bow already in hand, a gull-fletched arrow notched and ready.

"Wait," Jehrid murmured as Sollis turned to signal his brothers. "There's another. One you can't see. It'll be the youngest, small enough to be easily hidden. Kill these and he'll be blasting a horn a second later."

Sollis's lean features remained impassive, though a slight tightness in his voice told of a marked impatience. "This matter requires resolution," he stated. "One way or another."

"Their prisoner, if they truly have one, will die the instant that horns sounds."

"The matter requires resolution," Sollis repeated in the same clipped tone.

Not here to rescue, Jehrid realised. *Only to silence.*

He returned his gaze to the sentries, then scanned the surrounding grassland. This was not his usual hunting ground. Smugglers and wreckers tended to keep to the east, close to the main roads leading to northern towns. *Where would he have put me?* he pondered, eyes roaming the dim country. *The falls are loud enough to mask all but the strongest blast. He would need me close…* His gaze came to rest on a small mound near the edge of the spray-damp ledge next to the falls. It would have been easily taken for just a clump of grass in the gloom, but the shape was subtly wrong, the lean of the grass not quite the correct angle for the wind. *He grows careless with age.*

Jehrid turned to his sergeant, nodding at the loaded crossbow in his grip and beckoning him closer. He lay at the sergeant's side and pointed out the mound. "You have it?"

The sergeant braced the crossbow against his shoulder, settling his cheek against the stock, fingers poised on the lock. "Clear as day, milord."

"He'll stand when the others go down. Don't miss." Jehrid inclined his head at Sollis. "As you will, brother."

Sollis raised a hand to make a series of complex but rapid signs, seven brothers immediately rising in response and moving to the edge of the copse. They crouched in unison, arrows notched nocked and bows drawn, all without the barest rustle or creak of straining wood. There was no further instruction from the Brother Commander, he simply drew, aimed and sent his arrow into the chest of the left-most sentry, the man caught in mid-fall by another arrow before disappearing into the grass with barely a groan. Six more bowstrings snapped as one and Jehrid had a scant second to witness the demise of the remaining lookouts before a slim figure jerked upright from the tell-tale mound, a long sailor's horn raised, back arched as he drew breath. The sergeant's crossbow snapped and the slim figure had time for a spastic final twist before collapsing from sight.

Jehrid surged to his feet and sprinted for the falls, sparing a glance at the sentries to confirm none still moved and coming to a halt beside the one with the horn. His features were pale in the gloom, youthful prettiness rendered slack and ugly in death. There was something familiar about the set of his eyes, the smoothness of his brow stirring yet more unwelcome memories. *Aunt Tilda's eyes,* Jehrid thought, scanning the boy's body. *A good mother would have spared him this.*

"Just a boy," a voice whispered at Jehrid's back. He turned to find Sister Cresia staring at the corpse, eyes wide and face white. Something glimmered in her right hand, something sharp judging from the way it caught the meagre light. She blinked, noticing his gaze and quickly concealed her hand in her robe.

Jehrid crouched and lifted the boy's limp arm, pulling back the sleeve to reveal two black circles tattooed into the flesh alongside three vertical lines. "Two wrecks and three kills," he told Cresia. "Youth is not the same as innocence, sister. Not on this shore."

Brother Lucin led them to a notch in the cliff edge where a series of narrow steps had been carved into the rock, so weathered and softened by the seaward winds as to be barely visible. The climb down to the ledge below was short but not without peril, the damp steps and gloom making for some unnerving slips, though luckily there were none in their company sufficiently clumsy to completely lose footing, a deadly mistake judging by the roiling waves visible below. Sollis drew his sword and took the lead as they proceeded towards the falls, the cascade of water arcing down like a fluid glass curtain. The Brother Commander held up a hand to halt them in place and moved on alone, disappearing into the gloom behind the curtain. A second later came a faint sound of clashing steel then Sollis reappeared and beckoned them forward.

Behind the falls the ledge opened out into a grotto, much of it fashioned by hand judging by the worn but plain chisel marks on the rock. Sollis stood at the grotto's deepest point, running his hand over the rock as if in search of something. Another sentry lay nearby, sword in hand and blood streaming from a deep gash in his neck. Jehrid was impressed he had managed to draw a blade before Sollis cut him down.

Lucin moved to Sollis's side and peered closely at the rock, fingers probing for something. Eventually, he grunted in satisfaction and moved back, murmuring something to Sollis which Jehrid could barely catch, "Locks from the inside."

The older brother gestured at Cresia, leaning close to her as she came forward, his words too soft to hear above the tumult of the falls. Jehrid saw the girl give a reluctant nod before moving towards the rock, laying both hands against the damp stone, her form becoming still, face blank with concentration. She remained like that for some time, the two brothers standing by with evident impatience. Eventually Lucin moved to whisper a question at which the girl turned to him, face flashing anger as she voiced a harsh rebuke. Jehrid expected the brother to respond with some form of admonishment, but instead he merely sighed and moved back, gesturing for Sollis to follow.

"Our sister may be young," Lucin said, moving to Jehrid's side. "But she is well versed in ancient lore regarding these tunnels. To open the entrance requires pressure in one particular spot. She'll find it soon enough."

Jehrid's gaze lingered on the girl, noting she had resumed the same statue-like stillness, her hands flat and unmoving on the rock. Abruptly she stiffened, leaning closer to the wall, eyes closed and head cocked at a slight angle. Her features betrayed a brief spasm before she stepped back, flexing her fingers, and a three foot wide section of rock swung inward to reveal a narrow passage. The sister stepped back, face paler than before though lit with a triumphal grin as she offered them a bow and bade them enter.

...

The width of the passage would permit only one entrant at a time and Sollis insisted on taking the lead. Jehrid ordered his Excise Men to remain and guard the entrance before taking his place at Sollis's back, expecting some objection. However, the Brother Commander merely glanced at him and drew his sword before disappearing into the passage. Jehrid followed with Brother Lucin and Sister Cresia at his back. He had suggested they remain with his men but they merely shook their heads and fell into line, faces tense but, to Jehrid's eyes, not so fearful as they should be. The passage was dimly lit with torches set into the walls every twenty paces, guttering in the breeze from the entrance. The walls were roughly hewn, displaying only the most workmanlike skill in their fashioning. Whoever had crafted these tunnels had displayed scant interest in artistry.

Sollis set a slow pace, keeping his steps soft to prevent any betraying echo. Jehrid noted a slight downward slope and a gradual but increasing curve to the walls, indicating they were following a spiral course deep into the bowels of the rock. The curvature of the passage became more pronounced the deeper they went, obscuring the way ahead sufficiently for Sollis to flatten himself against the wall and move forward in a sideways shuffle. He stopped at the sound of voices, softly spoken but echoing well in the tunnel. There were two voices, both male, engaged in some form of argument, the words indistinct at first but becoming clearer as Sollis began to inch forward once more, now moving in a crouch, sword-grip reversed so the blade rested against his back. He stopped when the voices became clearer, turning to Jehrid with a questioning glance.

Jehrid felt his hand dampen with sweat, knuckles suddenly white on his sword handle. Two voices, older men, one he knew, though it had been many years since he heard it.

"... speak to me of promises," it said, a rich voice possessing the broad vowels of the shore-folk, but coloured by a faint note of scorn. "Promises were made to me also. Promise of gold and jewels. Instead we risk much to scavenge no more than spices and silk. A tidy profit, to be sure. But hardly worth drawing the Lord Collector's eye."

"Gold will be forthcoming," the other voice replied. It was mostly toneless but with an odd accent, the vowels distinctly Renfaelin but the cadence similar to the harsh babble of Volarian sailors. "When you give me what I came for. And don't forget, without me you would have had no wreck to plunder."

Jehrid frowned in surprise as the other voice fell silent. *Since when did he ever fail to find a rejoinder?*

After a pause, the first voice spoke again, this time betraying a discomfort barely masked by angry defiance. "We've talked of this enough. She's mine. And she stays mine until you pay."

There came a sound then, so harsh and grating Jehrid took a moment to recognise it as a laugh. "What do you imagine you are, little smuggling man?" the second voice enquired when his mirth had subsided. "What cards do you think you hold? You are no more than a maggot feasting on the dead before the tide comes to wash you away. You have seen what I can do. Give me the woman unless you would like another demonstration."

A long, frozen pause. *Now for blood,* Jehrid decided. The insult and the challenge were too great to ignore. Jehrid could picture him standing there, face stricken with fury, fist no doubt clamping hard on a dagger, his other hand clutching a cudgel. 'The Dance of Hard and Sharp' he had called it; the traditional smuggler's fighting style. In an instant all would be chaos and confusion. The perfect moment to attack. Jehrid inched closer to Sollis, readying himself for the rush.

So it was with no small amount of shock that he heard the frigid silence broken by the first voice. "Bring her."

He's afraid. Jehrid found he had to contain a gasp of amused realizsation. *He's actually afraid.*

Footfalls echoed through the tunnel then another long pause, silence reigning until they returned. "Ah," the second voice said, now tinged with a tense anticipation. "I was expecting some-one... older."

"She carried the amulet you described," the first voice said, hard and sullen. "Worthless bauble though it was."

"Show it to me." Another pause, then a satisfied chuckle. "Worthless to you perhaps, but not to her." The voice switched to Alpiran, coarse and harshly accented, but still fluent enough for Jehrid to follow. "*Isn't that right, my dear? It must have taken a remarkable effort to earn Rhevena's Tear at your age. Most don't until they're nearing dotage. Is your gift so powerful? I imagine not, since you remain bound by this scum.*"

A female voice, tremulous but also defiant, the cultured accent contrasting with her interrogator's grating vowels. "*Free me, and I'll be happy to show you.*"

"*Don't trouble yourself, honoured lady. I'll shortly discover its nature for myself.*" There came the scrape of a blade being drawn as he switched back to Realm Tongue. "Hold her still."

Brother Lucin came forward in a rush, his steps drawing a loud echo from the stone, the bleached concern on his face betraying a desperate urgency. "He will do it!" he hissed at Sollis. "We cannot delay."

An enquiring shout came from beyond the curve; Lucin's footfall had not been missed. Sollis straightened, reversing the grip on his sword and glancing at Jehrid. "Secure the woman and take her out of here. Leave the others to us."

Then he was gone, blue cloak trailing as he charged from sight. Jehrid surged after him, the multiple echoes of the brothers' boots like thunder as they followed. Beyond the curve, the passage opened out into a large chamber, near twenty feet across with bunks covering the walls and several side channels leading off in various directions. Standing in the centre were three figures, an olive-skinned woman of perhaps thirty years of age, her arms bound behind her back, and two men. The man on the right was of middling years and unkempt appearance, his wiry frame clad in ragged, threadbare garb.

But it was the man on the left who captured Jehrid's attention. He was older, of course. Hair now grey and thinning when it had once been thick and dark, face clean-shaven and lined with age, though he stood just as tall as Jehrid recalled and his waist seemed as free of paunch as ever. As expected, he had armed himself with a cudgel and dagger, swirling to face the intruders in a crouching stance, lips drawn back in a snarl, one that faded as he caught sight of Jehrid.

"Cohran Bera!" Jehrid called to him as he charged clear of the tunnel. "Stand and await the King's Jus—!"

He ducked as one of the Red Breakers sprang from the shadows on the left, something fast and sharp cutting the air above Jehrid's head. Another appeared on the right, axe raised to swing at Sollis and falling dead a heartbeat later as the brother's sword delivered a single expert thrust to his throat. The Breaker confronting Jehrid was clearly a traditionalist, coming at him with a cleaver in one hand and a cudgel in the other, aiming well-timed blows at his head and legs. Jehrid sidestepped the cudgel, swayed back to evade the cleaver and brought his blade up and down to hack through the Breaker's hamstring before he could recover for another swing. This smuggler was not easily cowed though, despite being forced to one knee and yelling in pain, he managed another lunge with the cleaver before Jehrid's sword point sank into his chest.

Jehrid spun, sword levelled at Cohran Bera, now moved to the centre of the chamber, eyes locked on his. "You've grown," he said in a low growl before turning and issuing a shrill whistle. Only a bare second's delay then a tumult of pounding boots, a dozen or more Breakers appearing from the side tunnels at a run, all armed. Four went down almost immediately, tumbling to the floor as the brothers' throwing knives flickered in the torchlight. Those who managed to get close enough to exchange blows were scarcely more fortunate, most falling in the space of a few sword strokes though the momentary confusion allowed their leader time to run for the nearest passage, three survivors at his back.

Jehrid shouted in frustration, a familiar red tinge colouring his vision as he started forward. It was the woman's shout that stopped his pursuit, his gaze swivelling towards her, now standing rigid and head drawn back, the wiry man's fist in her hair, his other holding a thin-bladed dagger to her throat. Jehrid had time to catch Cohran Bera's final glance, oddly sombre and lacking in hatred, before the shadows swallowed him.

"Oh no!" the wiry man barked, addressing his words to Sollis as the brothers quickly surrounded the pair, closing in with swords levelled. He jerked the woman's head back further, the edge of his blade pressing hard against her skin. "I require your consideration."

Sollis held up a hand to halt the brothers, lowering his own sword to take a single step closer. Jehrid noted Sollis's free hand twitch as it caught something that slipped from his sleeve. "Release her," Sollis commanded in a flat rasp. "If your life has value to you."

The wiry man replied only with another grating laugh. Jehrid frowned at the genuine humour he heard in that laugh, and the lack of any real hostility on the man's face. For all the world he seemed no more than a man responding to a particularly well executed prank. "Ask him," the wiry man said, nodding to Brother Lucin emerging from the passage with Sister Cresia at his side.

"What value does his Order place on life? Did they bother to warn you what you'd find here? I'll wager they didn't."

It was Brother Lucin who spoke, face grim and gaze steady as he regarded the wiry man, his voice now possessed of a cold, unwavering note of command. "Kill him."

"Brother..." Jehrid stepped towards Sollis but the brother had already begun to move. His left hand seemed to blur, something small and metallic catching the light as it flew free. Jehrid shouted in alarm, knowing a killing blow might cause the wiry man's arm to tense with dire consequences for his hostage. Sollis, however, had chosen his target well. The throwing knife sank hilt-deep into the wiry man's wrist, the knife falling from his spasming grip. The woman twisted, tearing herself free and falling to the floor. Jehrid quickly moved to her side, sword pointed at her now prostrate captor.

His gaze met Jehrid's for a moment, bright with pain and fury, then softened as it shifted to the throwing knife embedded in his wrist, and he began to laugh anew.

"Kill him, brother!" Lucin commanded in a yell, his voice suddenly shrill with panic.

Sollis moved to the wiry man, sword drawn back, then stumbled to his knees as the floor shuddered beneath his feet.

"You put too much trust in these deluded mystics, master," the wiry man said, blood now streaming in rivulets from his nose. "Far too much trust..."

A great booming sound shook the surrounding rock, a jagged crack appearing in the floor, stretching the length of the chamber. Jehrid saw Lucin grab Sister Cresia's arm and drag her towards the passage as the chamber shuddered again, the floor becoming a jumbled matrix of cracks, the brothers reeling from multiple fountains of shattered rock. The wiry man was laughing again, writhing on the shuddering floor in uncontrollable mirth, blood now streaming from his mouth and eyes. Sollis lurched towards him, sword raised for a slash at his neck… and the chamber floor exploded, stone shattering all around into a fog of dust.

Jehrid had time to catch hold of the woman before the floor gave way beneath them, air rushing past his ears as they plummeted, swallowed by the welcoming dark.

…

The docks once again, his only reliable dream. It was always the same. The same pier, the same hour just before nightfall, every detail perfect and vivid even though the memory was over twenty years old.

He crouched behind a wall of stacked barrels in a quiet corner of the South Tower docks, peeking out at the end of the pier. There were people there, dim shadows glimpsed through twilight mist, four standing and one kneeling. The kneeling figure was bound, face concealed with a sack tied at the neck. Even so Jehrid knew whose face lay beneath the sack, knew without any shred of doubt the face of the woman who knelt with head bowed in numb expectation of her fate. Just as he knew the name of the man who drew a knife and stepped to her side.

He turned away then, knowing what was coming, reeling through the streets as his gorge rose to spill his guts on the cobbles. His treacherous ears caught the sound of a body tumbling into harbour waters, the splash carrying well in the clammy air. He ran, through the streets and the city gate and out into the fields beyond, blinded by tears, running until his lungs turned to fire and his legs gave way. He lay out in the fields until morning, and when the sun rose to wake him with its warmth, he got to his feet and started north. The road was long, and he grew to know hunger and danger as close friends for the wild country was ever rich in threats, but eventually, a thin, ragged boy staggered into Varinshold and sought entry to the Realm Guard.

"Has to be your real name, boy," the sergeant told him, quill poised over parchment, a somewhat wicked glint in his eye as he added, "King Janus wants only honest Guardsmen…"

He awoke to the taste of blood, iron, and salt stinging his tongue and provoking a convulsive retch as his senses returned. His dulled vision, hampered by eyelids that now seemed to be fashioned from lead, could see almost nothing save a faint impression of tumbled rock, though the sound invading his ears prevented any return to slumber; a muted but continuous, echoing torrent of rushing water.

"*Not alone after all,*" a voice muttered nearby, a female voice, speaking in Alpiran.

It took a moment before he made her out, crouching in the gloom, on her knees, arms still bound and eyes pinpoints of light behind hair hanging in damp tendrils over her face.

Jehrid paused to spit the blood from his mouth, tongue exploring where his teeth had left a ragged impression on the inside of his cheek. "*Nor, it seems, are you, honoured lady,*" he replied in his coarse but functional Alpiran.

She straightened a little in surprise, then spoke in accentless Realm Tongue that put his Alpiran to shame, "Would you mind?" She turned, crouching to proffer her bound wrists.

Jehrid realised realized his hands were empty, his sword no doubt lost somewhere in the fall. He fumbled at her bonds, grunting in frustration at his shaking hands, forcing himself to draw a series of deep breaths until the tremble subsided, though the cause was obvious. *He laughed. He bled and he laughed… He did this. He brought down the chamber.* The mystery of it all was absolute, but for one signal and reluctant conclusion: *The Dark.*

The woman gave an impatient sigh and Jehrid mumbled an apology, shuffling closer to work on the binding cord. The knots were well crafted and it took a protracted effort before the cord came loose. She issued a loud groan of mingled pain and relief, slumping forward with hands cradled in her lap, a soft curse coming from her lips. The words were mostly unfamiliar but he caught the name *Rhevena* among them.

"Rhevena's Tear," he said aloud, remembering the wiry man's words. "Goddess of the shadowed paths, is she not? Protector of the dead."

The woman's posture became guarded, her hand moving unconsciously to her bare neck. "I thought your people had no truck with gods," she said.

"Knowledge does not equal worship." Jehrid took a moment to flex his legs, confirming the absence of broken bones or torn muscles, though they did ache considerably, and his hands bore several painful scrapes. He levered himself upright, taking a closer look at their surroundings. They were in a narrow passage, the walls even more crudely made than the tunnel under the falls, dampened by a constant trickle of water. He stood at the base of a steep gravel slope, formed no doubt from shattered rock and providing enough of a break in their fall to prevent a bone-crushing landing. To the right the passage was completely blocked by fallen stone, leaving only the leftward course, illuminated by a faint, bluish light.

"Can you walk?" he asked the woman.

She nodded and got to her feet, ignoring or failing to notice the helping hand he offered. "Your comrades?" she asked, peering about.

Jehrid glanced at the wall of stone blocking the passage, then lifted his gaze to the black void above. *How far did we fall?* "I doubt we'll see them again," he said.

He took the lead, the dim luminescence growing as they followed the passage, the sound of rushing water increasing with every step. "You were held here for days," Jehrid said. "Have you any knowledge of these tunnels?"

"The route from my cell to the main chamber only. They were careful with me, my hands were always bound."

He found it odd Cohran would have exercised so much caution, and restraint, in confining her. Wreckers rarely took captives and the fate of those that did fall into their hands was never pretty. "*You are so dangerous then, honoured lady?*" he asked, dropping into Alpiran once more.

She frowned and shook her head, gesturing impatiently for him to move on.

"*That man, back at the chamber,*" Jehrid persisted, halting to face her. "*He paid them to take you, didn't he? Paid them to wreck the ship carrying you. Why?*"

A mix of anger and grief passed over her face before she mastered it, meeting his gaze with stern resolve. "Did your father teach you Alpiran?" she asked, once again keeping to Realm Tongue. "You speak it with much the same accent. He told me he had been a sailor in his youth, learning many tongues and sailing to many ports. You have much the same face, and the same bearing. He *is* your father, is he not?"

Jehrid found himself mastering his own surge of anger. "In name," he muttered, turning and continuing along the passage.

"And what is your name? You have yet to tell me."

"Jehrid Al Bera, Lord Collector of the King's Excise. At your service, my lady."

"Lord Collector… He spoke of you, said you would come one day. The thought seemed to make him sad. Now I see why."

Jehrid felt an abrupt need for a change of subject. "And your name, lady?"

"Meriva Al Lebra."

"Al Lebra is an Asraelin name."

"My father was an Asraelin sailor, obliged to forsake his homeland when he met my mother."

"Obliged?"

"She was a junior priestess to the temple of Rhevena in Untesh. Paying court to her required a certain… adjustment in his beliefs."

"He forsook the Faith for marriage?"

"For love, my lord. Has not love ever forced you to an extreme?"

There was a new note in her voice, clearly mocking but also gentle enough to remove any anger from his reply. "I have always found hate a better spur to useful action."

The passage soon grew wider and a dim glow appeared ahead, the pitch of cascading water deepening further. They found a body a few yards on, a slumped, cloaked bundle of twisted limbs. "May the Departed accept you, brother," Jehrid murmured, crouching to peer at the man's face, recognising him as one of the archers who had taken down the sentries above. He was plainly dead, features drained of all colour and his head pressed into his shoulder at an impossible angle. However, he had somehow contrived to retain hold of his sword.

"The Sixth Order," Meriva said, her tone soft but Jehrid could hear the fear it held. "You answer to them?"

"I answer to the King." He hefted the sword and held it up to the sparse light. *An Order blade*, he thought, seeing the telltale pattern in the steel, a facet of their secretive forging arts. *The strongest and keenest blades in the Realm. Doubtful they'll let me keep it.*

"Then why are you here with them?" she pressed.

Jehrid bent to remove the brother's scabbard from his back, a difficult task given the contortions of his body. "I came for the Breakers," he grunted, turning the corpse over and working at the buckles. "They came for you."

She made a small sound, half a laugh and half a groan. "To rescue me, no doubt."

"Their mission is their own." He tugged the scabbard free and buckled it on, around the waist rather than the back, sliding the blade in place. He straightened, staring at Meriva until she met his gaze, eyes shrouded and posture guarded, as if she might turn to flee at any second. "I will allow no harm to you," he told her. "But I will have the truth. Why do they want you?"

She sighed, her stance becoming a little more relaxed, though her gaze told of a lingering mistrust. "To hear the message I carry… Or ensure my silence."

"You carry a message? From who?"

She looked down, clearly fighting a deep reluctance. Jehrid stood and kept his eyes locked on her face. It was a favoured trick when dealing with reticent informants, stillness and silence always stirred the tongue better than outright threats. "From the gods to the godless," she said eventually, raising her gaze once more. There was still fear there, but also an overriding defiance. "I have said all I will say. Now, I suggest we move on. Unless you intend to stand and gawp at me forever."

He held up the only other weapon found on the brother's body, a hunting knife of good steel. "Do you know how to use this?"

She hesitated and reached for the knife, clasping it tight. "No. But I will, if needs must."

...

Twenty paces on the passage opened out into a cavern, the ceiling lost to the darkness but the walls speckled with pinpoints of light, each no brighter than a match but combining to provide a clear view of the spectacle before them. A torrent of water arced down from the black void to continually replenish a broad pool in the centre of the cavern. Jehrid saw there was a slow but definite current to the waters, his gaze tracking to the right where the cavern narrowed into another passage, water foaming as it was channelled deeper into the rock.

"There must be a fissure," Jehrid mused, gazing up at the cascade. "Siphoning off the river waters before they reach the fall."

He watched Meriva peer at the cavern wall, her fingers playing over one of the pinpoints of light, tracing dark tendrils across the surface. "Some kind of lichen," she mused. "Fed by the water and giving off light as a reward." She paused, then added something in Alpiran, voice pitched low in reverence, as if she were reciting a catechism, "*May the goddess accept my thanks for her beneficence.*"

Jehrid was about to take a closer look at the channel on the right, assuming it led out to sea, and therefore might offer some avenue of escape, but paused when Meriva clasped his arm. She pointed at something in the pool, something limp and man-sized, trailing a blue cloak as it drifted in the shallows.

Jehrid plunged into the water and waded towards the body, heaving it over to reveal a lean face and greying hair. Sollis's eyes remained closed but his features twitched as Jehrid took a firmer grip on his shirt and began to haul him from the pool. *Still alive,* he thought with a certain grim resignation. *Of course he is.*

Meriva helped him drag the Brother Commander clear of the water and away from the damp rock fringing the pool. They rested him against a relatively dry patch of wall where Meriva pressed a hand to his forehead. "Chilled almost to the point of death," she said. Her eyes went to Sollis's right arm, his hand dangling from a twisted wrist. "And that's certainly broken."

Jehrid nodded agreement and reached for the brother's forearm, squeezing hard. Sollis came awake with a shout, trying to raise his right arm as it sought the empty scabbard on his back. He tried vainly to rise, ice numb legs giving way and leaving him flailing against the rock.

"It's all right," Meriva said, casting a reproachful glare at Jehrid as she placed a calming hand on the brother's shoulder. "We are friends."

Don't be too sure, Jehrid thought, watching the realisation dawn on Sollis's face, the lean features tensing against the pain, and a sharp calculation returning to his eyes.

"My brothers?" he said, gaze switching from Meriva to Jehrid.

"We found no others alive," Jehrid told him.

Sollis closed his eyes momentarily, face as immobile as the stone behind him. When he opened them again there was no grief, no sorrow, just firm decision. "I need a sling for this," he said, patting his broken arm.

Meriva tore a strip from the brother's cloak to fashion the sling and tied it in place, Sollis gritting his teeth against the pain as she pulled it taught. They helped him upright and moved to the channel at the far end of the cavern. Jehrid peered into the gloom beyond the foaming waters, seeing no ledge or other means of navigating such a treacherous passage.

"We could just jump in," Meriva suggested. "Trust the gods to see us safely free of this place."

Sollis gave a rasping grunt that might have been a laugh, drawing a scowl from Meriva. "They have preserved us this far," she said.

"Blind chance has preserved us," the brother replied, though his tone softened as he regarded the channel. "Though, in truth I see little option."

"The current is too swift," Jehrid stated. "And the course may well lead further underground before it reaches the sea. If we aren't dashed to pieces we'd most likely drown. And if we were to make it out, we'd find ourselves flailing amid the Blades in the dead of night."

He turned away from the channel, eyes roaming the cavern and finding a patch of dark a good way back from the pool where the glowing lichen didn't cling to the walls. He moved towards it, far enough until the shadows swallowed him. He could see nothing ahead, just blank emptiness, his hands finding only air as he reached out to explore the void.

"If we had a torch," he murmured. "A candle even. Just the barest flicker of light..."

And the black turned white. It was so sudden he found himself reeling, stifling a shout of pain and shielding eyes now streaming with tears. He blinked and cautiously looked again, finding the way ahead illuminated, a soft beam playing over the rock like a shaft of sunlight caught by a lens. The beam moved, revealing a tall, broad passage leading away from the cavern. Jehrid followed the course of the beam, tracking it back to Meriva, standing with her arm extended, and light streaming from her hand, held out flat like a spear-point.

The Dark, he thought, feeling his mouth hang open in an appalled gape. *Free my hands and I'll show you... Light born of the Dark... This is impossible.*

His gaze shifted to Brother Sollis who seemed markedly less shocked than a servant of the Faith should be, standing back from Meriva with evident surprise but also a certain grave acceptance. *Perhaps he knew what he would find after all.*

Meriva walked towards Jehrid, arm still outstretched, the light beam bobbing as she moved. He saw a wary impatience on her face as she came to his side, avoiding his gaze and nodding at the way ahead. "I can't do this forever."

...

She kept a few steps ahead as they moved, a slim silhouette framed by the light she cast forth. It gave off no heat, no threat that he could see, and yet Jehrid found he had to force himself to remain close to her as Brother Sollis struggled on behind.

There can be no room for the Dark in a Faithful soul, he recited inwardly, recalling a sermon from a Second Order missionary his mother had once dragged him to. *The Dark, as practiced by the Deniers who lurk in our midst, brought the Red Hand down upon us. Never forget this, and always be vigilant. Only evil can come of the Dark.*

There is no evil in her, he knew, watching Meriva guide them on, her impossible light playing over the jagged vault of the passage. *So then,* he wondered, his gaze going to Sollis's hunched form. *What truth is there in the likes of him?*

Meriva came to an abrupt halt, shoulders sagging a little and her light flickering as she tried to hold it steady. "Something there," she said in a strained whisper. Jehrid moved to her side, his eyes tracking the faltering beam to some kind of mound. A mound that glittered.

Meriva issued a pained sigh and lowered her hand, darkness descending as her light died, though the glittering mound ahead was still visible, lit by the faint orange glow of multiple torches.

"Give the brother your knife," Jehrid told her, stepping forward and drawing the Order blade. "Stay behind us."

He paused to meet her gaze, seeing a great fatigue there, and a trickle of blood falling from her eyes. She held his gaze for a moment, then blinked and wiped the red tears away.

"Does it hurt?" he asked her.

She smiled faintly. "It... tires me."

"Wasting time," Sollis grunted, taking the knife from her and moving on.

They kept close to the passage wall, though Jehrid knew their presence would surely have been betrayed by Meriva's light. The glow of the torches revealed another chamber as they drew closer, a crafted place like the one from which they had fallen, the floor worked to a smooth surface and the walls shaped into a circle. In the centre sat the mound, glittering metal clustered around a tall stone column. Moving closer they saw silver plate stacked amid bronze figures and tangled jewellery, here and there the tell-tale gleam of bluestone, all shot through by chains of silver and gold, shining like gossamer threads.

"Gold and jewels," Meriva said, plucking a necklace from the mound and holding it up for inspection, three rubies set in a gold chain. "And still he wanted more."

"He was ever a miser," Jehrid replied. "And what miser doesn't want more?"

However, it wasn't the riches that most captured Jehrid's attention, it was the seven-sided stone column about which they were piled. It rose from the centre of the mound to a height of about twelve feet, etched all over with writing of some kind. Jehrid had learned his Realm letters at an early age, and could read Alpiran with sufficient effort, but these markings were unfamiliar, and the stone that held them clearly ancient. However, it did possess a form of decoration that made some kind of sense, a series of emblems carved into the top of the column on each of its seven sides. He began to circle the stone, finding each emblem to be different: a flame, a blazing sun, a book and a quill, an eye, an open hand… He paused at the sight of the sixth symbol, a figure holding a sword, deep holes where its eyes should be. *A blind warrior. Just like the one that sits atop the gate to the House of the Sixth Order, or the medallion every brother carries around his neck.*

"So the Faithful truly have builders in their ranks," Jehrid said, turning to Sollis.

Sollis said nothing, his stance unchanged and face as impassive as ever, though Jehrid noted he had managed to remove the scabbard from the knife. "There are six orders to the Faith," Jehrid went on, moving so he could view the final emblem, a snake and a goblet. "But seven sides to this stone."

Sollis merely returned his gaze and said nothing.

"These words." Jehrid jerked his head at the letters etched into the column. "What language is this? What do they mean?"

"It's Old Volarian," Meriva said. "The tongue spoken by the first Faithful to come to these lands."

"Can you read it?" he asked her, keeping his gaze on Sollis.

"It's been many a year since I had to." She placed a foot on the pile, dislodging a cascade of treasure as she leaned closer to inspect the letters. "The calligraphy is unfamiliar and the dialect strange. Far more archaic than any form I'm familiar with. But, I think..." She paused, lost in thought as Sollis and Jehrid continued to exchange stares.

"It's a narrative of some kind," Meriva said eventually, metal jangling as she moved to read more of the inscriptions. "Though it doesn't fit with any history I know, and much of the phrasing makes little sense."

"Read aloud what you can," Jehrid told her.

"'Armies clash beneath a desert sun... Blood flows in rivers, spilt by lies... The One Who Waits will face the Hope Killer's song...'"

"Stop!" Sollis commanded in a flat rasp, now turned so that his good arm was closest to Jehrid, shoulders lowered into a crouch, the knife now gripped tight.

"My lady," Jehrid said, backing away, sword levelled at the

brother. "Please get behind me."

Meriva hesitated for a second, then rushed from the pile, scattering trinkets as she placed herself at Jehrid's back.

"Something that will remain hidden," Jehrid said. "At what cost, eh brother?"

Sollis gave no response, moving to maintain the distance between them as Jehrid fought down the unwelcome memory of his skirmish with the Lonak all those years ago. *Sword against a knife,* he told himself, trying to stir a confidence he knew to be misplaced. *And him half-crippled.* But the memory was compelling, and still he backed away.

"What do those words mean?" he demanded, playing for time. "What is this place?"

"It's my home," a new voice cut in, rich and vibrant as it echoed about the chamber. "And you were not invited."

Cohran Bera stood perhaps twenty paces away, cudgel in one hand and long-bladed knife in the other. On either side of him stood two Breakers, perhaps the only survivors of his once fearsome band, both armed with crossbows. Jehrid whirled to face Cohran, nudging Meriva behind him, still painfully aware of Sollis's proximity but knowing this to be the greater threat for the moment.

"Fifteen of your cousins died today," Cohran told him. "You bring the Sixth Order to my door and destroy what took a lifetime to build. Have you no words of contrition, my son?"

"Fifteen wasn't enough," Jehrid replied, feeling a familiar, unwise sensation building in his breast. *The dim figures at the end of the pier, the sound of a body falling into the harbour…* "And don't call me that."

"Deny your blood all you want, *my lord.*" Cohran's face contorted as he spoke the title, like an ardent Faithful voicing heresy. "But I look at you and see no difference from that vicious little shit I pulled from a hundred dockside fights. The King chose well in you, a man who delights in slaughter and calls it justice."

"As opposed to a man who slaughters innocents to build a pile of riches he'll never spend."

"Riches." Cohran's voice softened a fraction as his gaze went to the mound of plundered treasure. "No. Power, boy. Power enough to buy a king's boon. He promised me, you see. Back when the wars raged as he built the realm. 'Soldiers need pay,' he said. 'Bring me gold, and there will be no more bounty-men. Bring me enough and one day, perhaps, I'll make a lord of you.' And, when he'd built his realm, paying his guardsmen with the riches plundered from this shore, what did he do? Have the Tower Lord spout empty promises at me for twenty years until he could send you."

Liar! Jehrid found the accusation dying on his lips as long-held suspicions tumbled into place. Al Serahl's lengthy and corrupt tenure in the Tower, tolerated far longer than anyone could have expected. The smugglers and wreckers able to buy immunity from the South Guard for years whilst in the north even the most petty corruption earned a swift execution. *The King took a loan from the shore,* Jehrid realised. *And now considers it paid, in me.*

"Doesn't have to happen, boy," Cohran went on, nodding at Sollis. "With this one gone, there are no other witnesses to gainsay whatever tale you choose to tell." He turned, gesturing behind him where the torchlight played on a series of irregular steps cut into the stone, ascending to a ledge far above.

"It's a steep and winding path," Cohran said. "But but it'll take you out of here. Keep the woman, if you like. I suspect she'll have little to say about all this. You have secrets of your own, do you not, my dear?"

Meriva moved to Jehrid's side, face set in a mask of determined fury. "Yes," she said. "I have secrets. But but this one I'll share."

Her arm shot out, straight and true, hand once again like a spear point. Jehrid closed his eyes as the light blazed forth, birthing an instant scream. When he looked again he saw the man on Cohran's right on his knees, crossbow forgotten as he clutched at his eyes, shrill panic and pain issuing from his mouth in a continual torrent. The Breaker on the left gaped at his fallen cousin for the briefest second, then at Meriva, his crossbow swinging towards her in a fear-born reflex.

Brother Sollis moved in a blur, doubling over as the knife flew from his hand, swift as an arrow as it described a perfect arc ending in the Breaker's skull, the blade sinking in up to the hilt. The Breaker remained upright for a heartbeat or two, mouth twisting around gibbered words and an odd, puzzled frown on his brow. Before collapsing, he managed to work the lock on his crossbow, the bolt missing Sollis by a clear foot before rebounding from the stone column and skittering off into the darkness.

Jehrid saw it all in the scant seconds it took him to close with Cohran. The Breaker chief was shaking his head in confusion, eyes moist and bleary, but some brawler's instinct provided sufficient warning for him to duck the slash Jehrid aimed at his head. He growled and whirled towards Jehrid, club and knife whistling, a large man of middling years moving with all the grace and speed of a youthful dancer. Jehrid parried the knife, ducked the club and knew in an instant Cohran was doomed. He was a killer and a fighter, perhaps the most deadly ever seen on this shore, but he wasn't a soldier. He had never faced a charging Lonak war band or hacked his way across a Meldenean deck. He fought for status or money, but never truly for survival. He had never seen battle, until now.

Jehrid anticipated his next attack with an ease that almost brought a laugh to his lips, the knife slashing at his sword arm whilst the club arced up for a strike at his chin. An attempt to stun and disarm, not to kill. Jehrid leapt and kicked before either blow could land, delivering the tip of his boot to the centre of Cohran's face, nose and teeth breaking under the impact. Cohran back-pedalled, trying to gain space for a parry. Jehrid slashed the knife from his grip with a quick swipe of his looted sword and drove a second kick into Cohran's guts, doubling him over. He tried a final, ineffectual blow with the club, Jehrid catching his wrist and twisting until he heard a crack, the club falling from useless fingers.

He stood back as Cohran stared up at him, face showing neither anger nor defeat. But pride. "Quite a dance, eh son…"

Jehrid drove the iron tine of his sword into Cohran's temple, sending him unconscious to the floor. "Don't call me that."

He turned at the sound of an echoing scream, seeing the blinded Breaker sprinting away into the darkness, his cries continuing to resound through the caverns until they were cut off by a faint splash. *He found the pool,* Jehrid surmised. *Carried out to the Blades, blind and mad. Nawen's Maw would've been a kinder end.*

He went to Meriva, now on her knees, shoulders sagging with exhaustion. He placed a finger under her chin and gently lifted her face, now so streaked with blood she might have stepped from a slaughter pen. "Will you be all right?" he asked.

Her eyes flicked to Sollis, now bending to retrieve Cohran's fallen knife. "*Will either of us?*" she whispered in Alpiran. "*This place, those words. They were not meant for our eyes.*"

Jehrid straightened, watching Sollis as he stood regarding Cohran's prostrate form. For once the impassive mask had gone, a sombre frown creasing the brother's brow. "He taught you to fight?" he asked after a moment, his gaze still lingering on the fallen outlaw.

"Yes," Jehrid said. "But war taught me more."

Jehrid detected a faint note of regret in Sollis's voice as he spoke again, "The pupil always steps from the master's shadow." Abruptly Sollis raised his gaze, all expression fading from his features as he briefly glanced at Jehrid and Meriva before gazing up at the winding steps with a critical eye. "Dragging him up there will be impossible. We'll bind him to the column, send your men for him later."

Jehrid gave a wary nod. "As you wish, brother." He bent to take Meriva's arm. "Can you walk, my lady?"

She sighed agreement and began to rise, then froze, her gaze snapping to the pile of treasure as it issued a jangling rattle, displaced metal sliding as something stirred beneath it. "No..." she breathed.

Something exploded from the mound in a fountain of glittering treasure, something wiry and dressed in rags, revealing pale flesh marked by many wounds, a feral grin shining in a face caked in dried blood. It screamed as it stumbled free of the pile; triumph, rage, and madness filling the chamber. A tremor thrummed through the rock beneath Jehrid's feet, both he and Sollis pitched onto their backs by the force of it, powdered rock spouting as cracks rent the chamber floor from end to end.

Jehrid saw the blind Breaker's crossbow lying barely five paces away and lunged for it, shouting in alarm as the rock beneath him lurched anew. The ragged thing issued another peeling laugh as a fresh crack opened to swallow the crossbow. Jehrid saw Sollis cast Cohran's knife at the laughing wreck of a man, but the juddering floor made it an impossible task, the spinning blade missing its target by a handspan.

The tremor faded as the ragged thing staggered, eyes tracking over them in evident satisfaction before settling on Sollis. Blood flowed from its mouth in a thick stream as it spoke, "Sorry to lose you so soon, brother. I always did find your cruelty so… entertaining." He sighed and raised his arms, head thrown back and his smile blazing anew. "I will miss this g—"

Something small and sharp streaked down from above, moving faster than any crossbow bolt or arrow, issuing a small whine as it sliced through the air to spear the ragged man through the eye. He staggered again, head swivelling about in confusion. Jehrid saw something metallic embedded in his eye, a dart of some kind, the needle-like point protruding from his skull as he reeled about, arms flailing like a drunk fighting imaginary foes. Another dart streaked down, a puff of red vapour spouting from the man's bony chest as it tore clean through his torso, drawing a piercing note from the floor as it rebounded and spun away into the shadows. The thing groaned and collapsed onto the mound, limbs soon slackening in death as blood streamed in rivulets across the gleaming metal.

Jehrid turned at a huffing sound, seeing Brother Lucin clambering down the crude stairway. Sister Cresia followed behind. "Brother," Lucin greeted Sollis on reaching the floor, a little out of breath as he moved towards the mound of riches, barely glancing at Jehrid or Meriva. Jehrid saw he wore a different face now, or more likely, felt no more need to conceal his true visage, free of any false serenity or deference. The face of a very serious man.

Lucin took a moment to survey the body slumped on the pile, eyes lingering on the blood-caked features though Jehrid saw no flicker of recognition. His expression grew yet more serious as he raised his gaze to the seven-sided column. "All too real," he muttered before turning away, addressing his next words to Meriva in Alpiran, no doubt assuming that Jehrid couldn't understand his meaning. "*You have a message for me, honoured lady.*"

Meriva took hold of Jehrid's proffered arm and hauled herself upright, wincing from the effort. "*Yes,*" she said, voice heavy with fatigue. "*The answer is no.*"

Lucin lowered his gaze in evident disappointment before inclining his head at the column. "*You read that, I assume?*"

"*Some.*"

"*Then I hope it provided an inkling of what your refusal will force us to do.*"

"*The decision was not mine. I merely carry the message. The Servants have spoken. Your war is not our war.*"

Lucin merely shook his head with a sigh. "*It will be.*" He nodded at Sister Cresia, now standing at the base of the stairway. Jehrid's gaze was immediately drawn to the brace of darts clutched between her fingers, darts that were identical to those that had dispatched the ragged man, though he could see no device on her that could project them with such force. However, any doubts that she had been the author of his end vanished at the sight of her face, bleached white and gaze fixed on the body laying amid the bloodied treasure.

"The first is always the hardest," Jehrid told her. She stared at him with moist eyes, no sign of a scowl on her brow. He saw that her hands were shaking.

"Sister," Lucin said with a note of impatience. "This matter requires resolution."

"No." Sollis stepped in front of Cresia, though his gaze was fixed on Lucin.

Jehrid saw Lucin's throat working before he found the nerve to reply. "Our Aspects are in agreement regarding the import of this mission…"

"Do not make an enemy of me, brother." The words were softly spoken, little more than a whisper in fact, but they seemed to linger in the air, caught by the cavern walls and repeated until they faded to a hiss.

A new voice came echoing down from above, the words indistinct but Jehrid recognised his sergeant's Nilsaelin brogue. "Lord Collector! Are you well?"

"Your men were kind enough to escort us," Sister Cresia said, the darts now vanished from her fingers and a distinct note of relief in her voice.

Jehrid's eyes tracked from Sollis to Lucin, noting how the elder brother's gaze was now averted.

"Quite well!" Jehrid called back, glancing at Cohran's still unconscious form. "Get down here! And bring rope!"

...

Cohran Bera stood gazing out to sea, a breeze stirring his thinning hair. It was a fine morning, barely a cloud in the sky and the rising sun a bright shimmering ball on a mostly becalmed Erinean. He favoured Jehrid with a fond glance as he came forward, then offered a respectful nod to Meriva. She failed to respond, arms crossed tightly beneath her cloak, face rigid. Jehrid had invited her out of courtesy, as the wronged party she had every right to witness the proceedings, though he had hoped she might stay away. *She has seen enough blood.*

Sollis, Cresia and Lucin could be seen on the crest of a nearby hill, all on horseback. The Brother Commander's arm still rested in a sling, the bones set and bound tight by the Fifth Order mission in South Tower, though the scabbard on his back remained empty.

"I'll get another when I return to the Order House," he said when Jehrid offered him the blade he had taken from the dead brother.

"I can keep it?"

Sollis shrugged. "It's just a sword, my lord. We have many." With that he strode to his horse and mounted up. Jehrid surmised this was the only farewell, or thanks, he was likely to receive.

"Cohran Bera," Jehrid began in formal tones. "You stand convicted of murder, theft, piracy, suborning the Realm's servants, and evading the King's Excise. Accordingly you will be executed under the King's Word in a manner deemed fit by the Lord Collector. As you have profited from the deaths of so many by casting them onto this shore, such shall be your fate."

He stepped forward and rested his boot on the pear-shaped stone to which Cohran had been chained, gaze fixed on Nawen's Maw as he tried to summon a face from his memory, one he thought he would never forget, one he hoped would be witnessing this event from the Beyond. And yet, though he strove to recall the dim figures at the end of the pier, seeking to stoke a hatred he had nurtured for more than twenty years, today he couldn't find it. *Why won't she come? Surely she would want to see this.*

"At least look me in the eye as you do this, son," Cohran said.

For a moment Jehrid found he couldn't lift his gaze, as if some invisible hand gripped him in place.

"You must have questions," Cohran went on. "Ask me and I'll tell you."

"You will earn no reprieve," Jehrid told him, still unable to meet his eye.

"I know. But perhaps I'll earn my son's regard."

Jehrid closed his eyes for a second, his boot slipping from the boulder, a great weariness pressing down as he stood back. He forced his eyes open and stood facing his father, seeing the fearsome wrecker now vanished, leaving behind the man he recalled from childhood, the prideful shine in his eyes as he beheld his son.

"Why did you kill my mother?" Jehrid asked him.

Cohran's smile faded slowly, the depth of his regret plain in the sagging, weathered features. "She was taking you away," he said. "She had grown tired of this life of danger and distrust, and fearful of the future. For she knew one day you would become what I am. She sold us out to the Tower Lord's men, not knowing they worked for me. She thought she was buying a new life in the north, with you. You know the code, Jehrid. Silence is the only law. And so I killed her, because my kin expected it, and because I needed to keep you with me... But you left anyway."

Jehrid's gaze returned to the stone, though he found he had no strength to lift his boot.

"It's alright, son," Cohran said. "Truth be told, I'd rather it was you than any other. Blood pays for blood. Let's get it done."

Jehrid was aware of the eyes of his men, all gathered to watch their Lord Collector's nerve fail. But still he had no strength today. Not for this.

"The ship you wrecked was called the Voyager." Jehrid turned to find Meriva at his side, face pale but determined as she stared at Cohran, suffering no reluctance to meet his eye. "Crafted in the yards of Marbellis near thirty years ago, funded by the honourable trading house of Al Lebra. For many years it was captained by my father and, when he became too old to bear the hardships of the sea, by my brother. He was a good man, an honest sailor who rose to captain at a young age, respected by his crew and loved by his family. When word reached him that I must sail to this shore, he insisted it be the Voyager that carried me, unwilling to trust the task to any other."

She stepped towards the stone, placing her foot on it, gaze still fixed on Cohran as she grated in Alpiran, "*I watched your scum slit my brother's throat, you piece of filth!*"

Jehrid turned away as she shoved the stone into the maw, hearing the rattle of chains and the crack of breaking bones. But no scream. *No,* Jehrid thought. *He never would.*

He waited for the faint splash, then turned to his sergeant. "Return to the Excise House. Double rum ration tonight." He glanced at Meriva, now staring down at the Maw as if frozen in place. "I'll be along directly."

He paused to watch Sollis turn his horse and ride away without pause, although his two companions lingered a moment. Jehrid found he didn't like the way Brother Lucin's gaze rested on Meriva, sensing far too much calculation behind it and experiencing a sudden wild desire to seize the brother and see him follow Cohran into the maw. Fortunately, it seemed Lucin sensed his intent for he gave an inexpert tug on his horse's reins and quickly disappeared from view. Sister Cresia loitered a moment longer, Jehrid gaining the impression of a smile as she raised a hand to offer a tentative wave. He waved back and offered a bow, seeing her laugh before she too rode from sight.

"It wasn't truly a man, was it?" he asked Meriva. "That thing we left in the tunnels."

She shook her head. "In truth I have never encountered its kind before. But I suspect whatever humanity it once possessed withered away long ago, and the world is enriched by its passing."

He nodded and pulled something from the pouch on his belt. "I believe this is yours, my lady," he said, holding up a small amulet; a single bead of amber set in a plain silver mounting. "Cohran… my father had it in his pocket."

Her gaze finally rose from the maw, a small smile curving her lips as she took the amulet. "My thanks, my lord," she said, lifting the chain over her head.

"Rhevena's Tear," he said. "Am I wrong in assuming it to be worn by all those… similarly gifted?"

"Different gods have different servants, carrying different signs. Though we all endeavour to serve a common interest."

"An interest best served by refusing whatever the Seventh Order required of you?"

"Seventh Order? What's that?" He saw her smile broaden as she moved away, going to the horse he had lent her. "Will you escort a lady home, my lord?"

"Gladly. Though only as far as South Tower. I'm sure the Tower Lord will meet the expense of finding a ship to take you home."

"South Tower is my home now. At least for the time being. The House of Al Lebra has many interests here. It was my stated reason for coming. It would seem odd if I was to depart so quickly, don't you think?"

"Certainly." He mounted up and fell in beside her as they followed the clifftop trail towards the distant tower. "Tell me, have you ever heard the tale of how Nawen's Maw got its name.....?"

Below the overhang the terns were already circling the spot beneath the maw, making ready to dive into the waves and claim the fresh bounty, for the southern shore had ever been kind to scavengers.

ABOUT THE AUTHOR

Anthony Ryan was born in Scotland in 1970. After a long Career in the UK Civil Service he took up writing full time after the success of his first novel *Blood Song*. His books have been published by Ace/Roc, Orbit, and Subterranean Press. Anthony's work has also been published internationally, being translated into sixteen languages.

For more information on Anthony's books visit his website at: anthonyryan.net.

Follow Anthony on:

Twitter: @writer_anthony

Facebook: www.facebook.com/anthonyryanauthor

Instagram: anthonyryan286

Lightning Source UK Ltd.
Milton Keynes UK
UKHW010607081222
413589UK00007B/190

9 781527 291799